LONG JOURNEY

LONG JOURNEY

A novel
by

JOHN FISHER

HODDER & STOUGHTON
ST. PAUL'S HOUSE, LONDON, E.C.4

To

NICK

Who will understand why

FIRST PRINTED . . . JULY, 1947

Made and Printed in Great Britain for Hodder & Stoughton, Limited, London
by Wyman & Sons Limited, London Reading and Fakenham

PROLOGUE

HERE WAS THE PROMENADE, with the palm trees and the great gingerbread hotels, and behind the town the green hills dotted with white villas stood against the blue southern sky. It was all a bit shabby, but less changed than he had expected. That woman with the shawl over her head looked pinched and under-nourished . . . and the old man on crutches glanced rather bitterly at the big car as it went by . . . but there were other big cars, sleek and shining, and smartly-dressed men and women strolling up and down or sitting watching the yachts out there on the vivid sea. You wouldn't think so much had happened. The War and Vichy, and the Germans and Liberation, and now all the hunger and sorrow and bitterness which were so carefully concealed from the tourists who were coming again with their foreign exchange. It was strange to be back in Europe, strange to be back on the shores of the Mediterranean. One had somehow never expected to be here again.

He glanced at Ruth. She was sitting back in the corner of the car, looking out at the sea and narrowing her eyes against the glare of the sun, and he suddenly realised how she had aged in the last few years. That grey hair under her smart little hat, the lines on her face, the thinness of her white hand with its reddened nails. Well, they were grandparents now, them-selves. Sylvia's eldest child would soon be five. She was born about the time Charles went away.

He looked back at the row of cafés, little shops all black and silver and expensive, big hotels, some of them still closed. This must be the one . . . yes, here it was. Still empty though, its high doorway boarded up, its shutters fastened. Rows and rows of green shutters behind the elaborate little iron balconies which had lost most of their paint. A queer, forlorn relic of the old Riviera of the 1900s, the Riviera of the Grand Dukes and the carriages and the cocottes. Those hideous caryatids supporting the doorway . . . and the overgrown little garden at one side, the terrace where an orchestra used to play.

He bent forward and rapped on the glass.

" Stop a moment, please."

The driver looked surprised, but pulled in to the kerb and stopped. Ruth looked surprised too.

" What is it, Harold ? "

" Nothing, really. I wanted to look at that hotel. That's where Father was staying, the last time I saw him. A lonely old man in a great elaborate suite of rooms . . . the place was pretty run-down even then. That chap Wilkins he had was very good to him . . . I wonder what's become of Wilkins. Father left him some money. I brought Charles, you remember, that time. It was in the spring of 1939, and I had to tell him that we were going to America and that we wanted him to come too. He said he would, but I never felt he really meant it. I remember an evening when we sat and talked in his room up there. Charles started asking him questions about the sea and ships, and I was rather surprised, I hadn't realised that Charles cared a button about such things. And I certainly never expected . . . oh well, there it is. But Father was obviously rather pleased to be asked about his early adventures. Round the Horn before the mast and all the rest of it. We'd none of us ever

6

taken much interest in his travels, even as children. I . . . I always felt shy and awkward with him. My mother . . ."

He paused. A little boy and his mother looking at picture-books in the hammock on the porch on summer evenings. London, Venice, Florence . . . we'll go there some day. The big room in the castle above the Italian bay, and the faded fans and ostrich-feathers and ribbon—tied bundles of letters, and that queer, gutteral woman . . . what was her name, Gregor, Nadia Gregor . . . with her beady little eyes. He crushed away that memory and went on.

"And Jim and Alice were only interested in his stories about gold and silver mines. Leadville, Cripple Creek . . . that was the only world they knew. That queer, dusty little town lost in the mountains . . . he must have wondered, sometimes, what an ex-sailor from Liverpool was doing there. In fact I think he wondered that all his life. Not only up there among the mountains, but later on, in the de-luxe hotels and the Italian villas and the château in Normandy. He always seemed a little bewildered somehow. Did you ever notice that?"

"Yes . . . I suppose so. He didn't show his feelings much."

"I didn't realise it, then. I always took him for granted. I knew, latterly, that he was unhappy about Alice, and that Jim had been a bit of a disappointment, and he'd never understood what Mother wanted, or what I was getting at. But I always assumed that he was pretty well satisfied on the whole. After all, he'd done what he set out to do. No one ever thought he would, either."

He stopped again, as another little memory flashed

up. The slushy wooden platform, the little train, the engine with its big cowcatcher and swinging bell, a group of men and women, stamping, laughing, making conversation, and a lonely-looking figure in an overcoat and an old Stetson standing on the step as the train pulled out again. A little boy looking at his mother and realising, vaguely, why her face was so white and hard and set.

"Yes," he repeated. "He did what he set out to do. But now, looking back, I can't help feeling that somewhere along the way he had discovered that what he set out to do, and did, was not what he wanted after all. God knows what it should have been. But I wish I'd tried a little harder to understand him. Oh well, we'll never know now."

He stared up at the peeling balconies and shutters, and tried to remember more about that last evening, the faces and the talk in that big ornate room. The tired old man with the faintly puzzled eyes and big, white, clumsy hands . . . he had been a boy, once, young and eager and certain about what he wanted, what he was going to do. A boy in Liverpool, who was going to be a sailor, as his father and his grandfather had been. One would like to know more about that boy, and how he became what he did.

CHAPTER

I

IT WAS INEVITABLE THAT Roger Barton should go to sea, for his father and his grandfather had been at sea before him, and all his childhood in the Liverpool of the late fifties and the sixties was coloured by the nearness of the river and the ships. His grandfather had sailed with the privateers in the Atlantic and to the West Indies, had earned good prize-money and spent it all and had died little richer than he started. Roger's father had gone to sea at twelve as a cabin-boy and ended as first mate of a big emigrant clipper in the Australian trade. No wonder everyone took it for granted that Roger, too, had the sea in his blood.

He was the third child, but his two elder brothers died of measles when he was a baby, and after him there were no more ; in his early years he was small and weakish, but suddenly he began to grow, and soon people were predicting that he would be as big a man as his father, after all.

He could barely remember that father, a giant with scratchy, tobacco-smelling whiskers, who would arrive out of nowhere, poke his ribs, swing him up to the ceiling, and soon vanish again as suddenly as he had come ; he could barely remember standing beside his mother on a rainy wharf, and watching a big ship pass down the river, and jumping at the sudden bang of saluting-guns as the *Ocean Pride* sailed with emigrants, general cargo and Her Majesty's mails for the Colonies. The next thing he remembered was his mother weeping and putting on a long black veil, and people telling him that the *Ocean Pride* had been wrecked on King's Island off Port Phillip Heads and that his father had been drowned. Then there were days of vague uneasiness, vague calamity, and the furniture began to vanish, and little ferrety Uncle Henry from Bolton came and argued with Mother and went away again, and before long they moved into two dingy rooms above a draper's shop in a back street on the poorer fringe of Wavertree, and a new chapter of life began.

They had been left very poor, for Jim Barton had been a cheery, open-handed man who saved little of his pay ; life in those rooms above Mr. Pinker's shop was an endless scrape and struggle, marked only by acuter crises as rent-day drew near. Lucy Barton was clever with her needle, and went out dressmaking : gradually she built up quite a good connection among the rich families of Sefton Park and Wavertree : she would spend long days working in the sewing-rooms of their big, comfortable mansions, and often would bring home bundles of work to finish before going to bed. Roger would always remember a tired face bending over some black shining stuff in the gas-light, and the needle flashing in and out, and the ticking of the old clock, and the footsteps in the street below.

At first she found a beery, kindly old woman to come in and look after him while she was out, but later, as he grew older, he was often left alone ; he never minded those long hours of day-dreaming, staring out of the window, looking at old picture-books and drawing ships ; there was always her return to wait for, the door opening below, the voice calling up the stairs. His mother was a gentle, soft-voiced woman, with a firm, determined mouth and eyes ; she had a certain education, and was resolved to give her son a good start in the world. For a time she taught him herself ; later sent him to a little school kept by two ladies up the road. He was a good pupil, though always in a clumsy, dreamy way : quick at reading, fond of poring over maps, worried, himself, by his slowness at sums. Sums were important, he knew. He would need them for navigation. His mother nodded gravely when he told her that ; later he understood that she must have been wondering wearily if she would ever save enough to apprentice him to a good line and buy his outfit. She too took it for granted that he would go to sea.

So the months passed, and a year, and another, another . . . he grew into a tall, ungainly, untidy boy, big for his eight, his nine, his ten years : he went to a bigger school and studied and played and fought and scuffled, and came home to the sunny little room and his homework and his mother stitching and stitching through the long evenings.

And, as he grew, he gradually discovered another world, another life, very different from home. Soon half his days were spent in that world, the raw, exciting world of the docks and the river and the ships. Exploring it alone or with his friends, he felt his heart beat faster at the thought that some day he would be part of it, and yet that thought chilled him with a queer apprehension too. It was all so huge and strange and different ; bright and exciting, hideous and squalid, at once a lovely dream and a nightmare oddly sinister. The moan of fog-horns in the Mersey, the swirl of wide waters round the landing stage, the tugs and ferries and tall-funnelled liners and always the great sailing-ships. The clippers lay crowded in the docks, a bare forest of masts and yards high over roofs and sheds : they lay at anchor in long lines from the Sloyne to New Brighton, they went down the river behind their little tugs, came up again with cargoes from all corners of the world . . . the wide river, the wide grey estuary was alive with their presence, they gave the whole great city its life and character. Everyone—shipowners, clerks, shopkeepers and school-boys alike, watched them and talked of them and argued about them and laid wagers, big or little, on their passages.

Roger listened to this talk, gradually understanding what it meant and his part in it all. Sometimes an old friend of his father's would turn up : some ship's officer with a deep voice and hard red hands, polite and a little uneasy in the room above the Drapery : down the road lived old Captain Morris who had known Jim Barton as a boy and as a man ; he too would drop in sometimes to see how the youngster was getting on. The old, bald-headed man with hard blue eyes, barking abrupt questions.

" How old are you now, boy ? What are you doing at school ? Minding your books ? That's right. Get your book-learning while you can. You'll have plenty of other things to learn when you go to sea."

Sometimes too he would take Roger out with him, down to the waterfront. He would stump along, the boy trotting beside him, and now and then he would pause to greet some old crony, a grizzled sea-captain

like himself, a pilot, a shipowner. He would talk of
the men who had made Liverpool what she was : James Beazley, Henry Fox, young John Pilkington
and Henry Wilson of the White Star Line, little James
Baines, whose mother had kept the cake-shop in Upper
Duke Street, Baines who bought the old *Marco Polo*
for a song and was as surprised as anyone when Bully
Forbes took her out to Melbourne and back in five
months and twenty-one days. Baines of the Black
Ball Line, the clippers bought from the Yankees . . .
Lightning, Miles Barton, Sovereign of the Seas. . . .

Down on the landing stage he would begin to talk,
staring out at the river and the shipping and remembering a hundred other harbours round the world,
ten thousand other ships seen with a seaman's eye.
Ignoring the big black steamers with their screws or
churning paddles, which came trailing their smoke
across his clean sea-world.

From him Roger learnt more about the father his
mother tried to describe to him : heard of his pranks
as a boy, his promise as a second mate, his quickness
and clear-headedness that time the *Curlew* was dis-
masted off Mauritius, his last voyage in the Colonial
trade.

" I saw him just before he sailed that last time in
the *Ocean Pride*. She was a cranky ship, and he knew
it. He would have got a ship of his own after another
voyage or two. Old Williamson thought a great
deal of him. And now Williamson is gone too . . .
But there are other owners, boy, you needn't look so
glum. We'll see about it, in a year or two. And if
you're ever half the man your father was . . ."

The old man would make a gesture and turn back
to the grey, brimming river where the gulls screamed

and circled and drew your eyes after them towards the sea. Standing there together, the old man and the little boy, watching the pageant of the river's life, watching and commenting on this ship and that. A great clipper, perhaps, outward bound for Melbourne and Sydney, with waving and flags. Perhaps a Brocklebank from India, with her white-banded hull and square Whitehaven stern. Perhaps a graceful little Glynn fruiter, perhaps a Yankee packet from New York. There were the little colliers too, and the billyboys with their square mainsails and impudent, tailcocking jiggers ; there were the Mersey pilot-schooners going down to cruise off Point Lynas and guide the weary wanderers home.

Then they would walk along the docks—Canning Dock, Salthouse Dock, Wapping Dock—staring up at the bowsprits and calm-eyed white figure-heads, at the tall masts and wide yards. Winches rattling, stevedores shouting, riggers scrambling like flies in a spider's web among that tangle, which, as Captain Morris explained it, fell into order and symmetry. Royals and top-gallants and topsails and courses . . . it was strange to think of those bare yards crowded with sail, lunging before the Trades, of those figure-heads and bowsprits sliding gently into green harbours on the far side of the world.

Going back up the busy streets, past the public-houses blaring with voices, past ship-chandler's shops, mysterious with dangling oilskins and coiled ropes, the old man would talk about ships still. The Yankee packets, the other Black Ball line, the hell-ships with their hard-bitten officers and crews of vicious packet-rats. The ships of London River ; the great East Indiamen of the old days, the Blackwallers with their

smart Navy ways. The little Duthies, the trim green
clippers of the Aberdeen White Star Line. And
always the ships and men of Liverpool. Bully Forbes
driving his ship to "Hell or Melbourne," padlocking
his sheets, standing with levelled pistol to overawe his
terrified crew. Beazley's little *Vision* racing the *Cairn-
gorm* home from Foochow, neck and neck from the
China Sea to the chops of the Channel, passing her
samples to the tug off the Great Orme . . . the special
train waiting and the *Vision's* tea in London a day and
a night before her rival dropped anchor in the Thames.
Wooden ships, composite. Yes, and the iron ships
that were coming now.

"They'll do well enough, no doubt. But they'll be
hard ships, wet ships, dangerous. No, boy, I'm glad
I had my time when I did. You'll see some strange
things before you reach my age."

Roger nodding silently, his mind awhirl. There
was that whole wide, restless world of wind and sails
and sun and bitter darkness, the world which his
father had known, and Captain Morris—yes, and that
drunken seaman stumbling past in the gutter now !
the world which he himself would know some day.
It was always strange to come back from those after-
noons of wind and seagulls to the warm, quiet room
above the Drapery.

The months passed, the years, the strange, crowded
decade drew on. Across the seas, the Yankees had
stopped fighting each other with their big guns and
their ironclads ; the great bales of cotton were coming
again to the mills of hungry Lancashire. But old
Captain Morris shook his head sadly ; he mourned
the passing of a whole race of ships. The great American soft-wood clippers were ageing now, and with their

disappearing went the brave days of Melbourne gold and wild welcomes in Hobson's Bay. The race was passing to the wool-clippers of London. And behind them pressed the spectre of another age, the age of steam. There was the vast *Great Eastern* with her eleven-thousand horsepower engines, her endless row of masts, a monster, a monstrosity. There were more new Cunard liners and Collins liners, the Inman line. Even little James Baines was speculating, disastrously, with tea-kettles, and Bully Forbes's star had set. They said that he was on the beach somewhere out East.

One autumn day the old man caught a chill, went out coughing in a cold, blowy rain, came back shivering to his lodgings, took to his bed and died after forty-eight gasping hours. A married sister from Chester came and packed up his possessions, there was not much. A chest full of clothes, an old sextant, the models on which Roger had learnt the rigging of a ship. She arranged for the erection of an ugly stone over his grave in Smithdown Road Cemetery ; then she went away again, and soon there was no one in Liverpool who thought of Captain Morris save a few old wrinkled men who had sailed with him, and one boy who had walked with him along the waterfront.

His death left a strange gap in Roger's life, and that winter was shadowed by other changes too. For years his mother had suffered from rheumatism, a queer, paralysing stiffness that cramped her hands and arms and knees ; at first she had ignored it, then fought against it desperately. But now the time had come when she could fight no longer—when her stiff, twisted fingers could no longer hold a needle—and all her hard-won independence, all her hopes for Roger's future, shrivelled and warped like her hands. There was a dreadful evening when she sat crying at the table ; there was a long, anxious afternoon in a doctor's waiting-room among shabby, anxious women, there was a slow drag home through the rain. A few days later Uncle Henry came again, and clucked his tongue, stared about with pale, narrow eyes, sniffed, asked questions, made a grudging suggestion which could not be refused. In a few weeks they went to live in Bolton. A shabby trunk, portmanteaux, bundles : a thin, tired woman in black, a thin, long-legged boy in clothes too small for him, driving away down familiar streets to the station in an old four-wheeler that smelt of rotten leather and damp straw. Roger would never forget the smell of that cab, and the smoky, sickly smell of the train, and the sense of a whole familiar life and world changing, changed and gone for evermore.

Uncle Henry, Lucy Barton's brother, was a widower who had a big ironmonger's shop in the middle of the town. He was older than his sister, and his daughters were older than Roger : Julia was already married to a middle-aged corn-chandler, and Gracie was more or less engaged to a pimply young clerk in a cotton-firm. Uncle Henry had quarrelled with his servant, and was not sorry to have a sister, even a half-crippled sister, to take her place, but he was less pleased to be saddled with an overgrown, untidy nephew whose appetite was large and who made no pretence of liking Bolton or iron-mongery.

Uncle Henry was a parsimonious, suspicious, chapel-going little man, another race, another species from burly Jim Barton or Captain Morris or any of the seamen who were Roger's ideal : his ironmonger's business was his pride, and he had no patience with his nephew's eager interest in ships and seas. There would be no question of an apprenticeship now, that was certain : the little man bristled at the idea.

" If the lad wants to be a sailor, let him. But he needn't expect me to stump up forty pounds for him. If he has any sense he'll stay on dry land. There's a place for him in the shop, and a bed for him in the attic, and he couldn't expect more if he was my own son. He wants to follow in his father's footsteps does he ? Eh, well then, I'm not stopping him. He can go to-morrow if he wants to. But this afternoon he'll go down to the shop and work for his supper. Do you hear that, lad ? Then get along with you ! "

Lucy Barton would set her lips bitterly, but there was nothing she could say. Roger would glower, flush, hesitate, then do as he was told. Down to the dark, crowded, hateful little shop, long hours in the back, opening cases, rearranging stock, sweeping, scrubbing, under his uncle's sardonic eye. Long hours trailing round the streets with parcels, breathing the smoky air, deafened by the roar of wheels on cobbles, clatter of clogs on cobbles, dreaming of the great open river and the distant bursts of chantying as men walked round the capstan on some great clipper ready for the sea. Then home to the prim, airless little house, and Uncle Henry sniffing at his food and grumbling, Gracie looking virtuous and superior, his mother cooking, scrubbing, washing dishes, making beds, old now and tired and defeated, with her thin face and those stiff, twisted hands.

If it had not been for her he would have taken Uncle Henry at his word : at twelve, at thirteen he was sure he could find a berth as boy on some ship,

18

if only a dirty little collier-brig, if only a fishing-smack. Anything to be away from this. But he couldn't leave his mother alone to toil and drudge for Uncle Henry and for Gracie, with no one who cared what pain it cost her, no one to say a kind word . . .

So he set his teeth and stuck on, through the long, dark, foggy winter and the dusty summer that followed, and winter again. He helped his mother with the housework, lighted fires, polished fenders, carried coals ; he gulped his breakfast, rushed off to the shop and worked all day, came home, sat quietly all evening reading the improving books his uncle thrust on him or the tattered sea-stories he smuggled in . . . went up to his cold little attic, fell asleep and dreamed of the Mersey and Captain Morris and the screaming gulls. Days and weeks and months passing ; his father had gone to sea at thirteen, but he himself was fourteen, fifteen . . . soon it would be too late.

Rain and sleet lashed down out of the smoky sky, slush froze on the cobbles. His mother was bent now, and moved slowly, her face creased with pain. She did not go out much these bitter days, but one afternoon she had to hobble down to buy some tripe for her brother's supper, and, coming back, slipped, fell, hit her head against a doorstep and lay very still. The neighbours carried her in, fetched a doctor, sent down to the shop for Roger and his uncle. When Roger, white, breathless, shaking, burst into the little back room, he found half a dozen excited women there and a shabby little man in rusty black whose head-shake answered an unspoken question, without words.

The rest was a queer, unreal blur. The figure in the cheap coffin. Black clothes. A lean, sniffing clergyman. Gusts of rain over ugly headstones and gravel paths and a heap of earth : Uncle Henry pompous in his pot-hat, then another cab and an oddly familiar smell of wet straw, and people crowding into the house for cups of tea. Lucy Barton had left nothing but a few worn clothes and a few little trinkets : Roger found his cousin Gracie scornfully poking through them next day. Uncle Henry was out arranging for another housekeeper. The room would be needed when she came.

He returned in the evening, unsuccessful in his search, to grumble at Gracie's slap-dash cookery. When Roger announced that he was going, the ferrety little face sharpened, teeth snapped.

" I'm your guardian now. I'll thank you to remember that. It's no use you thinking you can make plans without consulting me."

Roger started to answer, then checked himself. It occurred to him that, after all, Uncle Henry did not like the thought of losing an unpaid drudge from his shop and his home. He went upstairs and sat on the bed in that cold little attic, staring at the flame of his candle-stump and remembering those warm, quiet evenings in the room above the Drapery at Liverpool. His mother looking up from her sewing to smile at him. When the candle began to gutter he roused himself with a start. There was not much to do. A couple of shirts, some much-darned socks, a yellowing daguerreotype of his father, the Bible that had been his mother's . . . they made a small bundle. Then he counted his money. A few shillings which customers had given him at Christmas, carefully hoarded against such an hour as this. Finally everything was ready. He blew out the candle and sat in the darkness, waiting till the house was still. Then he slipped downstairs and out into the empty street.

He tramped all night, slept for an hour or two in a haystack towards dawn, then plodded on, stiff, hungry, foot-sore, through a cold drizzle of rain. His mind was a turmoil of emotions—sorrow, anger, a queer exultant freedom and a shrinking sense of dread— which merged into one wild shaking, stumbling excitement as the houses grew thicker and sky greyer and the road went down into the familiar busy streets of Liverpool. He did not pause to turn off towards Wavertree and the street which had once been home : he stumbled on, forcing his aching legs to a sort of trot, along the crowded pavements that dipped towards the river. Suddenly the Pier Head, the Landing Stage, the Mersey, a ferry churning off to Birkenhead, a steamer at anchor in mid-stream. And, beyond her, upstream and down, moving behind their tugs or swinging to their cables, the sailing-ships he had so longingly remembered ; the long, lean hulls, the tall masts with yards outspread, the eager bowsprits and the figureheads. He stood a long time in the rain there, staring out at them, smelling the salt wind, while the gulls circled round above him, screaming a welcome or screaming a warning, encouragement or mockery. His throat felt dry and his heart thumped in his chest. The past was behind him now, and life lay ahead.

But his mood of challenge ebbed in the rainy dusk, as he tramped along the docks, among the drays, the crates, the cranes, the busy workmen and suspicious watchmen : as he timidly boarded this ship and that, peered round the dirty, unfamiliar decks, screwed up his courage to ask where the Mate was, screwed up his courage to approach some hard-faced, busy man.

" Do you want a hand, sir ? Do you want a boy, sir ? Any chance of a berth, sir ? " A stare, a head shaken quickly, perhaps a snarl. " What the Hell are you doing here ? No ! Get out of it ! "

By evening he was almost dropping, he stumbled back the way he had come half-sobbing with loneliness, disappointment, fatigue. At a squalid little eating-house he spent some of his money on a plate of greasy stew and a cup of scalding tea ; then he went on aimlessly along the streets, wondering where to go, what to do. He must save his money . . . perhaps he could find some sailors' boarding-house that would not be too expensive . . . the boarding-house keeper might help him to find a ship. . . . But he shrank away from the doorways where hard-eyed men stood watching the drunken figures shamble in : he wandered on, like a lost dog drenched and frightened, through the shadows and flaring gas-light of sailor-town. In those lights and shadows, figures, faces, were grotesque and sinister ; a reeling man with ear-rings, a great fat girl with paint-smeared face and uncovered breasts, a grinning mulatto, a great negro mumbling to himself. He would always remember with a prickle of horror that evening, and the night that followed, the night he spent huddled under the arcades of the Goree Piazza, the old Irish beggar-woman who came and crouched near him, staring at him through the shadows with bright eyes in a grey blurr of rags and hair. He might have slept a little, but he was not aware of it . . . only at last the darkness had melted to another grey, rainy dawn, and he could drag himself up and start his search again.

Only later did he realise how long that search might have lasted, and how lucky he was. It was early afternoon when he stood on that wharf staring at the big, shabby barque *Chester Rows*, and trying to pluck up his courage to board her and try once more. The rain was still falling : she was not a pretty sight in the grey afternoon, a few riggers scrambling about aloft, a few seedy men working on her harbour-filthy decks. They didn't seem to be doing anything special ; he watched them a little, and picked out a squat, long-armed Scotsman who must be the Mate. He was standing beside an open hatch, cursing all and sundry, and Roger told himself that it could be no good applying to him. There was a boy on board already . . . a scared-looking stripling with red hair ; the Mate was scolding him for something and ended his lecture with a great swinging cuff. A dockside lounger saw Roger's interest, and laughed at him.

" Wish you was in that boy's place ? Sailing for Calcutta in a day or two ? She wasn't a bad old barky in 'er day, the *Chester Rows*. Not as bad as she looks even now. They'll get 'er smartened up a bit once they've dropped Tuskar."

Roger murmured some answer and turned away. He ought to go aboard and try his luck—but he didn't dare. It would be no use . . . He was dragging off over the greasy cobbles when he heard a thin crash and a thin cry, and swung round again. The lounger was staring, all agog. It was, he said, the red-haired boy. Fallen down the hatchway.

The boy was hauled up again—a dangling red head, a white face with a smear of blood on it, a white spear of bone through a trouser-leg ; he was taken away on a barrow, and what became of him Roger never learnt. Before he knew what he was doing, he was standing on the deck, stammering at the Mate, and a pair of hard blue eyes were raking him.

"Na, he'll not sail this voyage, the wee fule. So you want to step into his shoes do you? And what use do you think you'll be to us?"

Heart thudding, tongue clumsy, stammering an answer. Willing to do anything, not afraid of work, know the rigging of a ship . . . Captain Morris . . . My father . . . The *Ocean Pride*.

"So your father was First Mate of the *Ocean Pride* was he? And you know the rigging of a ship—on a wee model anyway? Man, it's not the rigging will concern you. Can you clean out a pig-pen? That's all we'll want from you. We can sail the ship for ourselves, you understand."

Another mumbled answer. The hard eyes still searching. A long, breathless wait. At last the answer.

"Oh, well, you canna be worse than yon other dirty little keelie. Ten shillings a month, you lucky wee devil. And don't come whining to me when you begin to wish you were back on dry land."

Blood pounded in his temples and a warm glow flooded his body—only for a second did he remember the dangling red head, the blood-stained face of his predecessor. He had a berth. He had a place in the world—To Hell with you Uncle Henry! To Hell with you!

*   *   *   *

They let him sleep on board while the *Chester Rows* was finishing her loading; for two bewildering days

24

he toiled from dawn to dusk, scrubbing out water-tanks and harness-casks, cleaning pantry and galley, white-washing that pig-pen, carting heavy cases of cabin-stores, ordered about by a dozen imperious voices, cuffed by a dozen heavy hands. Who half these people were he never knew ; there were only a few that he learnt to recognise besides the Mate ; there was a little scowling Welshman who was Second Mate, there was a slow, sleepy Yorkshire carpenter, there was a tall, grey formidable figure with bushy eyebrows who appeared from time to time, staring about him, and who proved to be Captain Daniels, the Old Man himself. Back-breaking days of scurry and confusion, quick meals snatched in a grimy eating-house near the docks, brief, exhausted nights on a pile of old rags in a corner of the galley with the grizzled, silent watchman . . . time flying as it had never flown before. The day came when he was sent to a crowded room off Water Street, where, in a blare of voices and scrum of unwashed bodies, he was signed-on with the rest of the new crew ; he was given an advance-note for ten shillings, found a shop-keeper who cashed it at a heavy discount, bought what he could in the way of outfit, came back to a last restless night of excited dreams. Next morning they sailed.

He would never forget that morning ; the darkness draining away to leave revealed the untidy docks, the wet wharves and roofs of sheds and scummy water of the dock ; the Mates bustling about and barking orders which he tried desperately to understand and obey. He was cold, hungry, yawning and shivering, and there was a queer lump in his throat which he could not swallow away.

25

The crew came on board, reeling and singing or sleepy and bleary ; a few blowsy women turned up on the quay and shrilled down dirty jests or tearful farewells ; Roger remembered his childish dreams of chanties and swelling sails and romance. Bustle and confusion increased ; there was the Old Man talking to a whiskered, top-hatted figure who must be the Owner, there was the Mate pushing and hustling the dazed, snarling hands, there was a little Irish urchin who seemed to be the other Boy . . . The *Chester Rows* warped out into the basin, gates open, a tug backed in. As the hawsers tightened, as the wharves and waving figures slid away, Roger knew that at last his life—his real life—had begun. It seemed a queer, drab business at that hour.

The morning blurred into afternoon as the once-familiar landmarks—Seacombe, Egremont, New Brighton—passed in slow procession and were gone ; as the Rock Light passed, and Crosby, (how often had he heard those names !) and Formby Lightship. The Mates cursing and shouting, the wet decks lifting and dipping to the sea, the sea-wind cold and salty ; orders and running and oaths and hauling at heavy ropes . . . swabbing of decks, fixing of chafing-gear, a knot of men forward rigging out the long jib-boom. Point Lynas, the Skerries . . . afternoon and dusk and darkness all one nightmare of sea-sickness and misery. The sea was rising and the little tug streamed and laboured ; long before Tuskar was reached her whistle began to blow. Dimly he heard more orders shouted, saw figures aloft casting off gaskets and loosening sails, added his weight,—insignificant, ignored—to the men who were walking aft the topsail halliards,

and, through his sickness, was stirred by a sudden
burst of chantying.

> " Then up aloft the yard must go,
>   Whisky for my Johnny !
>   Whisky is the life of man,
>   Whisky Johnny ! "

Sails spreading and filling and a strange new lift
and kick and thrill of life in the planks underfoot.
Three long blasts, the hawser cast off and dragged,
heavy and dripping, in ; the little tug swinging away
and vanishing. Sails set . . . all hands mustering
aft. As the Mates picked their watches, as Roger
heard his name called, he felt a queer desperate
panic. But he was in for it now.

CHAPTER
II

IT SEEMED A LONG time now since the *Chester Rows* ;
and that Scots First Mate, and Bosun and Chips
grumbling away together in the Half-deck ; old
Kelly with his stories of the time he struck it rich in
the Australian gold-fields and drank champagne-
wine in the best hotel on Collins Street ; little Pat
Riordan with his broken teeth ; the old Swede who
read a Bible in the Dog Watch ; all the crowding and
bewildering horrors of a boy's first week at sea. The
cold, the wetness. The sickness, the crawling, drenching hours on watch. The shivering hours of half-
sleep, the taste of pork or salt junk fighting with the
taste of sea and the sour taste of vomit ; the noise, the
rack and scream of wood, rattle and squeak of gear,
howling of wind . . . the angry voices bellowing
half-comprehended orders. " Get on there, you boy,
you there ! Jump to it, I say."

He could smile now, looking back on that boy
going aloft for the first time, his body weighing a
ton as he dragged it out over the futtock shrouds ;
he could smile as he remembered the boy drinking in
the tall stories the old men told him in those quiet,
ghostly, moonlit nights of black and silver in the tropics,
and how he gaped and marvelled at the Hoogly and
the ships in Garden Reach and all the sun and dust

28

and dung and withered flowers and gentle, brown, half-mocking faces of his first foreign port.

The memories of that voyage were mixed up with memories of other voyages now ; it had taken him back to London River, and he had sailed again from there each time since. The little barque *Jane Withers* with general cargo for Jamaica ; flying fish again, and women in Kingston leaning over old green balconies, and, on the voyage home, long-faced Mr. Foster, the First Mate, watching without expression as a proud young Ordinary Seaman—promoted from the swill-cask and the pig-pen—stood his trick at the wheel. First in the light breezes on the Line, and then in the great wild Westerlies that drove the old ship home. The seas racing and towering and following, and, through the kicking wheel, the feel of the whole ship from keel to maintruck, from foot to rudder, straining and fighting as her stern lifted to the waves. It would be so easy to blunder for a second—as another vast, shining, hissing shape heaved up astern—so easy to let the bows come round a little and then the *Jane Withers* would be on her beam-ends, broached to, the seas smashing over her. Terror in the thought, then terror melting into a queer, excited, glowing confidence.

And after the *Jane Withers* was James and Pollock's *Lady Mary* running her Easting through the wild Forties, raising Cape Otway Light one morning in the darkness before dawn. Hobson's Bay and Sandridge Pier, and the stevedores with their Australian voices screwing in the greasy bales of wool ; new hands shipped in place of those who had deserted—and how were they faring now, those deserters, on the sheep-runs beyond the River Murray or in the gold camps

29

of Bendigo ?—and the *Lady Mary* sailing again for London and the January sales. The Bass Straits and the cold South Pacific and the Horn ; the long run up past the Falklands to the Line. That was when the Old Man piled on all the sail he had : stunsails, a jib-sail, a second flying jib. That was the driving and racing that Captain Morris used to talk about ; it showed why men cursed the owners who supplied all those flying kites and the skippers who used them . . . and it showed the thrill of their use. The sight and feeling of the wide-spread, open-winged giants of canvas, taut, straining, twanging and hum-ming, driving the *Mary* like a racehorse across the long hiss and bubble of the waves.

But sea-life wasn't usually like that. It was lime-juice and slush, boils and sores and nagging restless hunger. Long oily calms and endless hauling at the braces, watching the catspaws, cursing and grumbling, the days dragging away. It was the Channel in mid-winter, the cold and the sleet and the head-winds and the great black steamers looming through the darkness out of the squalls. And the end of every voyage was always just the same.

The wharf sliding nearer and the ship suddenly crowded with strangers ; agents, boarding-masters' runners, tailor's runners ; glib, shabby men with cockney voices and quick eyes. " Clean up the decks." Then the little pause, the mate giving his final word. " That will do the crew." And the crew picking up their traps and vanishing, no handshakes, no farewells, no one bothering. You had lived and sweated and shivered and cursed and yarned together for half a year or more, but now it was over. Another voyage done, and this was London. It would be just the same if it was Cardiff, or Glasgow, or even Liverpool. The pubs and the whores and the grimy eating-houses and the gin palaces and music halls, the gas lamps shining on the wet cobbles and the drift of faces passing, the crowds, the crowding strangers who cared less than nothing about another sailor home from sea.

Each time he had come ashore full of good intentions and firm resolutions. He was going to live prudently, saving his pay, studying navigation at the classes held in the Seamen's Institute. If he was going to get his ticket now or never was the time to try. A few years more and it would be too late—there would be nothing before him but what he already had. Each time he meant to make an effort, but he didn't. Somehow when it came to the point it didn't seem worth while. And when his money was gone there was nothing for it but to find a ship again.

The *Paladin* was a full-rigged ship like the *Lady Mary*, bound for Sydney with general cargo and a few passengers. Her lines were good, and she had made some fine passages in her time, but she was old now and had come down in the world ; her present owners were an obscure cheese-paring little company who sent her out under-manned, ill-provisioned and " parish rigged." For a week or two Roger cursed the fate that had brought him into this old tub ; then, like everyone else, accepted it with grumbling resignation. There were better ships after all, but there were worse ones too.

They made a slow run to the Line, and lay for days in the doldrums, sweltering in the oily calms and hot, drenching showers, the sails of other ships on the horizon changing position strangely between dusk and dawn as the great hidden currents twisted the windless surface of the sea. The South East trades were light and uncertain, with calms and sudden squalls ; there was endless making and shortening of sail, endless trimming of yards. Tempers began to fray ; the Old Man was sarcastic with the Second Mate, who came raging forward to take out his anger on the crew ; a thin little Irishman quivered and shrilled into defiance, was knocked crashing into the scuppers, kicked to his feet, again knocked down. His comrades watched under lowering eyebrows. Mick was not popular . . . and they hadn't thought the little mate had it in him . . . but one or two low voices began to suggest, later, that something ought to be done about the little swine. Accidents had happened before now, in a sudden squall maybe, on a dark night. Mick, spitting through broken teeth, kept a silence more dangerous than threats.

But after they found the Westerlies and started running down their Easting there was no more trouble of that sort, no time for it. The Old Man was determined to make up for lost days and weeks ; he kept his royals on till even the silent Mate was roused to expostulation ; he watched unmoved as sheets parted or belaying-pins snapped, and the watch, with half-admiring curses, struggled to save the wildly-flapping sails. It was the old, familiar, ever-unfamiliar blur of misery ; the drenching green seas cascading over the rail, the black hours aloft wrenching and straining at iron-hard canvas ; it was the sodden blankets, the cripping walls of the fo'castle, the flooded galley and uncooked food, the cold, the biting cold. Day after day and night after night on the drive of the great mile-long seas, past the Crozets, past Amsterdam Island, past the South Cape of Tasmania, up again

into the sun. At last, a hundred days out, Sydney
Heads in a bright soft dawn.

It was good after all to be alive that morning, to
see the sun rise over the great bay and the city shining
out of its green background, to feel the ship sliding
up through the bright water and hear the cable
thundering out as the anchor went down . . . to
stare out at the wharves and houses and shipping, and
make plans for drinks and meals and girls ashore.

Sydney with the tall clippers lying in the Cove or
crowded round the Circular Quay ; crack wool-
clippers so smart and spick and span and shining,
brass-work glittering, yards squared . . . Sydney with
the little steam-ferries bustling off to Neutral Bay or
Manly, the passengers lining the rails to wave at
another ship just in from the Old Country . . .
Sydney with the coasting-steamers, and the mail-boats,
and the Island schooners whose crews were brown
Kanaka boys. Ashore—when liberty came at last—
was the warmth and dust and rawness of a new land
again ; the busy city streets where you were conscious
of a wide world of bush and mountain. Where you
were always conscious, too, of the sea. Townsmen,
old women, pretty girls . . . tall, brown-faced farmers,
bearded men with tales of Bathurst and the gold-mines
. . . sea captains with sober eyes, drunken seamen,
apprentices cocking their caps and joking with the
shop-girls and fighting with the seedy larrikins. Food
in a Chinese eating-house on George Street, aimless
wandering and gazing, nobblers here, nips there,
gaslights and darkness blurring into a strange, distant
pageant . . . another warm room, harsh music, the
soft thick lips of a girl. That was as squalid as the
fo'castle, in its own way.

C

Most of the crew deserted. Roger thought of going with them, but didn't. They wouldn't really be any better off, he knew. A few days' freedom, a few boasting plans, an evening of drinks, a boarding-master watching and calculating . . . morning and splitting heads, empty pockets, in the fo'castle of some other ship no better than the *Paladin*. He shrugged his shoulders and stayed where he was. When the cargo was discharged they loaded ballast ; then, one sunny morning, cast off from the Quay. Behind their tug down the Harbour, past Bradley's Head, past the Middle Harbour, past the North Head to the open sea, and up the coast to Newcastle. They were to load coal there, for Callao. Well, Callao would be something new. . . .

There were more desertions in Newcastle ; many new faces in the fo'castle, new voices grumbling and quarrelling, when, after filthy days of heat and toil and coal-dust, they sailed again. Down through the Tasman Sea into the wild South Pacific, into the cold grey days and black starless nights of crashing seas and screaming winds. Flooded decks, flooded galley, aching cold and misery.

Most of the new hands were elderly, disillusioned men who had left their ships in Sydney, worked ashore, starved, broken stone on the highways, slept among the larrikins under the bushes of the Domain, and finally come back to the fo'castles which were their only homes. They were soft and underfed, and their thin clothes were not meant for the South Pacific ; the Old Man opened his Slop Chest and drove hard bargains which they accepted with bitter complaints. One or two, battered wrecks who had been " faked up " by the boarding-master, broke down completely into shaking helplessness and sickening open sores. They were not pleasant company in the narrow, airless little fo'castle.

A few were better; gay, hard young devil-may-cares; a boy from Bathurst who had run away from home to see the world; young Tommy Thompson from London whose adventures would have filled a book. With him Roger struck up a warm friendship at once. Tommy, like himself, came of a seafaring family that had seen better days; his father had been an officer in a crack Blackwaller, and if all had gone well Tommy might have gone to sea as a smart Blackwall midshipman. But things had not gone well (what had happened, Roger never learnt) and Tommy, at fourteen, had shipped as boy in a little brig trading to the Baltic. That was six years ago, and since then he had knocked about all over the world. The Baltic, the Mediterranean, a crack Aberdeen wool-clipper, finally six months as A.B. on a steamer in the Australian coasting trade.

"That was pretty good," he said. "Slap-up food, plenty of time ashore, seven quid a month and overtime. God knows why I chucked it. Tired of steam, for one thing. Wanted to sail deep again. Wanted to see the Old Country again, maybe. The good old Smoke—wait till we get there! I'll show you things about London that you never guessed."

He was a small, tough, grinning youth with freckles and reddish hair, hard as nails, always cheerful, treating the *Paladin*—and all life's up and downs— as a colossal joke. And yet, Roger found, he had some education, and somewhere in him was a deep, secret ambition such as Roger himself had once had, and lost again, until now. For Tommy, at nineteen, swore that it wasn't too late to make something of yourself.

" Other men have done it, why not you, or me ? Hell, we're both of us better now than that little Manx cat of a Second. Better than any of those snot-nosed apprentices, anyway. When this voyage is over we'll get to work and show 'em all what we can do. I know an old man over in Rotherhithe who'll be glad enough to coach us up a bit. . . ."

His jaw set aggressively. Roger felt a sudden eager surge of confidence.

" By God, Tommy, I think you're right ! We'll show 'em ! We won't rot away like this all our lives. After all, my own father. . . ."

Tommy laughed, hit him on the shoulder, swung away.

After seventy days they reached Callao and anchored in the harbour. The lighters came alongside, the dolly-winches were manned, the long, grimy toil began, hour after gritty, glaring hour, day after day. Thirst and sweat and coal-dust and burning sun . . . the yellow shore, the yellow town shimmering in the heat across the blinding water. There was a rumour that they were to go on to the Chincas to load guano, and old hands spat sourly as they described the islands, the armed guards and the convicts, the yellow, permeating dust, the stench that killed taste and smell. But then the word went round that they were going up in ballast to Frisco, to load grain. Frisco . . . well that was not so bad. More days more dollars. The Barbary Coast was worth seeing too. . . .

When the coal was discharged and the ballast taken in, they were grudgingly given a run ashore. Roger came back with a vague impression of dust, smells, painted, peeling buildings, sallow men in rags and sallow men in ornate uniforms. This time, with Tommy, he steered clear of the drinks and the women, and came back early to the ship. In the morning the rest of the crew straggled aboard, bleary-eyed, battered, with lurid tales of the dives of the Calle Puna ; the ship was made ready, topsails and topgallants set, cables hove short ; then, on the offshore breeze of evening, they put to sea.

It was a peaceful voyage, rolling light in ballast up northward through the sunny Trades. They were carrying one passenger this trip, an American who had come on board at Callao, he was said to be a rich man and to have been in Peru on some business connected with silver-mines. A big, fat, friendly-looking man who lounged about the deck, smoked cigars, watched with benevolent interest the working of the ship. The steward reported that he was generous and open-handed, popular with after guard, and, wondered what a bloke like that was doing as a passenger in an old tub like this. Roger, looking at him with an interest he couldn't quite account for, wondered too.

And then one golden evening in the second Dog Watch, Mr. Thatcher—that was his name—came down from the poop and sat beside him when he was lounging on a hatch. He made a remark about the weather, in a slow American drawl, looked up at the sails and asked a question or two, nodded thoughtfully.

" Well," he said. " She's a pretty sight, this ship of yours, with her sails set. Even if she does need a lick of paint here and there. Last time I came up

37

this way was in a dirty little steamer out of Panama. Loaded down to the guards, so crowded you could hardly find a place to sit. San Francisco in 1850 . . . we'll never see a sight like that again. Four hundred ships rotting in the harbour—crews, mates, skippers, all cleared out for the goldfields. All sure they were going to strike it rich, poor fools."

He laughed shortly. Roger glanced at him.

" Some did though, didn't they ? "

" Some did, sure."

Roger hesitated. Ventured :

" You did yourself? "

The other laughed again.

"Oh, me. Not then, son. Not that time. I made my pile fifteen years later. Washoe silver. The Comstock, that's where I was lucky. Well, we'll never see a sight like that again either. Virginia City . . . you don't know about all that ? "

Roger shook his head. The sea was bright in the sunset, the ship lifted gently, dipped gently, forging on. Murmur of sea, soft creaking timbers, swish and chafe of sheets and halliards, rattle of blocks. Against that familiar background the slow, un-English voice describing a world wild and different and strange. San Francisco of the gold-rush days, the saloons and gambling-houses, the muddy streets, the gun-men and the Vigilantes, Cora and Casey dropping from the gallows as the bells tolled for James King. Then the gold-fever waned—and beyond the Sierras Comstock silver started another boom. He described the bare, dry, tortured slopes of Sun Mountain, when the shafts went down and down under the crazy, high-perched sprawling city of wood and brick and tin. He named the famous mines—Ophir, Savage, Gould

and Currey, Choller, Yellow Jacket, Potosi ; he spoke
of the mine-owners, Stewart, Terry, Mackay, who
had been poor men, too, once. Silver, silver . . . the
mills roaring, the bullion going guarded across the
mountains to San Francisco. Gould and Currey
producing six million dollars in a year. Then the
shafts breaking into black boiling water that no pumps
on earth could handle.

" Old Washoe's not played out yet though. Whether
Sutro gets his tunnel through to drain it or not. When
you get to San Francisco you'll see what Comstock
silver has done for the city. Ralston's new bank on
Sansome and California . . . and his house out at
Belmont . . . Go down to the Stock Exchange and
watch them gambling in Comstock. Men, and women
too . . . yes, women curb-brokers, you won't see a
thing like that anywhere else in the world. Yes, son,
just wait till you see . . ."

He laughed, stretched, fell suddenly silent, and
after a minute or two got up and went away, leaving
Roger's head in a whirl. Later he tried to tell Tommy
about that conversation, but Tommy was not
interested.

After that though Mr. Thatcher often came and
talked to him. Talked of his trip to Peru, and the
silver-claims on which he had taken options, and what
he would do when he got some backing : Ralston
might be interested, he guessed. Ralston, Croker,
Stanford, Huntington, Lick . . . apparently he knew
them all. Ranching, railroads, gold-mines, silver-
mines.

Interested, flattered, a little puzzled, Roger could
have listened all day.

" At your age," said Mr. Thatcher, " I was landing

in California with two dollars in my pocket and the soles falling off my boots. My God, that seems more than twenty years ago."

Roger mumbled some answer. Again that strange, restless dissatisfaction was stirring in him.

And one evening Mr. Thatcher abruptly began to ask him questions about himself. His boyhood? How did he like this life? What was he paid? Shyly and clumsily he tried to explain that he wasn't going to spend the rest of his life before the mast, that he was going to sit for his Ticket, find a berth as Third Mate, Second Mate . . .

" What does a Second Mate get ? "

" I dunno. About six pounds a month."

" Thirty dollars. Christ, a mucker in a Comstock shaft earns that in a week."

Roger flushed.

" Some day I might——"

" Get a command of your own? Yep, you might, at that. A ship of your own and sixty or seventy dollars a month till you're too old to sail any more. And then a room in a Liverpool boarding-house and maybe a widow marrying you for what you've saved. Well—it's not everyone's life."

Roger made no reply. He felt a prickle of irritation, for which he could find no words. You couldn't just look at it that way, in terms of dollars and cents . . . And yet, that night during his watch on deck, he remembered what Mr. Thatcher had said. They were nearing San Francisco now ; the sky was overcast and there was a sharp, fresh breeze before which the *Paladin* was running under all plain sail. He remembered a thousand other nights—warm, sleepy nights when it was an agony to stay awake ; drenched, black,

icy nights when it was an agony to be alive at all.
Nights in the forties, hungry nights, wet blankets,
" All Hands," sleet and spray. The maggot-crawling
biscuits, the rancid pork, the slush. The old men with
their open sores, the foul-mouthed young bullies, the
scared boys. That was before the mast. And if you
were an officer . . . Mr. Foster on the deck of the
Jane Withers, staring out at the slushy London wharf,
another voyage over, nowhere to go, nothing to do,
till sailing-day came round again. His own father
had lived this life of toil and squalor—and when the
sea took him his widow was left to scrape and pinch
and work herself to death. " At your age I was landing in California with two dollars in my pocket . . ."
Mr. Thatcher had taken the road which led to fortune.
Palace hotels, fine horses, ranches, mines. And he
was not the only one. The smart hotels of Sydney and
Melbourne were full of men who had come ashore in
rags : it was the same in Frisco . . . Mr. Thatcher
had said as much. He knew what he was talking
about. It was all very fine for Tommy to laugh. What
in Hell did Tommy know about it, after all ?

*   *   *   *

They reached San Francisco two days later. As
they came through the Golden Gate, Roger found time
to look at the great Bay, the city sprawling over its
hills. Someone pointed out landmarks : that was
Mount Tamalpais up there to the north, that island
was Alcatraz, that was Goat Island—Yerba Buena—
there was Telegraph Hill. A great, noisy, bustling
modern city—queer to remember Mr. Thatcher's

stories of the tents and huts and mud-holes he found when he first came here, only twenty years ago. The Bay was alive with ships, clippers, barques, steamers, tugs. There was a big liner warping out of dock . . . there were crowded white ferries churning away to San Mateo or Oakland . . . there was a queer old South Sea whaler with a gilded, windowed stern, a high-cocked jibboom, little brick try-works on her deck . . . there was a graceful little schooner from the Islands, there was an English barque ready for sea.

They came to their anchorage and let go : rowing-boats came bumping around, a swarm of agents, tailors' touts, boarding-house runners, flashy, hard-eyed shouting men. Mr. Thatcher appeared, the steward behind him smirking as he carried up big valises : he must have got a good tip to make him grin like that. Mr. Thatcher, in a big overcoat and a wide, high-crowned, western-looking hat, was shaking hands with the Old Man and the Mates, cracking a last joke with the apprentices, ready to go ashore. He paused by the gangway, saw Roger, and beckoned to him.

" So long son," he said. " And good luck to you. If you do ever want to try your luck in California, come to the Occidental Hotel and ask for me."

Then he turned quickly and was gone down the ladder before Roger could reply. Tommy was standing near. He had not heard, but he had watched suspiciously. As the boat drew away he spat glumly over the side and avoided Roger's eye.

They lay for a few days at anchor, the hard blue bay and brown hills sparkling in sunshine round them or vanishing in a sudden white fog alive with smacking paddle-wheels and blaring fog-horns. The runners' boats hung round them, and one man after another slipped over the side in the darkness and disappeared towards the dives and saloons of the Barbary Coast. No one saw them again, everyone knew what would happen to them. A hocussed drink or the swing of a black-jack, another dazed Limey waking up in the fo'castle of some Yankee hell-ship bound for the far side of the world. " Poor bloody fools," said old Pete wisely. " I know where I'm well off, if they don't. Those Frisco crimps don't catch me as easy as that." Next morning he too was gone.

They were towed across to Port Costa on the Carquinez Straits. Ballast was discharged, holds cleaned and lined, hard-bitten stevedores loaded the heavy sacks of grain. Bare dusty hills behind ; the narrow blue channel through which the steamers for Stockton and Sacramento went ploughing up into Suisun Bay. Over there was Benicia, where Heenan came from, the Benicia Boy who beat Tom Sayers. You could still see his hammer in the forge, so they said. But there was no time to go and look at it now. Cargo in, hatches covered, sails bent, time to go again. A dozen new hands, ragged, dazed, blear-eyed, bundled aboard by the boarding-master, kicked forward by the mate. A last night at anchor in the Bay : they would be sailing on the tide about noon. It was only by chance that Roger found himself standing an anchor-watch just when he did.

The ship was very quiet. It was raining a little, and the lights of the shore, the riding lights of other ships were blurred through the mist. He huddled alone at the break of the poop, shivering, his collar

43

turned up against the rain. To-morrow they would
sail again. More gales, sleet, cold, furling sail off the
Horn, scraping paint and tarring rigging for grilling
hours on the Line. Hardtack, pork, slush and lime-
juice. " Sixty dollars a month till you're too old to
go to sea any more, and then . . ." Mr. Thatcher
would be asleep now, in a warm, soft bed at the
Occidental Hotel. " When I was your age I was
landing in California with two dollars . . ." Tommy
had laughed at him, but Tommy was wrong. And
what about his own futile plans, that old man in
Rotherhithe who taught navigation; was there really
anything to hope for that way ?

He stretched his chilled limbs and looked over the
side. Something was moving out there. He watched
as it came shaping itself out of the night ; a boat,
two men rowing slowly and quietly. It was no surprise
when the low voice called up to him :

" Limey ! Ahoy there, limey ! Want a trip to
the shore ? "

For a second his voice stuck in a dry throat. He
looked round in a sort of panic, his heart thudding.
Familiar shapes of hatches, deck-houses, a gleam of
white paint ; the familiar smells of galley and tar
and bilges. The feeling of masts and spars like great
living creatures, standing silent and watchful in the
darkness overhead. No sound from the cabins aft,
or from the half-deck house. No sound from the
fo'castle where the hands were sleeping off their last
wild night ashore ; where Tommy was asleep . . .
Tommy would get the odds and ends in his sea-chest.
Tommy . . . but the dim figures below him were
backing their oars, the boat was nudging gently against
the ship's side. He had enough money in his pocket

to pay them. And Mr. Thatcher would fix him up in the morning. Find him a job, a new start in the new world. It was all a dream anyhow. But here he was, swinging over the rail and dropping into the boat below.

CHAPTER

III

THE STEAMERS CAME UP the muddy San Joaquin River to Stockton, through the green swamps and narrow sloughs to a sleepy city of wooden buildings, stagnant canals and slowly-turning windmills. In the summer, with the mosquitoes and croaking frogs under the smoke of burning reed-beds in the tule-lands, the tourists would arrive in their dust-coats and sun-glasses to drive round the streets, gape at the wind-mills, admire the huge Insane Asylum which was the town's chief monument, and then go on their way to Merced and Yosemite. But in winter the town relapsed into torpor again, and the horses fretted in their stalls in Steadman's Eagle Livery Stable, while endless games of euchre and pinochle went on in the little room at the back.

Old Bill Jackson didn't care much for pinochle, he preferred to watch and spit tobacco-juice and talk of the roulette and faro of the mining camps. He was a bald, wrinkled little man, always whittling aimlessly on a piece of wood, and to Roger his talk was a dis-torted echo of a half-forgotten voice in a fo'castle telling of Ballarat and nuggets, Collins Street and champagne. Old Jackson too, by his own account, had made his pile in the gold mines and lost it again.

46

Listening to Mr. Thatcher had caused enough trouble—only a fool would want to hear any more fairy stories about mines. Sometimes instead of telling tales about his own adventures old Bill would want to ask questions, and all that dreary, humiliating story would have to come out again.

" Yes, I jumped my ship in San Francisco. Thought I knew a fellow who would help me to find a job. He'd left town though. Then I was on the beach."

Better to forget that rainy morning, and the two dapper clerks in the opulent hotel lobby, sneering at the draggled young sailor who had come blundering in. " Mr. Thatcher? He pulled out two days ago. Said he was going to New York." Water dripping off soaked clothes on to the soft carpet : blood caked on his cheek still—the boatmen had beaten him up and taken all his money—the great, unfriendly alien city swarming and rushing and roaring outside. The thought of the *Paladin* going down the Bay, the thought of Tommy . . . " Gone to New York? " " Yep. And we don't want you in here, son. Get going now. On your way."

" I guess I could have found another ship. But, I dunno, I thought I'd see what I could do ashore. It was pretty tough at first . . ."

Keep away from the crimps and doss-houses. Tramp about the streets, ask strangers for work, sleep among the hoodlums in the Sand Lots—it was like that night in the Goree Piazza again only a hundred times worse. Pick up a job here, a job there. Smashing crates in a warehouse, washing glasses in a saloon, pushing round trucks piled with stinking hides in a tannery, sleeping in flop-houses that made the old fo'castle seem like paradise. Drifting with the restless

47

world of Western labour—battered old men and hard-faced youngsters as rootless as a lot of sailors, wandering from job to job, from town to town. Irishmen spoiling for a fight, gentle little Mexicans, thin consumptives from the East, leathery old-timers like Bill. The sawmill in Oakland ; that was a good job, he'd saved some money, then got restless and drifted on. The brief, killing, sweat-blinded spell of summer heat working on an irrigation-ditch near Stockton here. Up to the knees in mud, in a cloud of mosquitoes, under the sultry summer glare. After that the big wheat-ranch up the valley, at harvest-time, when there were jobs for anyone. That was pretty good too, in its way. Burning days of heat and thirst and labour, meals wolfed at long tables by the kitchen door of the ranch-house, nights of heavy sleep in a log shed full of the smells and snores and gruntings of half a hundred men. The sun coming up over the distant mountains and another day begun.

The great black horses, twitching under their fly-nets, drove the great header through the sea of grain : blades swung and swung and lopped heads went down the apron into the wagon which followed alongside ; the big steam thresher shook and puffed and devoured, the sacks swelled and filled. Perhaps the *Paladin's* cargo had come from these very fields. Perhaps this grain would fill some British ship, go rolling round the Horn in her, up to the Line, up to Queenstown and Tuskar and Liverpool. The pilot-boats with their numbers on their sails waiting off Point Lynas. . . .

Sometimes the owner of the land would come, driving a pair of matched bays, and watch a little, and drive off again. He owned not only this ranch, but the next and the next, thirty or forty thousand

acres in all; over their pipes, in the grey, weary
twilights, men reckoned up what he must be worth.
Someone had heard that his ranches brought him in
three hundred thousand dollars a year. Now Roger
spoke of that to old Bill Jackson, who grunted and spat.

"Yeah," he admitted, "They might, at that. But
he's one of the lucky ones. And how long do you
think it took him to grab all that land? No, son,
there's only one place worth a damn, and that ain't
California. In Colorado, now. . . ."

Colorado. He was always talking about that high,
sharp-aired mountain world. Scarlet canyons, pine
trees straggling up to timber-line, and the snowy
peaks standing over all; raw new towns, roads and
railways invading the lonely valleys, mining-camps
plastered on breathless hillsides, stamps crushing the
gold-laden ore.

"Yep," said the hoarse voice. "You ought to go
there sailor. There's a real country. Why sit in this
swamp when you could be living a man's life up in
the mountains? Wait till you see it . . . But you're
ten, fifteen years too late now. Denver—hotels,
schools, theatres, concerts. Concerts! Hell, I remember a few little cabins along the creek. I remember
the time when they buried a man a day, every one
with his boots on. I saw Chivington and his boys
come back from Sand Creek after they'd wiped out
that bunch of Cheyennes. Killed five hundred of
the bastards, they did, braves, squaws, children . . .
Riding back into the town cheering and yelling and
waving the scalps they'd lifted . . . The Indians let
us alone after that."

The little man laughed, spat, went on.

"Those were the days when a poor man had a

D

49

chance. Gregory Gulch, South Park, California Gulch. One man I knew, he took out sixty thousand dollars in a single summer. Any tenderfoot could make twenty dollars a day. Placer mining, that's the only game for a poor man. Oro City in the boom days . . . boy, we'll never see a thing like that again ! That's all over now, I guess. It's all Blackhawk, Golden, Central City. Quartz-mining. Stamps, smelters, mining experts with College diplomas, Eastern capitalists running everything. No room for an old Fifty-niner like me, I hear they're even building a railroad up to Golden now."

He shook his head, sighed deeply, then brightened again.

"Just the same, there's more gold in those mountains than anyone's ever dreamed of yet ! They've only scratched the surface—some day they'll find the real thing. The real lode, the Mother Lode, that'll make all their bonanzas look like two cents. And the man that finds it won't be any Eastern expert with a string of letters after his name. It'll be some old pick-and-pan prospector—like me. Maybe it will be me. I'm thinking of going back and having another try. Or I might go up to Montana. Or up to the Black Hills—I hear there's something doing there. If it wasn't for some dam-fool treaty with the Indians . . . Yeh, that might be worth having a look at. But I got a kinda feeling I'd rather go back to Colorado. Down San Juan way maybe . . . look at here, son. . . ."

He bent forward, intent and solemn, scratching little maps with a stick in the dust. Roger watched and listened, amused, a little pitying—and yet, in spite of himself, a little stirred. These wild stories were hard to swallow—but just the same, stranger things had happened in this country, and were happening every day. Even a ragged, tobacco-spitting old man like this might, as he claimed, have seen fortune shining up through the sand and water that swirled in his pan. Might, as he dreamed, see fortune shining out again. Stranger things were happening every day.

California had seen a million miracles which the sober-minded found it hard to believe. Roger remembered Mr. Thatcher's stories—they had sounded far-fetched, on the deck of the *Paladin*, but now, day in, day out, he heard similar tales of the good old days. Dutch Flat, Grass Valley, Downieville, Sierra City, Placerville, Mormon Bar. The days when Stockton's now-sleepy streets were alive with miners, freighters, pack-trains, when the sixty miles of road to Columbia were lighted like a city street by the camp-fires of the eager multitudes. From Mexican Sonora five million dollars worth of gold came in one summer—and that was only twenty years ago.

Now the poor man's day was over in California too. There was no room for an eager boy with a pan and a pick-axe, between the great companies whose flumes straddled the mountains, whose flying jets of water ripped away whole hills, and the patient Chinamen in wide hats who washed a thimble-full of gold a week from the tailings of long-deserted mines. No chance for a tenderfoot to make his fortune here. But further east, beyond the Sierras, beyond the deserts, were those great peaks and canyons of the Rockies, those sage-covered uplands, those white buttes and bluffs above the rivers, and there were whole empires still half-known, waiting to be conquered.

51

When he could listen to old Bill Jackson no longer he would get up and wander out into the long, dim stable to be alone. He had lost his sailor's distrust of horses now, and had learnt the mysteries of feed and harness and curry-combs. In a queer way these horses reminded him of ships ; like ships they had their ups and downs, their cranky little ways, their patient willingness. He would look down the row of stalls at the restless quarters and switching tails, he would look at the long, sad faces, the soft noses dropping to the water-trough, and he would compare this beast and that with ships he had known or heard about. Old Paleface, the big, battered chestnut, had been a rich man's darling once, and was wretched and forlorn and puzzled in this ignoble, hard-worked livery-stable old age ; to look at him was to think of the once-proud *Paladin* with her lovely lines and peeling paint. And old fat Mary, plodding along the dusty streets in the shafts of an old buggy, was like the old *Jane Withers*, broad-beamed, patient, slow. Big grey Challenger with his bared teeth and rolling eye was a dangerous horse, a killer if he got the chance ; there were ships like that too, hoodoo ships, man-eaters. And then there was the big black mare, so clumsy, so ungraceful, with her big shambling feet and big square head. People shook their heads when they were offered her, but there was no horse in the stable who could go as she could, striding out, pulling, mile after mile, hour after hour. Like Baines's old *Marco Polo*, that square black ugly box of a ship whose passages startled the whole world.

Old, weary horses most of them, like ships which had seen better days. But sometimes a rich rancher would drive in and stable some crack team among them for an hour or two, while he shopped, drank, argued with his banker. Sleek, shining, well-groomed horses, twitching disdainful little ears and stamping restlessly ; lovely and trim as Blackwall frigates, as crack China clippers, as *Norman Court*, *Thermopylæ*.

The *Thermopylæ* . . . That seemed a long time ago now. Were the clippers still racing home with tea, or had the steamers, the canal at Suez, spoilt all that as people said they would ? They would be somewhere on the seas, the clippers, at any rate. Running their Easting down to Melbourne, screwing in wool, sailing again for London and the January sales. Round the Horn, up through the Trades, a good slant of wind, stunsails set aloft and alow. Queer how you forgot the cold and wet and curses, the maggots in the biscuits, the slush. . . .

There were steamers going every day down Suisun Bay and the Carquinez Straits to San Francisco and the sea-world again. He had saved some money, he could keep clear of the crimps and boarding-masters, he could wait to pick his ship carefully—an English ship, homeward bound. Homeward bound for Liverpool Town . . . Tuskar, the Skerries, Point Lynas, the Mersey. His mind filled with homesick little pictures of the river, the docks, the grey, busy streets ; with echoes of friendly Lancashire voices and clattering Lancashire clogs. But really, he knew, it wouldn't be like that at all.

When Spring came he moved on. Eastward, across the Sierras, towards the mountains he had heard so much about.

*　　　　*　　　　*　　　　*

For a time he worked in a sawmill in Truckee. The little town was full of the shrill voices of saws ; yards and streets were piled with timber, day after day the trees were felled on the mountains, came down to feed the sawmills, went on as props and timbers into the black tunnels of the mines. Up there, a few miles away, was the great bare mountain tunnelled and gashed and laden with the wild life of Virginia City ; along the river, at Carson, men were toiling and dying to drive Sutro's tunnel into its boiling black heart. At Truckee all the talk was of Ophir, Crown Point, Belcher ; of Ralston, Sutro, Fair, Mackay ; of vast bonanzas and vast swindles ; of floods and fires in shafts five hundred feet below the surface and tunnels that broke into great chambers of fantastic wealth ; above all of the battles of the giants on the stock-exchange. Everyone was gambling in mining stock ; a hundred eager voices urged him to join in. " How about it, sailor ? You'll never get rich this way. Don't you want to take a flyer ? Only this morning I got a real hot tip. . . . " But somehow nothing here caught his imagination, the odds against an outsider were too long. Towards the end of the summer he started on his wanderings again.

The tall, awkward, silent young man, sitting quietly in the long railroad car that crashed and rocked on, through darkness, sunshine, darkness, towards the East. Dust in hair, eyes, mouth, dust in the food at the little eating-houses by the line, dust and flies. Tired women with bundles and babies, wailing children, men arguing, grumbling, boasting, drinking out of bottles, sleeping open-mouthed in the swinging yellow lamplight, mumbling in the dark.

Dust and heat and shimmering mirages on the grey

sage of the deserts ; the long, barren spaces of Salt
Lake, and a ripple of interest, broad jokes about
Mormons and Brigham Young ; Ogden and a long,
dragging wait ; another train crawling on, into the
mountains, into the mountain air, across the backbone of the Continent. Evanston, Granger, Carbon,
Laramie, Cheyenne.

As a third train went rocking down by Greeley and
Evans—in Colorado now—Roger forgot for an hour
or two his weariness and uncertainty. He knew not
one soul in all this huge new land ; his savings were
nearly gone, autumn was the worst possible time to
arrive in a new place and look for work. From the
mines and ranches a thousand men would be pouring
into Denver every week . . . there were some on
this train now, loud-voiced, jingling a summer's
earnings, eager for the joys of the city as sailors home
from a six-months' voyage. He would have to compete
with them, and with hundreds like them, all more
experienced than himself. He would have to find
work—or starve.

He knew all that—but he forgot it for an hour or
two, as he stood on the little open platform of the car,
breathing the tingling, electric mountain air and looking out at the great tumbling sprawl of mountains
that filled the West. Perhaps it was that air which
gave him such confidence.

An old man came and stood beside him, a beard
whipped by the wind. He spat tobacco-juice and
shouted through the crash of wheels ; pointed out
landmarks along the way. This river was the South
Platte, that mountain was Longs Peak. He asked
Roger questions and tried to sell him mining-claims ;
then, finding himself ignored, went away again,

grumbling about stuck-up English tenderfeet. The sunset burnt away over the mountains ; rich golden light flooded bare foothills, bare plains, creek-beds and clumps of yellowing trees and little ragged farms. Then a great shadow spread out from the mountain-range and the world slipped into dusk.

In the Denver station, among the jostling strangers, in the shift of shadows and glaring lamps, Roger felt his confidence collapse as quickly as it had swelled. He picked up his case and forced his way out to the street, through a mob of brazen-voiced hotel-runners and hack-drivers ; took a few steps—and then stopped. Here he was. This was Denver. A thousand, fifteen hundred miles of plain and mountain shut him off at last from the sea. What in God's name was Jim Barton's son doing here ?

After a minute he picked up his case again and went on.

* * * *

By spring the memory of that night had faded, and the memory of the first long, hungry, money-counting week dragging round the Employment Agencies and staring at Help Wanted columns in the Rocky Mountain News. By spring he felt as if he had always lived in Mrs. Vance's boarding-house and worked in Potter's Hardware Store.

Little Joe Potter was a Yorkshireman, who had come to America thirty years ago ; at home he would have had some tiny shop like Uncle Henry's, but here his business was glittering and growing, and his son Sam, about Roger's age, was all American. They were a friendly pair, an elderly, chirpy little sparrow and a chirpy young sparrow, and Sam, who had none

of the airs and graces of the boss's son, took a fancy
to Roger and helped him a lot in his first days in this
unfamiliar world. Sam worked as hard as any, in
the warehouse, behind the counter ; he was the only
son and the business would be his one day.

Roger often wondered what Uncle Henry would have
thought of the mining-tools and wolf-traps and giant
powder which jostled the pots and pans on the shelves
of Potter's store, or of the brown-faced men in battered
Stetsons who came to buy and remained to gossip in
slow Western voices about water-rights and the price
of silver, about barbed wire and repeating rifles and
deer-shooting. They belonged to the frontier which
still made itself felt in this glittering modern Denver
of offices and theatres, street-cars and hotels ; through
their anecdotes of Shorty This and Big Bill That ran
a scarlet thread of violence and gun-play, and sooner
or later the talk would come back to the gold mines
and the silver mines. Caribou, Bobtail, Gunnel,
Pelican, Dives, Silver Plume. Famous mines and
others which would be famous, or ought to be.

"There was a fellow in from Baxter the other day.
He was telling me about McCormack's 'Redman.'
They're doing pretty well, by what he says. Putting
a ten-ton smelter down in the canyon . . . the high
grade ores smelt out round $125 a ton. . . ."

Roger, snatching a moment here and there to listen,
caught a dozen more glimpses of this new world.

". . . Ready to quit. Then they decided to try
once more. Drifted ten foot North and broke right
into a six-foot lode."

"Those telluride mines up in Boulder County are
shaping pretty well. I hear the new smelter at
Alma. . . ."

Someone throwing down on the counter a few little specimens of ore. Men picking them up, peering, fingering.

" Galena, eh ? From San Juan ? Is that so ? Looks pretty good. What does it assay ? I hear a couple of fellows have made a big gold strike down that way too."

The voices rambled on : young Sam Potter, who hadn't much time for prospectors trying to get grub-stakes, listened as impatiently as Tommy had listened to Mr. Thatcher. When they had gone he would turn to Roger and grin.

" Well brother, I saw you drinking it all in. I suppose you think it will be your turn next to go and find a silver mine."

Roger would smile and say nothing. In the evening he would go quietly home to supper, up to his books in a chilly little room. History, politics, economics, geology, mining and engineering, business management. Mrs. Vance approved of him ; she thought he was a fine, steady young man, her own sons would have been like that.

But they were killed in the Civil War, and Mrs. Vance's health broke down and they had come from peaceful Connecticut to raw Colorado, and he had died and left her to get along as best she could alone. A small, thin, white-haired woman with deep lines in her face. She liked Roger best of all her lodgers— the industrious young Scot from the flour-mill, the elderly bank-clerk, the freight-agent, and his wife, the exotic little Monsieur Duclos with the beard, who was said to have had an important position in Maximilian's Mexico—she looked after him and mothered him during the winter—grey days of blizzard, dazzling

days of sun and snow and sleigh-bells and white
mountains against blue sky—and her face fell that
day in the spring when he came back and showed
her the newspaper headlines about the gold strike
at Arastra. It was what Old Bill Jackson had always
talked about—free gold, placer-mining, the only
chance for a poor man. A thousand men were already
staking their claims and panning wealth from the
creek bed, and thousands more were pouring in, in a
stampede such as Colorado had not seen since the old
days of California Gulch. And there was grizzled
Cy Williams coming into the store—an old-timer
like Bill Jackson who knew all the ropes and was
willing enough to take along a husky young tenderfoot
who had enough money saved to buy an outfit for the
pair of them. Mrs. Vance tried to dissuade him ;
old Joe Potter tried too, and offered to raise his wages,
Sam shook his head dubiously. But Roger wouldn't
listen to any of them.

CHAPTER
IV

HE CAME BACK ONE golden afternoon of summer, about the turn of the decade. Six years was a long time, and he hesitated once or twice as he went along the once-familiar streets under the cottonwoods. The street had changed, empty lots had been built upon, there were new big houses shining in fresh paint beyond their new lawns. Probably, he told himself, Mrs. Vance would be gone and her house pulled down.

Things were changed, and he was changed too, immeasurably changed from the raw young tender-foot who found his way along this street for the first time seven years ago. He was young still—but he didn't look it, he knew : he remembered the reflection he had seen in the window of a store on Larimer Street just now. A big, tall, fleshless man with a serious face, a weather-beaten face, hard lines round his mouth and wrinkles round his eyes. A clumsy, ungainly man in the stiff new suit and stiff new shoes, the collar that chafed his neck and the big grey hat that marked his forehead. No longer a boy but a man, no longer a raw English sailor but a Coloradan, no longer a penniless adventurer but a moderately-prosperous, moderately-successful citizen. There had been a hundred men like himself on Larimer Street this afternoon : ranchers, storekeepers, editors of little country papers, country lawyers, come to the city for a day or two. Lines and wrinkles and hair a little thinner, a new suit of clothes, a suit-case checked at the depôt, two thousand dollars just deposited in a bank . . . that was what he was bringing back from those six strange years.

In those six years, he reflected, how many men had rocketed from poverty to millions? Leadville and its silver, Leadville and its millionaires. Tabor, Chaffee, Moffat, Fryer, Stevens, Riche . . . others and others, some of them men he had known, men he had worked with, men to whom he had lent money when they were broke, men who had been living on beans and bacon in the spring and were rolling East in private Palace Cars before the Fall. Two thousand and a new suit . . . it wasn't much to show for six years.

The street was changed—all Denver was changed. That was what Leadville silver had done! His footsteps faltered and he nearly turned back, but then he went on. No harm in seeing, anyhow. Old Mrs. Vance was kind and friendly, in the old days. It was almost a shock to see the little yellow house unchanged, with its picket-fence in need of paint still and the curtains very white, the windows very clean in the peeling window-frames. He rang the bell and waited . . . then the door opened. Mrs. Vance, whiter, thinner, older, staring at him with realisation slowly dawning in her eyes.

" Why it's Roger Barton! For goodness sakes where have you been all these years? Only last week I was thinking about you, and wondering why you'd never come back as you said you would! Come in, come in, and tell me what you've been doing. I was

61

beginning to think you must have got yourself shot in one of those nasty mining-camps. And where are those nuggets you were going to bring back, young man ? "

She searched him with her quick old eyes where mockery masked welcoming affection, and as he followed her into the little parlour he had a queer, wistful sense of home-coming. Nothing was changed. Could it really be six years ?

But a good many things were changed, he found, as he sat and listened to her quick, familiar voice again. She was older, much older, he saw, and her hands shook a little as his mother's hands used to shake. The furniture looked shabby, her black dress was a little rusty, the lines in her face were deep.

" No," she was saying. " They've all gone, the ones who were here in your time. That Scotchman, he got married. And old Mister Dewclo died five years ago. Remember how he used to talk about Mexico ? I suppose you're staying at the Brown Palace these days. You aren't ? Well, if you want a room . . ."

" You said you would always have a room for me."

" So you remember that, do you ? I should hope so. Yes, I've got a room for you all right. There's the little back room Mr. Dewclo had . . . I've only got two boarders now . . . Well, I can't get round the work the way I used to, and that's the truth of it. Still, I might be worse off than I am. The Johnsons —Miss Johnson helps me a lot. And her father is a real nice little man, though he has his weaknesses. Polite and well-meaning and gentlemanly, though he never knows where anything is, hardly remembers to put on his necktie. A little like Mr. Dewclo, in some ways . . . dreamy, always living in the past. They're from back East originally, but they've travelled round so much they hardly know where they are now. Hard on a girl to be brought up that way. No home, no time to make any proper friends, living in hotels and boarding-houses, looking after her father. He's an artist. Paints portraits and gives drawing-lessons and that—it's all they've got to live on, as far as I know. I'll show you some of his paintings by and by. Lovely paintings—well, anyway, you have to tell him so, poor man." She laughed quietly, and broke off, at the sound of the front door opening. " I believe that's Mary now. She just ran down to the store for me."

The old woman got up and went out of the room : Roger stood by the window, looking out. The sunshine flooded the bare, burnt strip of grass and the ugly wooden house next door, poured in at the window, poured across the worn carpet, touched the ugly chairs and little tables, gleamed on ugly china ornaments. The door had closed behind Mrs. Vance, and he heard voices in the hall ; idly he wondered if it was as a tribute to his new suit that she had brought him into her little-used front parlour. There was the gilt and marble clock which had been a presentation to Mr. Vance when they left their home town in Connecticut to come West. There was that picture (how well he remembered all these things !) of ladies in eighteenth-century costume sewing the first American flag. He turned to look at the picture more closely, and then swung round suddenly as the door opened again and Mrs. Vance ushered in a girl. A girl, or rather a young woman, twenty-one or twenty-two he thought, with a pale, thin, serious face and dark hair. As she came

towards him, urged forward on the old woman's
explanations and introductions, he felt a sudden
burning shyness, felt large, clumsy, awkward, wished
to God that she had stayed away. It had been pleasant
enough, gossiping with Mrs. Vance. But this young
woman was another matter. Their hands touched,
he mumbled a greeting. He blundered backwards
again. Old Mrs. Vance watched, amusement snapping
in her eyes.

Somehow they were sitting down, Mrs. Vance was
talking . . . Mrs. Vance was asking him questions.
Where had he been? What had he been doing all
this time? Mary Johnson sat very quietly in a corner,
looking down at the carpet : he found his voice again
and tried to answer the quick incisive demands. That
first gold-camp, Arastra. Yes. Yes, it petered out
pretty quickly. No, we didn't strike it rich there.
Old Cy Williams guessed wrong to start with.

" I didn't know the difference then, of course. I've
learnt a few things since then."

He stopped. There it all was, but you couldn't
describe it. The wagons and four-horse stages jammed
in the streets of roaring boom-towns, the lonely mining-
camps sunk in canyons, the pack-trains creeping along
the cliffs like ants along a wall. Patient men washing
the sand by forgotten creeks ; hammer testing the
rock and water swirling in the pan. Buckets going
down black, dripping shafts, roar of machine-drills
and reek of shot-firing, thud of stamps and rattle of
crushers, hot blast of furnaces. Yes, there had been a
lot to learn before a raw young sailor knew his way
about the West.

Silver Cliff and Rosita, Lake City and Silverton,
Del Norte and the Rio Grande, back to Leadville

. . . just too late. That was something again you couldn't describe. The new, sprawling, swarming town filling the valley, thrusting up the gulches, lapping over the hills. The hills riddled with shafts, smeared with dumps, bristling with chimneys, restless with flames and smoke and jets of steam. Sunset fading over the great mountains above, and the lights blazing out along Chestnut Street and Harrison Street. The shouting of the barkers and the clamour of steam-pianos and the swirl of the crowds through the dance-halls and saloons.

Mrs. Vance asked a question, and he hesitated, made a little gesture, before answering.

" No," he said. " I didn't strike it rich. I got on to one or two pretty good things—a claim on Fryer Hill for instance—only there was a lawsuit and I hadn't the money to fight. No, Mrs. Vance, I'm no Tabor I'm afraid. Still, I came out richer than I went in, this time. And after all, it's all experience."

" And now I suppose you're going to go back and try again ? "

" I don't know. Maybe I'll try some other district. I'm going to think things over."

He looked at his watch, and stood up.

" If you'll excuse me, I'll go down to the depôt and get my bag. But I'll be back for supper."

He paused a little uncertainly, wanting to add something more. Something to show how glad he was of the welcome she had given him, this little feeling of home-coming. He fumbled for a phrase but could find none, and yet Mrs. Vance seemed to understand. Her face softened for an instant, and then wrinkled formidably again.

" All right. But you'll have to hurry. You'll get

E

your supper if you come back in time. And no supper if you're late ! "

She laughed, flapped her hands at him, shooed him out of the room. He just had time to jerk an awkward little bow at Miss Johnson, and to receive a polite, self-possessed little smile.

Her father was at supper too. Roger, having heard that Mr. Johnson was an artist, had expected vaguely a big, jovial, eccentric man with a flowing cloak : he had never seen an artist, but imagined they were all like that. It was a surprise to find this shabby, mousey little creature with darting eyes and a ragged Vandyke beard, a restless little creature tittering and chattering nervously all through the meal. The others were rather silent ; Mrs. Vance, between visits to the kitchen, watched her guests with a sort of ironic amusement. Miss Johnson listened to her father a little impatiently.

He gobbled his food and fired questions at Roger in a high, squeaky, cultured voice : what about Leadville, what about all those shooting-scrapes and lynchings, what about the new millionaires ?

" I have met some of them myself," he declared. " You mightn't think so, but I have. When they ' make their piles ' the first thing they think of is to have themselves immortalised on canvas. Oh yes, I have painted the portraits of several silver-kings. Fine subjects too, some of them, though not easy to satisfy. They have their own ideas as to what constitutes a good likeness."

He gobbled a mouthful of pie, gulped his coffee, chattered on.

" And now, of course, their wives and daughters must be immortalised too. And the daughters must

66

learn Art. Learn to sketch, to dabble in water-colours like any young lady of culture. I have a little sketching-class—we go out on the prairies for all the world as if we were on the Roman Campagna. They must also learn to play the piano. To strum elegantly on the piano. That I cannot teach them, alas ; that is my daughter's province, is it not, my dear ? "

Roger glanced across the table.

" You give piano lessons ? "

" A few."

" Mary is an excellent teacher. An excellent pianist. She has, I am told a fine Touch . . . like her dear Mother. I remember when we lived in New York there was a Hungarian pianist in the same establishment . . ."

The little beard wagged, the story rambled on. Mrs. Vance looked a little sardonic.

" . . . And again in California . . . You know California, I believe. We met a number of your fellow-countrymen—or ex-fellow-countrymen should I say ?—out there. I remember Lord and Lady . . . Delightful people, cultured, travelled. They were enthusiastic about Mary's talent. And also were kind enough to approve of my own efforts in my own field of art. They had been up in the Yosemite Valley —I showed them some sketches I had made up there. You can imagine the sort of thing, the Bridal Veil, el Capitan . . . They were most appreciative. Insisted on buying them, to take back to their ancestral home in Kent. Though I am afraid that beside their Constables and Turners . . ."

He made a deprecating gesture. Roger, bewildered, mumbled some reply. The high voice stuttered on at him, and he pretended to listen. Miss Johnson, he

67

realised, wasn't listening at all. She was looking at him, in a queer, searching, appraising way, and when she felt that he was aware of her watching she blushed a little and turned to speak to Mrs. Vance.

*　　　*　　　*　　　*

After supper, while Mrs. Vance and Mary Johnson were washing up, Roger and Mr. Johnson sat in the little arbour at the end of the backyard. It had been a pleasant place at one time, but now it was overgrown and untidy, its wooden seat half broken and the creeper untrimmed. But the cool soft twilight was agreeable, and the feeling of the whole tree-shaded neighbourhood relaxing in the dusk. Families settling themselves in rocking-chairs on porches, young men and girls murmuring and giggling together on the steps, children playing on little lawns. The water was tinkling in the irrigation-ditches along the street ; there was a smell of wet dust, wet grass, damp and coolness : the sky was still bright, though sun and shadows had already gone.

Mr. Johnson chattered on for a few minutes, and then quite suddenly fell silent, got up without a word and went off towards the house again. He looked frail and small and down-at-heel as he stumped up the path towards the door : Roger watched him go, and wondered what secret of failure and disappointment lay behind those nervous moods of garrulity and gloom. His daughter must have had a strange childhood—a strange life for her, this. No wonder she was quiet and anxious and thoughtful. The little white teeth nervously biting her lip . . .

She was still quiet when she came out with Mrs.

Vance later, to sit and rest a little in the twilight, the washing-up done. Her father had gone out, she said : she spoke flatly and casually, but Mrs. Vance's eyes narrowed at the words. They were silent for a time ; then Mrs. Vance asked him some questions about Mr. Potter, and he answered.

" Old Mr. Potter is dead now. Sam's got the store. Married and doing well. The old man was always very good to me when I worked for him. I suppose partly because he came from England too. And from the North—Yorkshire, it was."

Mary Johnson looked up.

" Yorkshire. York. There's a Cathedral there, isn't there, that's very wonderful. My father has told me about it. My, but I'd like to go to England ! "

" You've never been ? "

" No. We were always going. But we never went."

" You have travelled a lot in America, though."

" On yes. First thing I remember, we lived in Connecticut. " Father taught drawing in a school in Hartford. Mother was dead by then—I hardly remember her."

Her voice checked for a moment, then went on with a sudden confiding quickness. Roger saw Mrs. Vance look across sharply, as if surprised.

" I liked Hartford. You've never been there of course, Mr. Barton. When we had to—when we left there and went to New York, I hated it. Noisy, dirty, ugly . . . But we didn't stay there long. We went to Chicago. When we got there it was still just a heap of ruins after the fire. No one had any time for drawing-lessons then. So we went on out to California. San Francisco—that's a nice place, you've been there, haven't you ? Did you see the sea-lions out at the

Cliff House? One summer we were up at Calistoga, another we were at Merced. That's when father was painting those pictures up in the Yosemite. Then we came back, here. I wonder sometimes where we'll go next."

" You won't go anywhere," Mrs. Vance's voice made them jump. " You'll stay right here and settle down."

" I wonder. I'd like to . . . Though I'd like to see more of the world too. England—and Europe. Paris. Rome. Maybe Greece and Egypt and the East. India."

She ended with a breathless little laugh. Mrs. Vance laughed too.

" You are a restless young lady. Well, if you're interested in India, here is someone who can tell you about it. Didn't you go there once, when you were a sailor ? "

She shot the question at Roger, and Mary Johnson stared at him quickly.

" You were a *sailor*, Mr. Barton ? I didn't know that ! Tell me about it."

Roger laughed uneasily.

" Not much to tell. Yes, I was a sailor of sorts, once upon a time. My father was a real sailor though, Chief Mate of one of the crack Liverpool emigrant-clippers. I grew up in Liverpool . . . except for a few years in Bolton. When I was old enough I ran away and shipped as a kind of cabin-boy in an old barque bound for India. Calcutta—I don't remember that anything very exciting happened while we were there. After that I made three more long voyages. One to the West Indies, two to Australia. Finally I swallowed the anchor in San Francisco."

" You what ? "

" Came ashore for good. Gave up seafaring. I wasn't in 'Frisco long. Then I got a job in Stockton. You must have gone through Stockton on your way to Merced, didn't you ? "

" Yes . . . I think so. But why did you give up the sea ? "

" I don't know. It's not much of a life, before the mast. I wasn't getting anywhere. I wanted to try my luck ashore. A passenger had filled me up with stories about Washoe and the Comstock bonanza-kings. I was going to be another Ralston."

Mrs. Vance chuckled drily.

" Perhaps you will be yet, young man. Another Tabor, anyway."

Mary Johnson was staring at him through the dusk, her brows puckered in concentration. Abruptly, she demanded.

" Are you ever sorry you gave up the sea ? "

He hesitated.

" Sorry ? No . . . No. Not really."

" I wonder. The way you said it . . . I think I should be, in your place. You were in sailing-ships of course. I remember on the way to Calistoga, going over on the ferry from San Francisco to Vallejos, we used to pass big sailing-ships at anchor, or being towed out by tugs. Men scrambling about up in the rigging—sometimes you'd hear them singing. You'd see the ship getting smaller, going out through the Golden Gate . . ."

She made a little gesture. Roger looked away, down the weed-grown little yard, at the old house blurring in the twilight. The soft mountain twilight . . . funny how you suddenly felt those thousands of miles of mountains and deserts between you and the sea.

" What are those songs they sing ? "

" The chanties ? Oh, all sorts. They don't sing them as much as they used to. But they still do, when it's the right sort of ship and crew. ' Reuben Ranzo ' and ' Whisky Johnny ' and ' Stormalong.' ' Stormalong ' is supposed to be about old John Willis—he was a great clipper-captain in his day. His son is a famous ship-owner. Or was ten years ago, I don't know about him now. Yes, there are all sorts of chanties. Capstan-chanties, topsail-chanties . . . chanties you sing when you're homeward bound . . ."

He stopped suddenly. The hazy sunshine on San Pablo Bay, and the crash of voices as the muddy chain came clanking in.

> " We're homeward bound for Liverpool Town.
>   Good-bye, fare-ye-well,
>   Good-bye, fare-ye-well . . ."

For a moment he almost thought that someone was singing it now, somewhere near. Mary Johnson was looking at him through the shadows. He could see, indistinctly, the little white face, grave and thoughtful. She gave a tiny nod.

There was a pause : he moved uneasily : he didn't want to be asked more questions about ships and seafaring. He wondered why not, wondered why it was such a relief when Mrs. Vance's dry voice said :

" So you came to Colorado to make your fortune."

" That's right, mam."

" And when you make it "—Mary Johnson's voice was still grave and questioning—" what will you do ? "

to the old yellow house and the arbour where Mrs. Vance and Mary Johnson were still sitting quietly in the dusk.

They sat and talked there most evenings ; once or twice little Mr. Johnson joined them, chirping away about pictures and Italy and Michelangelo, falling suddenly into glum, nail-biting silence. An infuriating little man, yet a pathetic little man too, with his ragged beard and his stained fingers. Roger could not understand the cause of those stains at first ; only later did he learn, from Mrs. Vance, that besides his portraits and his sketching-classes Mr. Johnson was assistant to a photographer.

" That is what they really live on, I guess," she said. " Those portraits he paints—well, he's only done two, and I don't know that he was ever paid for them. And the sketching-class doesn't amount to much. He earns something in Hermann's Photographic Studio. And he has other jobs too. Teaches hand-writing—calligraphy he calls it—writes cards and tickets to go in the windows of stores, I don't know what all. But of course he won't tell you about that. He's ashamed of doing that kind of work, he had to think of himself as a real artist and nothing else. Poor little man, there's some good in him, if it wasn't for his failings."

Roger agreed absent-mindedly. He was sorry for little Mr. Johnson—but he was sorrier still for his daughter, that quiet, worried girl with her big eyes and determined little mouth. He had never known a young woman of her kind before, and he was still shy and blundering in her company. Yet more and more often, as the days went by, he found himself at unexpected moments thinking about her, hearing

75

her voice, seeing her face as he had seen it that first afternoon in the dusty sunlight, that first evening in the dusk.

There were many other evenings talking in the dusk, under Mrs. Vance's friendly, observing eyes. Evenings when Mr. Johnson was there and Mary sat quietly in the background ; evenings when he was out, and she suddenly found her voice again. It was not so hard to talk to her after all, and to answer the questions. Questions about Liverpool and London, about Calcutta, Jamaica, Melbourne, the Equator or the Saragossa Sea. Odd, he noticed, how she never asked him about his adventures in the mining-camps and mountains, how she changed the subject when he spoke of Arastra or Boulder or Leadville. It was the same, what was more, if Mrs. Vance spoke, as she sometimes did now, of the Connecticut from which they had both come. Mary would answer vaguely : " Yes, I suppose so. Yes. Is that so ? Oh, I hardly remember. I don't know . . . " All her interest was for distant countries and great cities which she had never seen. That was pathetic too, he thought. It was unlikely that she would ever know the London, Paris, Rome she dreamed about.

In the mornings, now and then, some gawky girl would arrive with a bag of music, and Mary would give her a lesson on the tuneless old piano in the parlour, scales and scales monotonously, patiently ringing through the warm summer-morning sun. Whether Mary Johnson played well or badly Roger could not tell, but once or twice her father made her play and sing for them in the evening, and he would sit and listen to her voice and watch her hands on the keys. She would sing the homely songs Mrs. Vance

76

asked for : " Swanee River " and " Lorena " and
" Home Sweet Home," she would sing the Italian
or German songs demanded by her father, songs
which she had learnt for him in a dozen dusty American
cities, and sung before strangers in a dozen boarding-
house sitting-rooms.

His time here was nearly over ; soon he would have
to go again. Back to the mountains . . . the little
narrow-gauge trains, the crowded stages, the ugly
wooden settlements sprawled beside rushing rivers,
the false-fronted wooden houses, the log cabins, the
saloons. Back to the shafts and the dumps of broken
rock, back to the mud and the empty tin cans, and the
flies. Back to the faro-tables and the mechanical
pianos and the fat, hard-faced girls with scent and
fuzzy hair.

Listening to that thin, clear voice, watching lips
and throat and hands on keys, he realised suddenly
how much he had been missing all these years. It
would be hard, this time, to go away.

Only a few days more now. She finished her song
and sat back ; then eyes met across the piano, and
suddenly he realised that she was thinking of that too.

CHAPTER
V

THE TRAIN CAME CLANKING down all the afternoon
from the high pass in the mountains, down the echoing
canyons and across the flats of rock and sage-brush,
down to the wide valley where the Curicanti River
swirled round the white and scarlet bluffs and tugged
at the willows along its empty banks.

It was all very familiar to Roger Barton, as he
travelled back that summer day in 1896. While
the dry, glittering landscape crawled past, he sat in
the smoker with big men like himself in Stetson hats
and ill-fitting suits, with dapper little salesmen and
tourists from the East. He puffed at a cheap cigar
and listened to arguments about the Party Conventions
and the Crime of '73 ; then the talk came back to
Cripple Creek again, and he threw away his cigar-end
and joined in. He'd just been up there, God Almighty
there'd never been anything like it, and hardly
started yet. God only knew how deep the veins went
down.

"Yes, I go there pretty often. Got a half-share in
one mine, the Horsefly, that ought to turn out pretty
well. Have to leave it to my partner, Jim Brady,
most of the time though. Of course in the mining
game you can never tell. . . ."

No, they agreed, you could never tell. They spat

and nodded and embarked on rambling stories of fantastic disappointments and breath-taking strokes of luck. Roger listened and capped their stories with others : stories of the old days, of Rosita, San Juan, Leadville.

"Yes, sir," he said, "I remember when Leadville was just half a dozen cabins, a few second-rate gold placers, all that was left of the old California Gulch boom. Haw Tabor kept a little store at Oro. They were all cursing a lot of heavy rock and sand that choked their riffles when they tried to wash the gold. I wish I'd been the man who thought of getting that stuff assayed . . . . Oh, well, there it is. When I got married I pretty well gave up mining. I own a hardware store in Curicanti, got three kids, pretty well settled down. Only of course I couldn't keep out of a bonanza like Cripple Creek."

"When I got married." That seemed a long time ago too. Mrs. Vance's house in Denver, and little Mr. Johnson talking about art, and Mary playing the piano and showing him all he was missing among the flies and dust of the mining-camps. He hadn't wanted to come away . . . and he'd kept thinking of her all that winter while he drifted round the Western Slope. And when he came back in the spring, he'd found that her father was dead, and she was as lonely as he was, and she'd been ready enough to listen to all his hopes and plans. He hadn't actually promised her the sunrise on the Alps and the gondola in Venice—or had he ? He'd stammered something about Curicanti, silver-mines, another Leadville some day with himself a second Tabor, another Denver, the Denver of the Western Slope. They were married in Mrs. Vance's parlour ; Sam Potter was his best man, and drove them

79

to the train in his Morgan Surrey, and they had come hopefully across the mountains to their new home. That must be fourteen years ago. He didn't feel so hopeful now, in spite of his half-share in the mine at Cripple Creek.

Around him the slow, yarning, arguing voices droned on. Glaring white rock threw back the screech of wheels and clash of couplings, wooden trestles rumbled, brakes protested on the curves. After a moment he brushed away his thoughts and plunged back into the conversation.

"Yes. Cripple Creek is the place all right. I remember Stratton when he was hammering nails and sawing wood in a carpenter's shop in Colorado Springs."

*　　　*　　　*　　　*

They arrived in the late afternoon, as the shadows were beginning to lengthen. On the bare wooden platform he greeted a few friends ; the ticket-agent in his shirt-sleeves, one or two loungers who had come down to watch Number Four pull in ; he heard the latest news of Curicanti and gave the latest news of Cripple Creek. Then he started up towards the town. It was all curiously quiet and empty after the great city and the booming gold-camp. The little depot, round-house, stock-pens, high-perched scarlet water-tank ; the dirt roads and grey bare lots and wide-spaced wooden shanties ; the little fire-station with its wooden tower ; then Main Street wide and formless, with false-fronted wooden stores or buildings of ugly brick. Dusty buggies and buck-boards, horses tied to hitching-rails . . . men in shirt-sleeves lounging outside their doors. Mr. Klein, the banker, locking

up his square brick bank ; Fred Bishop outside his
big grocery store, talking to Noble who had the ranch
up Aspen Creek, Doctor Whitman driving past in
his buggy, a group of drummers tilting back their
chairs and swapping stories in the window of the
Golden West Hotel.

There were no customers in Barton's Hardware
Store ; little Henry Miggs, who had not expected him
back till to-morrow, came forward tugging nervously
at his moustache to greet his employer and give an
account of his stewardship. He was accustomed to
being left in charge for weeks at a time ; as usual there
was no very good news to tell. Roger listened to his
glib, fluent explanations, poked round the dusty little
office and told himself that he must really check-up
more carefully on the books this time. He looked at
the new consignment of saws and hammers that
had come, and at the sample of some new stove-polish
that a drummer had left for him to see ; he heard
about the mix-up there had been over those rolls
of chicken-wire for Mr. Noble, and how young Cassidy
had come in and paid ten dollars of the forty-two he
owed. He looked round the untidy shelves and thought
of the great glittering aisles of Sam Potter's new building in Denver . . . then he grunted and went on.
Along Main Street again and down Western Avenue,
down the dusty little street fringed with cotton-woods,
its little wooden houses standing back in weedy lawns.
People sitting in rocking-chairs on porches waved to
him as he went by ; children looked up from their
games beside the irrigation-ditches ; his shadow
followed him, long in the setting sun. On all sides,
near or far away, there were the mountains glowing
gold and red.

His house was at the straggling edge of the town, where the street trailed off into a willow-fringed track which wound down towards the river. It was a big, scrubby-looking, rambling house of wood, with peeling paint and sagging porches, its yard a jungle of weeds, a few dejected-looking hens picking about under dejected-looking apple-trees. Behind was a jumble of sheds and outhouses, and on one side a paddock where two big rangy horses switched the flies. He went up to the gate and stood there, looking at Ute and Comanche and thinking of Sam Potter's new blacks that he had seen two days ago. They were he real thing . . . he sighed a little, feeling uddenly dejected and depressed. No one was about—they didn't expect him back till to-morrow. He ought to go in and find Mary. But he made no move.

Comanche came across and nuzzled at him over the gate : a long, ugly face, a soft nose thrusting at his arm. He stroked that nose absent-mindedly, still thinking of Sam Potter and his blue-ribbon thoroughbreds, thinking of the busy streets of Denver and Colorado Springs, thinking of those mines at Cripple Creek. If the Horse-fly came to anything . . . they'd got their shaft down nearly a hundred feet now, ought to find the real lode soon . . . If they did strike it rich . . . But the golden dreams seemed futile to-night ; it was an effort to be hopeful and to imagine what might be. It was very quiet here, in the sunset. . . .

Comanche jerked up his head and looked round ; a child's voice was calling shrilly, out behind the house. Alice, he thought. Alice was too old to go round making a noise like that. She must be twelve now.

The little boy, who had died after two days, would be nearly fourteen. Alice twelve. Jim ten. Little Harold—what—eight and a half? Nine?

As he tried to remember, the children suddenly appeared. A big, dark, noisy tom-boy of a girl, a big, untidy, freckled boy, a small, gentle, timid boy. Alice, Jim, Harold. They saw him and whooped and came running towards him, he kissed them rather awkwardly. A babble of exclamations, questions, news.

"We didn't expect you back till to-morrow. How's Denver, papa? And Colorado Springs? How's Cripple Creek? Have you got any nuggets to show us this time? Have there been any more strikes there? Any gun-fights? Did you bring us anything from the city? Was Number Four on time?"

"Yes, I brought you something. But you don't deserve it. Jim, what do you mean by letting the yard get in that state? I told you to clean it up, before I went away. Where's your mother?"

"She's in the kitchen. She's all right. We had a thunderstorm yesterday—gee, you ought to have seen the lightning! Harold was so scared he went and hid under the bed. . . ."

Harold had been hovering, timid and excited, in the background. As they turned on him he flushed scarlet.

"I did not either! I was just looking for . . . for something I'd lost."

"Oh, you little liar! You did too! Didn't he, Jim? He went and hid. . . ."

With a gesture Roger cut short their babble. He let Jim take his bag, he followed towards the house.

Alice still chattering beside him, Harold shyly dragging along a little way behind. Harold, small, quiet, deprecating . . . the poor little brat, he thought ; those two certainly do ride him pretty hard. Still, they stick up for him when the other kids round about come and try to pick on him. He takes after Mary's father in some ways. . . .

He went up the steps, across the front porch, through the house into the kitchen. Mary was bending over the stove. She swung round and looked at him.

"Well," she said. "So you got back to-day after all. We didn't expect you till to-morrow. And I didn't really expect to see you then."

Mary looked old . . . a middle-aged woman. Even her voice had changed, had a harsher, Western ring and turn of speech. The sight of her, pale and hot and untidy, gave him a little shock. All day he had been thinking of her as she was that afternoon fifteen years ago, when they first came here. She was still in the thirties—but she looked much more : forty, forty-five . . . thin, faded, her face lined and her eyes hard. That voice was hard and tired and bitter too.

He smiled at her and tried to make her smile, but she swung back to her oven again, and he was left talking to a thin, bent back. Yes, he'd got back a day sooner than he expected. Saw Sam Potter in Denver. Sam sent his regards.

"What were you doing in Denver ? I thought you went through Colorado Springs to get to Cripple Creek ? "

"Oh, I just ran up there to look at the old place again. It's changed a lot since we first knew it. Well, that's a good long time. How long is it since we heard of Mrs. Vance's death ? "

Mary didn't answer. He hesitated and added casually :

" I wanted to see old Sam, too."

" Why ? "

" Well, I had a little business proposition to put up to him."

She looked round sharply.

" Wanted him to put some money in that wild-cat mine of yours ? "

" Nothing wild-cat about anything in Cripple Creek. The Horse-fly is going to be a real world-beater. If we had a bit more capital. . . . "

" Did Mr. Potter think so too ? "

Roger moved uneasily.

" Oh, well, Sam was hit pretty hard in the Panic three years ago. He hadn't any capital to spare just now."

" So you'll have to close down the mine ? "

" Oh, no. Not yet, by a long chalk. We'll keep going. Brady agrees with me. . . . "

Mary had turned away again. Her back and shoulders stiffened. There was a long, uncomfortable silence.

He got up from the chair where he had been sitting.

" Well, I'll go and unpack my bag. The old train was as dirty as ever. Do you remember the first time you came over the Pass, Mary, how your nose bled with the altitude ? There was a woman whose nose was bleeding to-day."

Still no answer. He went slowly out of the room. In the hall he stopped and looked about. The place did look pretty tumble-down. An old, shabby house

85

like Mrs. Vance's. And Mary, thin and overworked, taking in boarders when she could get them, like Mrs. Vance. And himself, thin, stooped, middle-aged now, in this shiny, best, city-going suit. Things hadn't panned out just the way he had expected. He felt very tired to-night.

At supper, in spite of all his good intentions, the conversation came back to Cripple Creek again. Jim and Alice listening eagerly while they gulped and munched ; Harold watching his mother as she banged between table and stove, himself for the hundredth time talking gold.

" Gosh, Mary, it's the sort of thing we used to dream about when I was a prospector. It's like a great network of gold-ore coming up through the granite and porphyry where some volcano erupted in pre-historic times. Thirty thousand people there now, twelve hundred incorporated mining companies—a town, half-a-dozen towns sprung up round Bob Womack's cow pasture ! They reckon Stratton is getting a hundred and fifty thousand a month out of his Independence, without trying to work it to capacity. The Woods are going great guns at Victor. You heard how they found a rich vein of gold when they were digging the foundations for their new hotel, and turned it into a mine instead ? The total output of the area must be getting on towards a million dollars a month now . . . and they've hardly started yet ! "

He paused, and then, encouraged by Jim and Alice, went on. Suddenly eager and excited as he talked. Mary listened with pursed-up lips, but he didn't notice her. Gold, gold, Cripple Creek gold.

86

Gold found in that wide valley behind Pike's Peak ; found in a pasture beside a creek named after a lame cow. A crazy rancher who insisted on digging, and went on though everybody laughed at him, and started something that would change the whole history of Colorado—just when the silver mines had failed her, and the dazzling Tabor had found himself a beggar, all his mansions and his Opera Houses sold to meet his debts. The town growing. The shafts sunk, the railways coming ; the hotels, saloons, dance-halls, prize-fights of a roaring boom town eleven thousand feet above the sea. Breath-taking fortunes, wild strokes of chance. Winfield Scott Stratton, the dour, eccentric carpenter, going up on a twenty-dollar grub-stake, led by a dream to the great lode on Battle Mountain one Independence Day. Two Irish work-men, measuring out a tiny claim with a clothes-line, digging a shaft in secret, in the floor of their cabin, scooping out ore that ran thirty ounces, six hundred dollars to the ton. The city druggist spinning out a hat, digging where it landed, opening the great Pharmacist mine.

"Yes, things look better every time I go there. One carload of ore from the Portland was worth $50,000 ! Colorado would be in a bad way these days if it wasn't for Cripple Creek. And when the other two railroads get there——"

Mary looked up suddenly.

"I seem to remember you talking that way about Curicanti once upon a time."

"Curicanti—well. There are still rich mines round here. Only it's low-grade silver ore that doesn't pay the cost of smelting with silver the price it is. Since the repeal of the Sherman Act . . . . I've told

87

you a hundred times . . . Even so, if I hadn't given up mining. . . ."

"Given up mining! How many weeks of the year do you still waste up in the mountains? How much good money have you sunk in wild-cat mines all over the State? How many worthless prospectors have you grub-staked?"

Her voice was sharp as splintered glass. He tried to laugh.

"Never mind, Mary. After the Election this Fall, after we stop Wall Street from trying to run the country——"

"After this, after that! After Curicanti does become the Denver of the Western Slope, the way it started out to be! My goodness, the way you used to talk, the plans you used to make . . . I almost believed it myself, one time!"

She got up and began to gather together the dirty plates. Her face was turned away from him, but her back was still and angry. He saw Harold slip from his chair and go to her side.

*　　　*　　　*　　　*

That summer he spent even less time in the store. There was not much business—the rival Hardware Company, opened three years ago by a nephew of Fred Bishop, took most of what trade there was— and Henry Miggs could handle things all right. It was a relief to leave it to him and come home to potter round the house or sit in the little office and write letters to acquaintances in Denver or Pueblo who might be willing to put some money into the Horse-fly mine. The shaft was down a hundred and thirty

88

feet, and indications were promising. But sinking
shafts was an expensive business, and old Brady was
getting worried and wanted to sell out to an Eastern
syndicate. Only the price they offered would hardly
cover what had been sunk in the thing already. If
they could just go down a little deeper . . . one day
the luck would turn. He couldn't discuss it with
Mary ; she wouldn't listen, she would flush and flounce
away. Jim and Alice were too young to understand
the business end of mining, though they were wildly
interested in gold and silver, as they were in ranches,
trapping, cow-punching, all the life of the West.
They knew the stories of the mining-camps, the saloons,
the gun-play, the unexpected strikes—the shot deer
falling across an outcrop of rich ore, a tethered horse
pulling up a bush and uncovering a pocket of nuggets,
the lost mines waiting to be found again ; they knew
about California and the Fifty-niners in Colorado and
Custer's death on the Little Big Horn in Montana to
guard the gold-fields of the Black Hills. He would
talk to them sometimes about his own adventures
at Boulder or Leadville, and show them how to pan
the gravel, or build sluices and rockers, and describe
how the mercury picks up the gold and is vaporised
away again when its job is done ; he would read them
little articles about methods of stamping and smelting,
and speculate about the new cyanide process which
had been developed in South Africa, and which might
transform the whole gold-mining industry. Then
he would bring out the specimens of ore that he kept
in a cupboard in his dusty little office. Here,
Jim, take a look at this. That glittering stuff is
nothing—just pyrites. But this is gold—from Cripple
Creek.

" And this is silver-bearing galena. Lead ore of silver—it's from San Juan. Good stuff, but you have to roast it and smelt it. Leadville carbonates don't need roasting ; nature did that for us, hundreds of thousands of years ago. And the chlorides of silver, like they found at Silver Cliff, don't even need smelting. You can just crush them and amalgamate, like free-milling gold. This is tellurium—gold and silver both. Here's another carbonate. . . . "

The little jagged lumps of ore glittering on the table, and the faces bent over them, the thin brown fingers handling them. Alice with her hair falling forward round her sunburnt tomboy face, Jim winding his scuffed boots round the chair-legs ; both intent, fascinated. It was he himself, this summer, who would suddenly lose interest and throw the samples back in the cupboard. Somehow they didn't seem to matter. Nothing seemed right these days, somehow.

That trip to Cripple Creek and Denver seemed to have sharpened his perceptions, so that he saw himself and Curicanti and above all Mary with a new clarity. Mary and her neighbours . . . the shrewd, hard-faced women with shrill voices, the kind, eager, helpful women, enemies, friends. Arguing and gossip-ing and tale-bearing, exchanging recipes for preserves and advice for illnesses, reading Laura Jean Libby and Marie Corelli and looking at pictures of Gibson Girls and speculating about life in that East of the Marlborough-Vanderbilt wedding and bloomers, bicycles, rainy-day skirts, fantastic modernities. He realised that in this lost mountain-town as elsewhere the women drew their tiny, meticulous social lines ; that in Church Suppers and calls and gossip Mrs. Klein the Banker's wife or Mrs. Bishop the wife of the leading merchant looked down a little on their less exalted companions.

Mary, he realised, felt and resented this. She hated them, she hated Curicanti and poverty and taking in boarders and wearing old clothes. She hated Curicanti from the first . . . and though it had changed in these years, so that the early frontier days of gun-fights and lynchings were now almost a memory, she would always hate it with the same bitterness. Well, it was pretty wild when she first saw it. It must have been a shock, that day they arrived. . . .

She hated it still ; she hated Mrs. Klein and Mrs. Bishop, and even more she hated the poorer Miggses, Sauers, Ricketts, Bloggs. Ignorant, hard-working people, angular and ugly as their ugly, angular names. She hated the little brick school to which her children must go, and the sons and daughters of railwaymen and ranchers with whom they must sit in yawning tedium under the eye of withered young Miss Briggs ; she tried desperately to make up for all they were missing, and to fill in, herself, the gaps Miss Briggs' teaching left. Somewhere she had found an old piano and made him buy it for her ; on it the rebellious Jim and Alice must practice scales through long, sunny hours. Somewhere she had got together a strange collection of old books. *Treasuries of Knowledge, All the World in Pictures, Lives of the Great, Masterpieces of Art.*

" What is this picture, Jim ? Surely you remember ' The Last Supper,' by Leonardo da Vinci. Look, there's Our Lord in the middle, and Judas leaning towards him . . . I remember your grandfather telling me how he saw the original, in Italy, in Milan. It isn't really a picture, it's a fresco on a wall . . . And that statue—yes, that's right, Harold. The 'Apollo Belvedere'."

Harold always knew; Harold would sit for hours intent and solemn, turning the pages and staring at the pictures and spelling out the words underneath. Horses and chariots and galleys and elephants; knights in armour and frowning castles; kings in crowns and admirals in cocked hats; temples on Grecian headlands and fairyland towers on crags above the Rhine. Yes, one day he was going to see all that.

The other two would fret and yawn; they wanted to be out in the sunshine, playing with little Johnny Bishop or Herman Klein, with the little Miggses and Sauers. Wild Western games of pioneers and Indians, cattle-men and rustlers, the Pony Express, Jesse James. Or else they could go to the little shanty near the stock pens and talk to old Tex Clarke who had punched cattle in the Panhandle and shot a man in the wild streets of Abilene. Or they could hang about the switch-yards and watch the little switch-engine knocking the little red box-cars to and fro. Maybe they'd get a ride on the engine . . . or maybe the brakemen would let them climb into the caboose. It was like a little house on wheels, with its stove and its bunks and its observation-tower. There would be stories of wrecks and snowslides and fights with hobos . . . who the hell, they muttered fiercely, who the hell cared about old books?

They were annoyed—in a half-unconscious, instinctive way—when their mother scolded their father about his grub-stakes and his mines. They were thrilled by his stories of Leadville and Cripple Creek, and took it for granted that he would strike it rich some day. They even tried to plan what they would do then, the horses and guns and silver-mounted saddles they would buy. Mary would listen to their chatter with a hard, tired expression. Harold would listen too, a queer wonder in his eyes. It was hard to tell what Harold was thinking. But it wasn't till that day when lightning struck another of the trees by the creek that he realised how little he knew Harold. The blue-white electric flare, the crash and rumble of thunder, the rain streaming down. The barn door was open and banging and he was about to go out and close it : his slicker was hanging in his office and he went in there to get it first. In a dark corner, behind the desk, was Harold, huddled on the floor, white and trembling. He went over and tried to comfort him, but it was no use. When he bent down and touched that tense little body, Harold flinched, and twisted, then whipped past him like a terrified animal and ran away. Roger stood looking after him while the rain drummed outside. He realised that he had hardly ever touched Harold or spoken to him alone for years, and wondered hopelessly why Harold was scared of him.

*　　*　　*　　*

In the dusty store, in the saloons and barber-shops and on the street corners, they argued about the elections that were coming off this fall. Bryan trumpeting against the cross of gold on which Wall Street crucified all the little men in all the little Curicantis of the West—Bryan calling for the free coinage of silver which would bring the ghost-towns of the hills to life again. True, there was Cripple Creek . . .

but even Stratton, the king of all gold-kings, was backing Bryan ; he had bet a hundred thousand dollars on a Democratic victory. Stratton, with all his millions, snarling and brooding in a little frame house he himself had built when he was a poor carpenter, was always ready to help the under-dog. They said he had got Haw Tabor a job as a postmaster somewhere. Tabor who brought wood from Japan and stone from Italy to build his Opera House . . . Yes, it was a funny world all right, whichever way you looked at it.

*　　　*　　　*　　　*

The days passed, and the weeks of autumn. The children went to school ; Alice and Jim swaggering and elf-reliant, Harold shrinking and terrified among the blaspheming, stone-throwing roughnecks from lonely farms or shacks beside the railroad who mingled in the bare chalky classrooms with the more polished off-spring of bankers and storekeepers. Yawning, scuffling, slamming desks, stumbling through reading, writing and arithmetic, gabbling " Paul Revere," playing Pom Pom Pullaway in the muddy street, telling wild tales of back-alley pranks on Hallowe'en.

November came, and the Elections ; McKinley beat Bryan, gold beat Free Silver, Wall Street beat the West. The Horsefly Mine was full of water : the Horsefly mine was sold to the Syndicate who would hold on to it, with a batch of other ruined mines on that hillside, till they could drive in a drainage tunnel and get the whole lot going again. Snow came, piled on roofs, was shovelled in high walls off sidewalks ;

94

runners creaked and hissed and sleigh-bells tinkled
in the crystal sharp air. The mountains were a pattern
of bare grey rock and white snow ; the river a cold
black curve in the snowy valley. At Christmas a
present came for Harold from Doctor Whitman ;
Doctor Whitman who drove the fastest horses and was
the best shot in the country, who was the idol of Jim
and Alice and had hardly ever noticed Harold or
spoken to him. It was a copy of Kingsley's *Heroes* . . .
Theseus, the Argonauts, Perseus and Andromeda . . .
as he read it the bitter, snow-covered wilderness
glowed with warmth, the mountains dissolved to
reveal blue spouting seas and white cities and ships
with threshing oars.

Over his newspaper Roger would watch him reading,
lips parted, breath quick. Then he would turn to
the news again. Read about Cripple-Creek—producing a million dollars a month now—or about Tom
Walsh, the carpenter and prospector at Ouray.
Tom Walsh whose wife used to take in boarders. Tom
Walsh who had already taken nine hundred thousand
dollars out of Imogen Gulch, the Camp Bird mine.
It was always someone else who struck it rich.

*   *   *   *

Almost before they knew it it was spring again, and
summer. There were no boarders this year, but
Mary was kept busy just the same. Pale, headachy,
discontented, she dragged through the week's routine
helped by an Alice whose thoughts were far away in
dreams of horses and pack-mules and lost valleys
behind the mountains. Washing-day, ironing-day,
sewing-day, housecleaning-day, baking-day . . . then

95

Sunday again, and Church and a little rest, and another week begun. And after it there would be another, another . . . for ever. It wasn't much to look forward to. There wasn't much before the children. Alice would marry a rancher perhaps, and be happy enough in her way. And Jim would inherit the store ; he wouldn't like that much, he wanted something more adventurous. Already he was strong and restless, a good rider, a fair shot, always pestering you to lend him a rifle and let him go hunting with Jimmy Noble, spinning complicated plans of buying traps and setting trap-lines and making untold sums from the pelts of otters and muskrats and mink. A wild, hard, half-illiterate boy, leader of his gang in a dozen bitter battles with the shanty Irish and the Greasers who lived across the railroad-tracks. Roger would watch him at his games and his chores, and reflect a little sadly what a fine sailor that boy would have made. Tommy, he thought suddenly, must have been just like that once. The sea was a dog's life no doubt . . . but still . . . if Jim could have had a chance, if Jim could have gone as an apprentice . . . He had a sudden vision of half a dozen young brass-bounders swaggering up George Street in Sydney, caps tilted, laughing, joking, boasting about a record passage out, scuffling hungrily into a restaurant. You could almost see Jim among them. That was a better life, after all, than scraping on a mountain farm.

July came in, the Fourth with its banging fire-crackers, its flags, its Parade. The dust rose and fell again behind the little decorated floats, the horsemen, the band that blared Sousa marches down Main Street ; the sun set over the Picnic and Fish Fry among the scattered trees by the river ; rockets curved and flared in the darkness, and a drunken cowboy shot and wounded another in a brawl in Hennessy's Saloon. A fortnight later the Denver papers were full of the new gold-strike in the Klondike, ships coming into Seattle and San Francisco with millions of dollars worth of gold dust, with men who in a brief Northern summer had become millionaires.

Roger read the flaring headlines and close-printed columns ; he got out an old atlas and turned to the map. There was Alaska, there was the great Yukon curving down two thousand miles to the Bering Straits, there, almost on the Canadian boundary, were the little camps—Forty Mile, Circle City—where gold had been washed for years. And upstream, over the frontier, where the Klondike came into the Yukon . . . there was where the ragged prospector with his squaw wife had struck the bonanza of all time.

He picked up the paper again and read the names of those men who had been on the spot, who had dug the frozen gravel all winter and washed it in the spring, and come out now with bags and chests of gold-dust so heavy that they could hardly carry them ashore. Lippy, Stanley, Andersen, Hollinshed, Berry, Phiscator.

Four brothers on Eldorado Creek took out a hundred thousand dollars in two months. This man had been offered two million for his holdings, and refused. That man had two claims which were worth at least a thousand dollars a foot. Eldorado Creek had produced four millions. Bonanza Creek, over a million already. On Bonanza someone had panned twenty-four thousand dollars-worth in a day.

He looked at those figures, while excitement tingled restlessly in him. His mind went back—back to old Bill Jackson at Stockton, back to old Cy. They had always sworn that placer-mining was the only game for a poor man, and here were placers such as no one had imagined in his wildest dreams. Two hundred dollars to the pan. Eight hundred dollars to the pan. One pan—two shovels-full of sand—from Eldorado Creek had yielded two thousand dollars-worth of gold.

The news was flashing round the world; already from all Western America and Canada the rush was starting. There would not be much time, this year, to get in before the darkness and the ice clamped down. But in the spring there would be a stampede such as no man had seen since California in '49.

He put down the paper. Mary picked it up, glanced at it, sniffed.

" Do you believe all that stuff? "

" I don't know. Most of it. It's verified—look what the Dominion Surveyor says. And the Governor f the North-West Territory. And after all you can't get away from those two ships and the men—and women —coming ashore with bags and blanket-fulls of gold. A million dollars worth—more."

Mary stared at him.

" Maybe not." A pause. " I suppose you're sorry it's not in Colorado."

" Of course I am."

" Well, I'm not. I know how long you would remember your family, with a thing like that within your reach. I know how you would go—and I know how you would come back. No, the Yukon is a long way away. And it can't be too far away for me."

Roger said nothing. He got up slowly, put on his hat, went out into the hot, glaring afternoon, went down to the store. Henry Miggs was blinking over a newspaper too ; he was anxious to talk about this Klondike business, but Roger cut him short. He went into his little office, dropped into his rickety old chair swung his feet up into the desk and sat for a long time staring before him. The little room was stuffy, flies buzzed round the walls, a fly fought and buzzed in a big spider's web under the ceiling. He watched its struggles thoughtfully.

CHAPTER
VI

THE LITTLE STEAMER CREAKED and thudded, trailing a smear of smoke across the water. It was raining, and the cloud hung low over the cliffs and mountain-shoulders and endless pines of the Inside Passage ; rain sluiced down on the trampled decks and dirty paint-work and rattled against the canvas screens. Somewhere forward there was an aimless babble of whines and snarls and howlings from the dogs chained along the rail.

It was a relief to get out of the blaring, packed, tobacco-hazed saloon, but the decks were not much emptier. People huddled on wooden seats under shelter, people sitting on crates and bales in the open, collars turned up against the rain. Men wrapped in blankets, sprawled on the planking, a little knot of men round a hatch-combing, talking, arguing, spitting, rolling dice. Hard-bitten old men in Stetsons and mackinaws, flashy young men with big buttoned coats and cheap jewelled tie-pins, gaping country-boys dangling big red hands and staring at the sea, four giggling girls in huge, bedraggled hats and cheap fur coats, a pair of brown-faced old farmers chewing tobacco and spitting in methodical circles round themselves on the deck . . . even a baby wailing in the arms of a worried-looking young mother. He had

100

seen some queer gold-rushes, he reflected, but never one like this.

It was hard to believe that he was really here, with the wet, salty sea-wind on his face, in the crazy little steamer headed North. He and Charlie Dickson who was talking to a Swede in the saloon there now.

Planning it, back in distant Colorado, it had all seemed straightforward enough. You got a steamer from Seattle up to Dyea or Juneau. Then you packed your stuff across one of the passes to the headwaters of the Yukon. Build a boat—you had the tools with you—and float down the river to Dawson, getting there weeks before the river-steamers arrived from St. Michael on the Bering Sea. You would have time to look around, locate your claim, get started before winter set in. Work all winter—you used wood fires to thaw the frozen gravel—and clean up your dump when the water started to run again in the spring. By the end of the summer you would have made your pile, at last.

Whatever anyone said, there was no doubt that the gold was there. The official reports showed that. Thousands of miles of creeks and rivers, full of gold. Placer gold, the poor man's gold, not like quartz-mines that it cost thousand of dollars to develop. Though there must be quartz there too, the alluvial gold must have come from somewhere. Von Humboldt wrote, years ago, that he thought the great Mother Lode lay somewhere in the North. And anyway, quartz or no quartz, there were millions of dollars waiting in that gravel. And if anybody could find it, he and Charlie could. Hadn't both of them been mining gold and mining silver for nearly thirty years?

It wouldn't be a picnic of course, but you didn't expect that. No, the only real trouble had been the question of capital. Capital to buy an outfit, to pay your passage to Juneau, to keep yourself all winter till you could start cleaning up in spring. Fifteen hundred, two thousand dollars. It didn't sound much, but you didn't find two thousand dollars hanging from the nearest tree.

Thinking of that reminded him of a day he would rather forget. That day last winter when he came home and told Mary that he had mortgaged the store to Mr. Klein and was going to the Klondike with Charlie. Mary's face when she heard, and the silence in the warm little kitchen, and the old clock ticking away on the wall.

That hadn't been easy. It had been just as bad during all the weeks of preparation and packing, Christmas, the New Year, other people so excited about the *Maine* and Cuba and the licking the Spaniards were going to get from Uncle Sam. That last day and the friends seeing him off, full of good wishes and obviously convinced that he was crazy. Jim sulky because he wasn't coming too, and Harold scared and bewildered, and Mary cold and silent as a block of ice. Only Alice clinging to him, tears on her face, stammering hope and trust and confidence. Her wildly-waving handkerchief was the last thing he saw as the train took him round the curve by the water-tank.

At Seattle—gold-crazy, Klondike-mad Seattle— things had begun to look a little different. No time to stare across the harbour—masts, funnels, wheeling gulls, the sea again !—at the Olympics beyond the Sound. Chasing round madly with Charlie, trying to find somewhere to sleep, trying to book a passage, trying to buy things. Seattle was crowded to the doors, people sleeping on billiard-tables and in livery-stable hay-lofts, people left ten deep on the wharf when the ship at last sailed. They said fifty thousand were going North this spring. Some old timers in the mining-game, but most of them raw tenderfeet who had never been off a sidewalk before. Counter-jumpers, school-teachers, bank-clerks . . . women and children even.

The little steamer met a swell; rose, dipped, protested; the rain pattered down. Gulls swooped on a cascade of garbage, scuttles yawned out the blare of voices, the reek of engines, the smell of food and privies and bilges and unwashed bodies; he came back to the present and the fading Northern afternoon. Soon be time to go and fight for another meal, soon be time to go down to the airless little bunk with its smells and sounds and scurrying cockroaches, soon be the end of another day. It none of it seemed quite real.

He listened to the voices round him, talking, talking of what lay ahead. Skagway or Juneau or Dyea, maybe you could hire a Siwash to help you with your stores. The Chilkoot Pass and the Scales—was it true it would take you weeks to tote your stuff up there ? A thousand steps cut in the ice . . . they said the White Pass wasn't much better though. And after that you had to get down to Lake Bennett and build your boat—that was where the real fun began. They said those rapids. . . . They said if you lost too much of your grub the Mountain Police turned you back anyway . . . They said that the Yukon . . . But Hell, you didn't want to believe all they said. It stood to reason they'd try to scare you off. The gang that were there at the start, they were the lucky ones, they'd skimmed the cream . . . Skimmed the cream, like Hell they had, it had hardly started yet. The Dominion Government wasn't making things any easier though. Soon show the Dominion Government where it got off ; Queen Victoria would get a surprise if she tried to push this crowd around. And that went for this steamship company as well.

" Brother, when I'm on my way back they won't be treating me this way. If they try it, I'll just buy up the whole goddam company and throw them all out on their ear, from the directors to the stewards."

" When I come back." " When I've made my pile." " After I've struck it rich."

He tried to close his ears to the voices, and his eyes to the wet, grey, melancholy afternoon. He tried to think about home, and Mary and the children, and what they would be doing now. Jim and Alice had both left school—it would be harder than ever for Harold, without them to stick up for him—and Jim was helping Henry Miggs in the store. And Mary had another boarder, that would bring in a bit. Little Klein wouldn't be likely to allow much leeway on the interest-payments . . . No, the next few months weren't going to be easy for Mary, working and scraping and saving, all alone there, with everyone watching her and wondering and pitying.

She had thought he was crazy—everybody did, except Alice. It was a comfort, in a way, to remember Alice's excitement and confidence. How she had bombarded him with questions, advice, suggestions, toiled to mend his clothes and pack his bags.

" Have you got enough flannel shirts, Dad ? Have you got a good thick sweater ? What about socks ? What about the mosquito-netting ? It says in this book you'll need water-boots of walrus-skin. Will you get them in Seattle ? Or in Juneau ? And your parka ; will you get that in Juneau too ? It says you ought to take a little medicine-chest. Shall I ask Doctor Whitman what you'll need ? "

It was Alice who did all his sewing and darning and preparation, for Mary, thin-faced and tight-lipped, refused to help at all. It was Alice who washed out and aired and packed thick socks and flannel shirts and flannel underwear, Alice who hunted round the shelves of the store and picked out granite kettle and frying-pan and plate and cup. Alice who thought of putting in a fishing-line and hooks and sinkers and who, as a surprise, a parting present, made him a little case and filled it with needles, buttons, beeswax, thread.

It was something to know that at least one person believed in him. And yet that would make it all the worse if this didn't turn out right.

Near him a door banged open and Charlie appeared, short and stocky, his old Stetson pushed back on a sweaty red forehead, his quick little eyes looking up and down the deck. He saw Roger and came towards him, picking his way over the sleeping forms in their blankets, glancing at the two old farmers, automatically ruffling a little as he passed the four giggling girls.

" Gosh almighty," he said. " It sure is warm in there. I used to think you got some funny smells in a mining-camp bunk-house, but that's nothing to what you get here. And I used to think I'd seen some freak shows, but this mob beats anything Barnum ever rounded up. You know, I guess there's a few of everything on this ship. Iowa farmers with the manure still on their boots, and Eastern tourists and dry-goods clerks and tin-horn gamblers from every joint between St. Louis and the Barbary Coast . . . There's an Episcopalian clergyman, and an Englishman with a case full of shot-guns, and four old desert-rats that have prospected all over the South-West, and those hurgy-gurdy girls from 'Frisco, and a gang of boys who look like they're playing hookey from a grade-school in some hick town . . . Christ Almighty, man, what are we doing in a Noah's Ark like this ? "

He lent on the rail and spat down into the water, looking sombrely out to the grey oily swells that ran off to the cloudy shore.

" So this is the ocean, is it ? Or maybe you wouldn't call it the ocean proper. There's too dam' much water for me, just the same. And this old tub . . . I guess only the rust holds her plates together, eh ? Well, my old woman back in Denver told me I was crazy to come, and maybe for once she was right."

" You don't sound very cheerful, Charlie ? What's got into you ? "

" Oh, hell, I dunno. Been sitting in there all after-noon, listening to those dam'-fool tenderfeet talking about sailing down the Yukon . . . you'd think it was like taking a girl out in a row-boat on the pond in a city park. And then you get the others, the sourdoughs, who'll tell you what it's really like up North. That old Swede I was talking to—the old guy with the little beard—his name's Lindquist, he's been knocking round the Yukon for years. He was at Forty Mile when Carmack came back and told 'em about his strike . . . he knew 'em all, or so he claims. Hunker, Henderson, Joe Ladue. Old Lindquist didn't do so well, himself. Still, he made enough to treat himself to a trip back to Sweden to see his sister. Only he never got any further than Seattle. He's broke again now, and coming back to try again."

He gave a harsh little laugh, spat once more, went on.

"He was telling me a lot about life in Dawson. And there was another guy, who was there all last winter and only came out a couple of months ago. Drove a dog-team down to Dyea, in December, with a load of mail . . . he says you can earn big money hauling mail and freight, if you get a good team of dogs and know how to look after 'em. I guess you need money up there, at that. Last winter flour cost four hundred bucks a barrel. Candles were a dollar each. And with all this mob stampeding in, it will be worse than ever next winter. We'd better not waste any time about locating ourselves a good rich claim."

"What kind of wages do they pay?"

"Oh, fifteen, twenty bucks a day. Only you have to find your own grub. Unless you're a dance-hall girl with ideas. He was telling me how one girl, last fall, auctioned herself off for the winter. She went for five thousand dollars and her keep. Oh, it's a wide-open town that way, from all they tell. Saloons, gambling rooms, dance-halls . . . talk about Leadville in the boom days . . . and just the same, they say, there's hardly any gun-play. The Mounted

Police have got things taped. Last summer, on the Fourth of July, all the Americans started shooting in the air. The place was full of dogs who'd never heard a shot fired . . . it scared 'em so much they lit out for the woods, and it took days to round 'em up again. A gold-camp with no gun-fights . . . that don't seem natural either. Remember the early days in Creede ? "

" Hell, Charlie, you sound quite homesick."

" Homesick ?   I dunno.   Maybe that's just what I am.   All this darn country . . . it's too big, there's too much water, too many trees.   I don't like this boat, and the crowd on board her, and those dogs howling, and the rain.   I don't mind telling you I'd give a lot to be back in good old Colorado right now."

He gave a queer little shiver, and huddled down into his collar as a gust of wet wind came across the water.

" Oh well, what the hell.   What I really wanted to tell you was this.   That Lindquist . . . as I said, he's a real old sourdough, he knows the North.   But they cleaned him out good and proper in Seattle, and he don't know how he's going to get started again now. They don't even let you into the country unless you've got a certain amount of grub.   So I was wondering . . . how would it be if we kind of took him on as a partner, he'd be a useful man to have along.   He knows the country, and the trails, and how to travel, how to look after a team of dogs.   He knows the river and all those dam' rapids . . . he knows the likely places to prospect, when we get there, and he's got a lot of friends.   I know he'd be glad to join up with us, he's kind of looking round for a grub-stake.   But before I said anything to him I wanted to ask you. How about coming down and having a talk with him yourself ? "

" Sure, Charlie, I'd be glad to. It sounds a good idea."

Charlie nodded.

" I thought so," he said. " That old fellow might help us quite a lot. And if you ask me, we're going to need a bit of help. You and me . . . we may be old-timers back in Colorado. But when all's said and done, we're just another pair of dam' cheechakos up here."

Roger didn't answer. He looked out once more at the grey water, the clouds on the vast, dimly-looming mountains, the rainy afternoon darkening to dusk. But what he saw was the kitchen that sunny winter morning, and Mary's face when he came in and told her his plans.

He had argued with himself for weeks : sums, figures, calculations had wound and twisted through his brain night and day. He had tried to weigh the chances, he had tried to be reasonable and face facts. But only then, as he sat by the kitchen table, with Mary staring at him, only then had he realised all that he was staking on this last throw.

Up in the North, thousands of miles away, was a vast, unknown wilderness of snowy mountains and frozen rivers under a vast Arctic night. Somewhere in it lay a few little creeks whose frozen sands held gold.

The sun came in across the potted ferns in the window, the sun lay on the red-checked tablecloth and the plates and knives and forks. The old clock was ticking loudly in the tense, uneasy silence ; outside, somewhere, some snow fell with a heavy plop off the roof. It was warm in there, and quiet, and familiar, with that ticking clock and the smell of cooking.

If he never came back from that Northern darkness, he had realised suddenly, or if he came back emptyhanded, all this would go. A wheel spinning and a ball hesitating, dancing, and a moment of suspense with a fortune at stake. But it wouldn't be just a moment, it would be a year, two years. And it wasn't only his own security and happiness that were in hazard, but Mary's, Alice's, Jim's, Harold's. Was it, he had asked himself suddenly, too late to snatch back the stake ?

He had started to speak, but his voice wouldn't come. The wheel had already begun to revolve. If he had backed out, he would always have regretted it, he would always have hated himself, and Mary, and the dull, scraping, miserable life which would have been all he would have had before him for the rest of his days. It was no use talking any more.

As if she had known that too, Mary had said nothing. She had turned towards the stove again. He could still see the tired, hopeless stoop of her shoulders and her back.

The dogs down on the foredeck were still snarling and yapping, and a sudden guffaw of laughter came with the blare of voices through the scuttles of the saloon. Somewhere aft, out of sight, someone was playing an accordion. That tune about the Wabash that made you think of Fourth of July picnics by the river, of boys and girls on porches on summer evenings, of coolness and quiet and security. He listened till the tune died out in a discordant squeal, leaving only the yapping of the dogs, and the voices, and the thud and creak and rattle of the little steamer ploughing Northward through the rain. Then he knocked out his pipe and straightened himself.

" All right, Charlie. Let's go and see what your Swede has got to say."

CHAPTER
VII

NINETEEN HUNDRED AND THREE was nine months old when he came outside. As the steamer went thudding and throbbing southward towards San Francisco, people stared at him openly or covertly, nodded with deference when they caught his eye, nudged each other and spoke in low voices that held envy and respect.

" That's the fellow Barton I was telling you about. Yes, sir, he's made his pile all right. Came in back in '98. Landed up in Dawson with hardly the price of a meal. Now he's worth three or four millions. A New York syndicate has offered him three millions for all his holdings. Or that's the figure I heard. Someone was saying it was a lot more. No, he hasn't accepted yet, still dickering I guess. Well, I wouldn't mind being in his shoes. No siree ! "

It was strange to feel those glances and hear those low-voiced comments : the whole journey was strange as a dream. Listening to the beat of the engines, and remembering those days Northward bound with Charlie and Lindquist, and wondering what he would find at the end of this voyage. The world again—so changed no doubt in these four years !—and Mary, Jim, Alice, Harold, who would be no less changed.

Strange to come through the Golden Gate and look

out at the Bay, the shipping, San Francisco on its hills. Once, years ago, in another life, a boy had stood on another ship's deck and stared at all this. Mr. Thatcher. Tommy. It was very remote, all that. Only the thin, high screaming of the gulls was like an echo.

Mary and the children were in San Francisco : he had sent them money and arranged for them to meet him there. But they were not down at the dock to welcome him. His eyes searched the little crowd on the wharf, as the ship warped in and the strip of dirty water swirled and narrowed, but there was no sign of them. Strangers flocked aboard, asking him questions. It took him a moment to collect his senses and realise that they were reporters, that he was being interviewed.

He had talked to reporters often enough in Dawson : he knew how to smile and be genial and say the right things. Yes, this was his first trip out since he went North in '98. Yes, he was glad to be back, you bet he was. Yes, a great city, San Fransico. Oh yes, he'd been here before.

He might have told them more about that last occasion ; it was the sort of story they wanted. But he slid away from the subject quickly.

Yes, it was true that the Manhattan-Klondike Syndicate had made him an offer for his holdings. No, he couldn't give any figures, but they'd named a pretty good sum. What was he going to do, accept or refuse it ? Well, he hadn't quite decided yet.

"Yes, there were three of us went in together, Charlie Dickson and a Swede called Lindquist and myself. By the time we got to the Yukon all the best claims had been staked. We hung round a bit—went on one or two stampedes that came to nothing—nearly gave up. Then old Lindquist met another Swede who gave us a lay on a claim of his up Spruce Creek. We worked it all winter—you know, sinking a shaft, burning the gravel—and just above bedrock we made a nice little strike."

The reporters weren't much interested—they must have heard such stories a hundred times before. It didn't sound much, that way. The long, black, freezing winter, numbed hands, aching back, living in a stinking little cabin, wolfing beans and bacon and sourdough bread, going out to hack at the gravel in the reek of wood-smoke that made your eyes run. And at last—after nearly thirty years of searching —the gleam of nuggets when you washed a sample pan.

" By the time we'd got the dump worked out in the summer, we'd cleaned up about a hundred and fifty thousand dollars. Svensen got half—he owned the claim. We got twenty-five thousand each. Lindquist took his share and went to Nome—I don't know what became of him. Dickson had always hated the North —he wanted to go back to Colorado. He started off, but he never got there. He was slugged over the head and kicked to death in some dive in Skagway—he must have been flashing his roll a bit too freely. He was a good fellow . . . he always said there was a hoodoo on the North."

He skipped over that quickly : he still hated to think of fat, red-haired Charlie and what happened to him.

" He'd wanted me to come too : I'd just made enough to pay off the mortgage and get straight and start again, in Cripple Creek perhaps. I could have taken my family a trip to Europe . . . we'd have been fixed for life, in a quiet way. But that wasn't what I'd come for. So I took a chance and put the whole thing into a bench-claim on Bonanza. Drove a tunnel into the hillside, installed a boiler and used steam-points to thaw the gravel. I had to use hired labour . . . it cost me every cent I had, if things hadn't turned out right I'd have been worse off than when I got to Dawson. I'd have been flat broke this time. But instead of that I found more gold than I'd ever imagined . . . gold in the gravel, pockets of nuggets in potholes in the bedrock . . . I can still remember the look of them, shining in the candle-light. And the drifts of gold against the riffles when we started washing the dump in the spring. People came from all over to look at it . . . the foreman and I used to guard it with rifles at night. And after that I bought more claims and more claims, I used every cent I made to make more money, and it just seemed as if nothing I touched could go wrong."

No, you couldn't describe it—it was like being on a runaway horse, you could hardly try to control it. You just sat down in the saddle and let it go. You still felt a shiver of excitement when you remembered those wild days of power, success, achievement. But you couldn't make other people feel it. And already it was beginning to seem a bit unreal.

"Mind you, I'm not in a hurry to sell out of the Klondike. Don't you believe the people who tell you that the Klondike is worked out. Maybe there won't be any more spectacular bonanzas. But there

are thousands of medium-grade claims to be worked
still. Combined, worked on a big scale, they will
pay handsomely. And in any case the Klondike
isn't all the North. Millions of square miles of territory up there that have hardly been touched yet.
Not even explored or mapped. Probably a hundred
more Klondikes waiting to be found."

The automatic hopeful confidence : the pencils
scribbling. He wondered how many such interviews
the San Francisco papers had printed in the last
five years. These reporters must be sick of new
millionaries back from the North. His own plans ?
Well, it all depended.

" Probably I'll go back North in the Spring."

He escaped at last and went ashore, took a cab to
the hotel. The roar of traffic was bewildering, the
drift and swirl and blur of faces was bewildering, the
high buildings seemed to shut him in. Carriages,
wagons, street-cars with clanging bells, here and
there an automobile—a lot of them in fact. Glid-
ing along on steam or electricity, or spluttering along
on gasoline. He wondered if Mary would want
him to buy one of those contraptions ; he hoped not.
Were they really going to drive horses off the roads,
as the steamers were driving the white sails off the
sea ?

Here was the great hotel—four times the size of
that breath-taking palace where a shabby boy had
come quaking to ask for a Mr. Thatcher and find
him gone. Lights, warmth, expanses of soft carpet,
bell-boys running to take his bags, men in frock coats
bowing and rubbing their hands.

" Yes, Mr. Barton, everything arranged the way you
wanted. Our best suite, I hope you'll like it. Mrs.

Barton wasn't expecting you till this evening. We understood that your boat had been delayed. Made up time again? That's fine. She and the young lady and gentlemen are upstairs. Shall I send up and tell them you are here? Or would you like to go right up and surprise them? This way, if you please."

People watching out of deep chairs under little potted palm-trees. Water tinkling in a fountain. For a moment he felt self-conscious in heavy clothes and battered hat. Then he told himself that there was nothing to be embarrassed about, after all. San Francisco had seen many wilder figures than his, back from the mines and lumber-camps of the Sierras, back from the deserts of the South-West or the islands of the Pacific, with shabby clothes and bulging pocket-books.

The corridor seemed as long as a street, over-heated, over-carpeted. Here was the door, and the dapper man knocking . . . opening it and standing aside. Roger walked forward, into a sitting-room full of gilded furniture, and flowers, and mirrors. Mary . . . she looked older, a good deal older . . . he hardly knew her in that tight-waisted dress with all those bows and bits of lace and ribbons, with her hair piled up that way on her head. She glanced round, stared, sprang up.

" Roger ! "

But she seemed to shrink back for a moment as he went towards her, and her cheek flinched under his kiss. Before they could speak, another door opened, and Alice came in. An Alice he hardly knew either ; a young woman with her hair up, tight-waisted, long-skirted, in a white blouse with a high collar hard and tight round her throat. She ran towards him, tripping a little over that long skirt, and threw her arms round his neck.

" Alice ! Lord, you've grown up ! You're a young lady ! What would old Tex say if he could see you like that ? "

He tried to make his jocular as natural as possible, but he felt a queer embarrassed shyness, and knew that Alice felt it too. Behind her was Jim : a tall, broad-shouldered youth grinning awkwardly. His new suit seemed to fit badly, a hard collar obviously chafed his neck, his hands looked large and red below hard white cuffs.

" Hullo, Dad."

" Jim ! I hardly knew you either."

They shook hands, smiled at each other, stood back a little uncertainly.

" Well," said Mary. " We heard the boat had been delayed. But you got here to-day, after all. Did you have a good journey down ? "

*   *   *   *

It was all like that, awkward smiles and polite questions : it was no better when Harold came in. A thin, delicate-looking boy, self-conscious too in his brand-new clothes, biting his lip and flushing and mumbling a greeting and glancing at his mother, avoiding his father's eyes.

They sat round on padded chairs and made conversation : they gave him the news of Curicanti : Mary's flat voice made the place seem somehow unreal. The Store, Henry Miggs, the new Bank Building,

Mr. Klein. The house was shut up : the horses were out at Noble's ranch. Doctor Whitman ? Oh, yes, he was quite well. He wanted to be remembered. Everybody did.

There was a little silence. He looked at Mary and wondered if she was remembering, as he was, those vague dreams and plans in Mrs. Vance's arbour, the morning he had come to her, stammering and gruff and awkward, and promised her—had he ?—that one day they would have everything they wanted, that one day she should see Rome and Paris and the Pyramids. Well, he had made it come true after all. Somehow this moment ought to be more exciting.

Was this really the same Mary—this stiff, nervous woman in the frilly dress, with lace at her throat and her wrists, and her hair piled up that way ? Even her face looked different . . . the silk rustled as she moved, there was a faint whiff of powder and scent, she had been doing something to her hands. . . .

He had been sending her money at intervals during the last few years, enough for her to hire a girl to help with the housework and get what she wanted out of Mail Order Catalogues, but it was only during the summer that he had sent a real big cheque. There must have been a flurry when it arrived . . . he started to ask her what she had thought when she opened the envelope, but then something made him change his mind. Instead he turned to Alice.

" Well, how do you like San Francisco ? "

" Oh, it's all right."

What have you been doing since you got here ? "

" Shopping, shopping. Clothes, clothes, clothes. Fittings, dressmakers, hat-shops—I never want to see

119

myself in a mirror again. All those snooty women in black with pins in their mouths, smarming and simpering at you. " Yes, modom, no modom," and all the time you know what they're really thinking. . . . "

Mary frowned.

" Don't be ridiculous, Alice. You know you've enjoyed buying some nice clothes and things . . . any girl would. And of course it takes time, getting things properly. Especially when this is the first real chance we've had. That Madame Prince wasn't snooty, and she doesn't hold pins in her mouth. She has real good taste, and she's worked in all the best places in London and New York and Paris, and if you'd just listen to her instead of arguing and quibbling . . . Of course if you're going to behave as if you'd never been in a good shop before, people are going to look at you. And anyway, it hasn't all been shopping. You know you enjoyed it yesterday afternoon, driving round the Park and watching the people riding."

" Most of them looked as if they'd never been on a horse before."

" Oh for goodness sake, Alice, do you have to grumble about everything ? "

" I'm not grumbling. Only I don't like cities."

Harold gave a little hoot.

" Just how many cities have you seen, anyway ? "

She flushed, but ignored him. Roger looked at Jim.

" What do you think ? "

" Me ? Oh, I think it's swell. Gosh, those stores down there on Market Street . . . you can get anything in the world. Guns, saddles, clothes . . . and the people you see, all dressed up, coming out of the restaurants and the theatres. And even in the

Park there, some of the horses . . . there was one pair of matched bays, real high steppers, and there was a man riding a real English thoroughbred like you see pictures of in books. Out at the Cliff House you can have a meal on a balcony above the sea, and look down at the sea-lions, and the ships going out. We saw a Mail Boat starting for China. . . . And the way the cable-cars go up and down those hills. . . . There are a lot of automobiles around too—did you see them? I guess the automobile isn't just a toy, like everybody used to say it was. These ones seem to go all right. It would be kind of fun to ride in one . . . we could do that, couldn't we? I mean, we could get one, and play round with it ourselves? Oh, I think San Francisco's swell."

He grinned and stopped abruptly. Alice bent forward.

" Never mind about San Francisco. Tell us about the Yukon, Dad. About Dawson. Is it——"

Harold made an irritable gesture. Mary said :

" What can your father tell you that you don't know already? You and Jim have read about nothing else for four years."

" Oh, books and magazines ! They don't tell you anything. What is Dawson like now? Is it as wild as it used to be ? "

Roger laughed.

" No. It's not so wild now. There never was the gun-play there is in Colorado mining-towns. The Mounties had the place in hand from the start. Skagway was wild enough, though, if that's what you want. You've probably read about Soapy Smith and his gang. He came from Denver, as a matter of fact."

" I know. I read about him. Somebody shot him at last, didn't they? The Mounties are wonderful, aren't they? I read that they have the best dog-teams in the country. Is that so?"

She stared at him, her eyes quick with interest, and he tried to answer the questions that came in a flood. Dog-teams, trappers, miners, mines.

" Is it true there's a lot of discontent among the miners in Dawson? That the Canadian Government mismanages things up there? I was reading about the big concessions they give—and there's trouble about water-rights too, isn't there?"

Roger nodded. " How did you know that?"

" I read all I could get hold of. So did Jim. Dad— is it true there's a New York company that wants to buy you out?"

" They're going to make an offer, yes."

He looked at Jim, but Jim wasn't looking at him. Jim was sitting back in his chair, careful of his new, sharp, creased trousers, fingering his big bright new necktie and staring at his shining pointed shoes. It was funny that he hadn't asked any of the questions Alice did . . . you'd have thought he would have wanted to know everything he could. Five years ago he'd been crazy about gold-mining and prospecting . . . he had been a boy then, he was a young man now, with a high white collar and a tie-pin and his hair sleeked down on his head.

" Yes," he repeated, " They're going to make an offer. I've got to go East and see them, later on. Little Hargreaves, the head man of the Syndicate, was up in the Yukon a few months ago. Funny dry little fellow, always neat and tidy even in all the mud up there. Worth a lot of money, too. He's got a house on Riverside Drive in New York, full of antique furniture and old pictures . . . I expect they'll probably ask us to a meal. . . . "

Mary cleared her throat.

" You say that they are going to make an offer ? A good offer ? "

" Yes. I know that much."

" And of course you'll accept."

" I don't know. I haven't decided. It all depends. . . . "

His voice died away. He looked at Jim, who was still whistling quietly. He felt Mary's eyes on him, eyes at once hard and frightened, challenging and yet appealing, as they used to be. He moved uneasily, avoiding them.

" I don't know yet," he repeated. " We'll see. . . ."

He tried to change the subject, to talk about their more immediate plans. Whatever was decided, there would be time for a little vacation now.

" We'll see all there is to see round here. Might go up to Yosemite, Mary, and find out of it has changed since your father painted those pictures there. Then we'll go rolling back in style to Colorado, back home. . . . "

He saw Mary's expression, and stopped.

" You want to go back there so soon ? " she asked.

" Well—yes, I do. It's four years since I left, after all. Four and a half. I want to see my friends, don't I ? Doctor Whitman, Fred Bishop, Bill Noble. I want to see what Henry Miggs has been up to——"

" Henry Miggs ! The store ! Does that matter now ? "

He looked round the elegant, gleaming, silk-and-gilt-and-mirrored room. The big box of candy on the table, the roses, the shiny new books and magazines. Mary didn't know much about his business-affairs, but she did know,—even better than he did himself perhaps—the difference between being poor and being rich.

" Maybe it doesn't matter," he admitted. " Only— oh well, we'll see. We've got to go to New York, anyhow. We could even go to England if you want, to Europe."

Her thin, hard face softened suddenly. Her eyes brightened, Harold's eyes brightened : now it was their turn to lean forward and talk eagerly. New York. England. London.

" It's a shame we're not eighteen months earlier. We could have seen the Coronation of King Edward. Did you see the pictures of it ? He's a fine-looking man, isn't he ? And that lovely Queen Alexandra. It must seem funny for the English though, with Queen Victoria gone. It was too bad the Boer War spoilt the last years of her reign the way it did."

Alice started to say something, and checked herself. Harold looked across at her.

" Go on," he said. " Speak up. Tell us you think the Boers were wonderful. Like everyone else in this country."

" I wasn't going to say that, though as it happens I do think so. I was going to say, I don't see why Dad shouldn't go home if he wants to. Why should we go tracking off to New York and London, anyway ? "

" Well, if you want to go back to Curicanti . . . Buggy-rides with Johnny Bishop. . . . "

" What's wrong with Johnny Bishop ? "

"Nothing. Only *I* never want to see him again. And that goes for everyone else in Curicanti and the place itself too."

"Well, who cares what you——"

"Alice!" Mary's voice was sharp. Alice flushed and bit her lip. Harold turned to his father again.

"You meant that, didn't you, Dad? About going to Europe? We've been talking about it——" he gave his mother a quick, intimate little smile. "I got some folders from a steamship office in Market Street to-day. Cunard, White Star. . . . We were thinking that we could go to Italy first. Then France and Switzerland and places. Maybe even Egypt, and the Holy Land, and Greece . . . And then end up in England. . . ."

He stopped, his eyes shining. Alice gave a snort of impatience. But Roger saw Mary's hand go out quickly and touch her son's knee. Harold's thin white hand dropped to cover hers.

"Oh, well," he said slowly. "We must see how things turn out. No need to decide right away."

*   *   *   *

He left them, later, and went down to the barber's shop for a haircut and a shave. He was short with the barber, who seemed to know who he was and displayed a desire to talk about the Yukon; he grunted the fuzzy little man to silence and sat staring at his reflection in the mirror opposite. A long, thin, brown face, a greyish moustache rather stained and ragged, hair grey at the temples, dry and thin. Well, he reflected, he was nearly fifty now.

Some time in the next few weeks he would have to

decide what answer he was going to give to Hargreaves. It would be a good offer. Hargreaves had been impressed with what he saw. If the figure they named was anything like what was to be expected, it would be foolish to turn it down. A chance like this mightn't come again. Almost certainly wouldn't. Whatever you might say to the reporters, it was beginning to look as if the best days of the Klondike were over. High-grade claims worked out ; you could amalgamate, combine, work low-grade deposits on a big scale . . . but there were lots of snags in that. High costs, high wages, only a few months for working in the year. Above all the question of water. And in any case. . . .

The barber tilted the chair back, slapped hot cloths on his face, mixed lather in a mug. He relaxed, closed his eyes, felt the heat glowing against his face. He hadn't realised, till now, how tired he was. Tired and elderly and disinclined for more decisions, more risks, more hard work. It wasn't just the journey, and this strange, unnatural reunion that had tired him . . . it was deeper than that, it was a sort of accumulated weariness of years that had hit him suddenly to-day. Lying here, warm and sleepy, he felt as if he never wanted to move again.

It was true that the North was hardly touched yet. There were thousands of miles of creeks and rivers where no one but a few wandering trappers had ever been. And even in the Klondike there was a lot to do. If you worked with dredgers. . . . And you might do something with the quartz too, though no one had done much yet. But somehow, this afternoon, it didn't seem to matter much.

He was elderly and tired and sick of making plans and working. Sick of the North and the cold in winter, the heat in summer, the mud, the stenches, the flies. For thirty years, off and on, he'd been at it. Arastra and San Juan and Leadville, Cripple Creek, the Yukon . . . that was enough; time to sell out now, and rest a bit. Only, if he did that, what would Jim feel?

Jim had surprised him to-day . . . he had expected Jim to show more interest. But that was natural enough, all this had happened so suddenly, it had driven everything else out of his head. Picked up out of Curicanti and dropped down here with a pocket full of money and streets and stores all round him crammed with things and people he'd never seen before . . . he'd find his feet, in time, and go back to his old interests; he'd have to, there was nothing else he could do. He could to go College now, or to the School of Mines, perhaps that would be better. Or perhaps it would be better still to start him at the bottom. Shovelling dirt into a sluice-box, washing for colour along a creek, learning to trace up the float and find the ledge. Learning to load a pack-mule and throw a diamond-hitch . . . but he knew that already, learning to drive a dog-team, then, and make camp in a blizzard, and keep alive when the mercury froze in the bulb. He'd have to learn all that and a lot more. Assaying, milling, all these new processes, a whole encyclopædia of science, physics, chemistry, geology. Yes, he had a lot to learn. But he ought to do it all right, if he really wanted to.

No, you couldn't deprive him of his chance, if that was what he wanted. However tired you were, you had to go on till he was old enough, and knew enough, to take over. For if you didn't, or if he didn't want you to, Lord only knew what would become of him.

*   *   *   *

He went into the bar and had a drink, then he made his way upstairs again. It was supper-time, dinner-time, whatever you were supposed to call it. Mary and Alice had changed into other dresses, no less new and grand and unnatural. Mary looked at his heavy suit with disapproval.

" I suppose you'll be going to see a tailor to-morrow. You'll have to get some evening clothes. When we go to London you can get some suits made there. We will have to dress properly in England. We will be meeting all sorts of people, who notice that kind of things."

Her eagerness was a little pathetic, but he only grunted. He wondered how likely it was that they would meet anyone but tourists like themselves. Harold was looking eager too.

" I suppose there were a lot of Englishmen in Dawson ? "

" Oh yes, a good many. There was a little bar-tender in one of the saloons who claimed he'd ridden in the Grand National."

" Oh, that kind of person . . . I meant——"

" You meant blue-blood and coronets ? Well, there were a few of them too. Younger sons, remit-tance-men, most of 'em." There was one I used to see something of at one time, the Honourable Something Someone. He was a nice fellow, when he was sober enough to talk."

Mary looked pained. It was time to go down.

*   *   *   *

The lobby of the hotel was full of people, standing about talking, moving to and fro. Tourists, globe-trotters, California business-men, lumber-kings from Oregon and sugar-barons from Hawaii. There were elegant young San Franciscans too ; sons and daughters of those hard-fisted conquerors about whom Mr. Thatcher used to talk. Roger remembered how he used to gape as he listened to those names. Ralston, Sutro, Lick, Huntingdon, Crocker, Fair, Mackay. They werc dead now, most of them, the railroad-builders and the Comstock bonanza-kings ; Mackay was about the last, and he died a few months ago. Perhaps, he thought suddenly, somewhere in the city this evening a ragged boy was reading a newspaper article about Roger Barton who had made a fortune in the North.

The dining-room was a vast dazzle of lights on white table-cloths, on silver, china, flowers. Dark suits, bright dresses, bare shoulders, high-piled heads of hair. Head-waiters bowing and beaming, deferential voices against the music of an orchestra. " Good evening, Mr. Barton. Good evening, Madame. This way, please. This way."

Mary, he thought, was a little too dignified and stately. Alice was flushed and self-conscious, tripping over her skirt again. Jim looked large and red and out-of-place too . . . Harold painfully aware of them all. They settled down round a flower-piled table ; bowing men were proffering great stiff bills-of-fare, a wine-list. He left the ordering to Mary ; she knew what she wanted, so did Harold. So did Jim. Alice

I   129 pushed the card away like a sulky child. "I don't care. I'm not hungry." The wine-list was open at the page of champagnes.

The champagne came, cold and fizzing; Alice and Jim and even Harold had some too. They all raised their glasses in a vague, silent little toast, while the waiters beamed in the background as if they felt that here was a proper tribute being paid to success, wealth, five lives for ever changed. It was good champagne—but champagne for him would always be associated with Dawson, little curtained boxes round a dance-floor, muddy, tipsy men with girls on their knees. Charlie's comments after that last spree of his.

Jim and Alice did most of the talking, to each other and to him. Didn't he find things changed a lot in the world? Automobiles, this new wireless-telegraphy. Marconi had actually sent signals right across the Atlantic. Yes, a lot had happened since he went away. Funny to think what a lot. The War with Spain. Dewey, Schley, Roosevelt.

"Roosevelt and his Rough Riders," said Alice with enthusiasm. "A lot of them came from Colorado. They certainly showed the world that we know how to ride and shoot."

Harold made a faintly derisive noise. She whirled on him indignantly.

"Oh yes, we know what you think, little Mister Smarty. Who wants your opinion, anyway?"

Mary interrupted again.

"For goodness sake, don't let's start quarrelling and arguing this evening! Mr. Roosevelt comes of a fine old family in any case. Though of course it was terrible about poor President McKinley, wasn't it?"

Roger agreed that it was terrible. There was a little pause. He looked round the room, listening to the blare of voices against the gay music, smelling the warm richness of food and scent and flowers. Faces, faces . . . big, red, fat faces : delicate white faces. Women in evening dresses, with bare white arms ; women in big hats blossoming with flowers. Over in the far corner was a little bald man with a hard, elegant, fattish young woman : he watched them for a moment.

"There's old Sandy Heriot. The last time I saw him was in Dawson. He was wearing dirty mucka-lucks and ragged pants and an old mackinaw, and he was bumming round trying to raise the price of a drink. And now here he is ! How did he do it ? Oh, he got a grubstake from someone and went off on the first winter stampede to Nome. That must have been some journey. Blizzards, darkness, tempera-tures of fifty or sixty below. But it was worth it for Sandy, all right ; he struck it rich there. That's his wife. He met her in Nome. She was a waitress in an eating-house, though you mightn't think so."

Alice and Jim stared across the room with interest, but Mary pursed her lips distastefully.

"I would think so. That's just what she looks like, for all her new clothes."

There was another silence. Waiters changed plates ; another course ; Jim and Alice fumbling a little the many knives and forks. Jim said suddenly :

"I bet your partner, that Swede, is wishing he had stayed on the way you did. What is he doing now ? "

"Lindquist ? He went off to Nome too. I don't know what became of him there. He was a good

131

fellow. So was poor old Charlie. It doesn't seem right, somehow. . . ."

He made a gesture. Mary looked a little bleak. She had never met Charlie, but she had heard all about him ; the gun-fight in Leadville, the trouble in Creede. Again an awkward silence. Harold seemed to feel that some remark was expected of him now. He cleared his throat uneasily, and ventured :

" You never went to Nome, did you ? It's on the coast, isn't it ? Where they get the gold out of the sea-water."

Roger put down his glass suddenly.

" For the love of Pete ! " he exploded. " Gold from the sea-water ! He's lived all his life in Colorado, in the greatest gold-producing state in the country, and he doesn't know any better than that ! Listen, how often have I told you that alluvial gold is just the waste of quartz ledges, washed down and deposited in the bed of a stream ? At Nome, it comes from disintegrating glaciers. In the Klondike——"

He stopped short, aware that he had raised his voice more than he intended, and that people at nearby tables were looking round. Harold was scarlet and miserable. Mary's eyes were snapping with defensive fury. Jim and Alice glanced at each other knowingly.

" Oh, well," he said. " Never mind that. What do you all want to do this evening. Go to a theatre ? "

They did not want to go to a theatre, said Mary.

He could see that she was still furious with him, and he guessed that she was ashamed of these clothes of his. Clumsily he tried to make amends.

" So you want to go to Europe, do you ? Well, it mightn't be such a bad idea. There are some financiers in London I want to see. We could spend the winter over there, and by next summer we'll know better what we want to do."

Alice didn't look very enthusiastic. But Mary's whole expression changed as he spoke. She lent forward, Harold lent forward, both began to talk at once. Italy, hotels, couriers, the Alps, Paris, London. They had read, they had discussed it, they knew what they wanted. By the end of dinner it was all arranged.

CHAPTER
VIII

THEY SAILED ON AN English liner for Naples. It was
not actually very big, as modern liners went, but it
seemed enormous after those distant sailing-ships,
enormous even, after the little steamers of the Pacific
coast. There was a dining-saloon with a gallery and
a great domed glass skylight, and a lounge all blue
satin and gilt and yellow brocade ; the Barton's rooms
took up a whole corridor on A deck, and they sat at
the Captain's table and were made a fuss of by the
purser and the stewards.

The first few days were stormy, all the gilded woodwork shrieking and protesting as the ship battered
through the gales : Mary stayed in her cabin, waited
on by the stewardess and a rather yellow-faced Lucille,
and Harold stayed in bed too, the steward bringing
him trays. Jim and Alice came into meals, and tried
to pretend that they were hungry : in the big, half-
empty dining-saloon, with fiddles on the tables, the
red-faced Captain made himself polite to Roger,
and talked about his own son who had been a Conway
boy and was Fourth Officer of a P. & O. liner
now.

Then they came out of the storms into the warm
southern sun, and Mary was able to emerge from her

cabin and lie in a deck chair, muffled in veils and rugs, while Roger tramped up and down the deck with Alice and Jim explored the ship and made friends with a family from Baltimore which included two pretty daughters.

At dinner Mary was charming to the red-faced Captain and to Mr. Schultz the banker from Buffalo, and was careful not to be too effusive towards the white-haired Marquesa who had been born in California. Roger listened to her telling the Marquesa about her father who had been an artist and painted pictures of the Yosemite ; he watched her smile and nod and listen and file away little scraps of information about hotels in Paris and the Passion Play at Oberammagau. In her new evening dresses, with her hair done that way, she was fantastically unlike the tired, shabby woman who had cooked his meals and mended his clothes and gone out shopping through the dust or snow of Curicanti.

In the blue and golden lounge, after dinner, there would be more talk : talk of England and the Season, of Windsor and Sandringham ; Mary seemed to know all about Lady Londonderry and Mrs. Cornwallis-West, about grouse-shooting and the Royal Yacht Squadron. There was talk of Paris : she nodded understandingly when they spoke of Longchamps and the Crillon, of the Salon and Rodin, of the Duc de Sagan and Boni de Castellane. She nodded and listened and stowed it all away in her mind : Suffragettes and Carmen Sylva and Bayreuth and the peculiarities of the Tsaritsa and Franz Joseph's Frau Schratt ; the Battle of Flowers and the Tir aux Pigeons, what had happened at Mayerling and the truth about the " Malta Marriage," bac-

135

carat and Toulouse Lautrec and Lord Curzon and India . . .

When he could stand no more of it he would go down to see Harold, who would be sitting up in bed, with the tray on the little table at his side. A plate with the clean-picked backbone of a sole, a half-eaten roll and butter, a pile of grape skins and pips. It was queer to remember the black stinking fo'castle of the *Chester Rows*, and the hungry boys scraping out the old men's leavings in the mess-kids, the sour taste and the damp and the stench of paint and bilge. After a clumsy word or two to Harold he would get his coat and go on deck and stand there, watching the lights skip on the dark water, feeling the lift and throb and hurry of the liner taking them all into another world.

It was a strange time of transition ; ever since San Francisco it had been like that. They had stopped off at Curicanti on the way East : he had wound up his affairs there, made arrangements, said farewells. There would be a Barton library one day, and a new wing at the little hospital. Doctor Whitman had taken Ute and Comanche, more to please Alice than because they would be any use to him. Mr. Klein had bought the old house : he was going to pull it down and rebuild. In Denver there were interviews in the papers and a surprising number of visitors : men he had never seen but who claimed to have known him in Leadville or San Juan or in Arastra. Battered old men asking for a grub-stake, a little loan. Charlie's widow had appeared, too, fat and beady-eyed and tearful, to tell him about a mortgage on her home. He had given her money, but Mary was short with her.

136

New York was a hotel whose opulence dimmed even the one in San Francisco ; it was Tiffany's, Altman's, Wanamaker's, Gunther's ; silks and furs and shoes and feathers, pearls and diamonds and fitted dressing-cases. Mary got a French maid called Lucille, and Alice had to endure a lot of fittings, and Jim and Harold got new suits and hats and gloves and tie-pins. Jim bought a saddle with silver mountings, and began to take an interest in automobiles.

Little Hargreaves of the Manhattan-Klondike Syndicate made his offer : they had gone far higher than he had expected, so high that only a lunatic would have refused. It had been hard to explain to Mary why he had turned it down.

Sometimes, standing there on the deck in the darkness, he felt a pluck of panic at his heart. It was all very fine to make big plans for himself and Jim and the future, but too many things could go wrong in gold-mining. Not overnight of course . . . the claims were still paying, the manager in Dawson sent cheering reports each month—but in a year or two, if that claim petered out and there was no water to work this one, if they planned and panned along those new creeks without getting colour, then slowly, slowly but surely, all that he had would crumble away. Perhaps he was the fool Hargreaves thought him. Hargreaves had left his offer open. It was not too late, even now, to change his mind.

It was the thought of Jim that had made him refuse ; now he wanted to talk to Jim again, and find out what he really felt. But Jim always seemed to be busy these days, playing games, exploring the ship, making friends with passengers and crew. The sea grew

calmer and the sunshine stronger every day : Harold
recovered and came to sit beside his mother talking
and making plans and reading books about cathedrals
and palaces. Jim tried to make Alice join in games
of shuffleboard : Mr. Schultz told the world what he
thought about Roosevelt and the Trusts. They passed
the Azores, Flores and Corvo, high and green and lonely,
standing out of the sea. Roger stared out at them and
thought of all the ships that had passed this way,
clippers racing down under full sail to the Line, and
the South Atlantic, racing back again on the last
lap of their journey home. At Gibraltar they went
ashore and bought shawls and lace and tortoiseshell :
Roger was surprised by a strange little emotion he
had never expected to feel and could never explain
to his totally-American family as he looked at the
great grey hunch of the Rock and the warships anchored
out in the harbour. He had felt it once before, he
remembered now. In Dawson, when, ten thousand
miles from London, the flags on banks and government offices and police posts came down to half-mast
for the death of the old Queen.

The piled lights of the town, winking signal lamps
of the warships, dropped away in the darkness ;
morning showed the empty sea again, the windy blue
Mediterranean, dolphins plunging round the steamer's
bows. As those last days ended Roger was conscious
of a queer regret. He had half-dreaded this crossing,
and it had been dull and tiresome, and yet, he saw
now, he had enjoyed it too. He had been ready to
despise this liner and her steamship crew, and now he
would be sorry to say good-bye to her and them.
He wandered about the decks again, watching the
glint of sun on polished brasswork, slapping the broad

teak railings, feeling the wide scrubbed planking dip and lift beneath his feet. There was good stuff in this ship, he realised : honest, solid, reliable ; those builders of Clydeside had done their work well. Captain Dobson took him up to the bridge again ; he stood by the great compass and watched the chunky, stolid quartermaster at the wheel, and heard once more about Captain Dobson's son. Then it was time to dress for dinner. There were paper caps and favours, and a concert later, with lady-passengers dreadfully playing the piano and a Cockney steward singing comic songs. Mary gave a startled little gasp when she saw how much he was putting into the collection for the Seamen's Charities.

Alice sat glowering and self-conscious in the paper cap they had made her put on. When the ball began, she danced with Jim once : then he went off with one of the girls from Baltimore, and when the Assistant Purser came up to her smiling politely, she flushed and shook her head. Roger went and sat beside her and tried to make her talk and laugh. They watched—Harold watched too, with eyes queerly jealous—while Mary waltzed with the Captain, and the Doctor, and nimble, perspiring, gallant Mr. Schultz.

On the next afternoon they saw blue land ahead, and came into the Bay of Naples in a magic hour of sunset when Capri and Sorrento and Vesuvius were blue and gold under a golden sky. In the fuss of farewells and tipping Roger realised that Harold had disappeared. After a long search he found him alone up on the boat-deck, staring out at that great glowing panorama, his thin hands clutching the rail. He had to speak sharply, twice, before Harold heard him : it was like speaking to a sleep-walker; like a sleep-walker the boy followed him down, his eyes still bright with a queer, dreamy excitement, his answers absent-minded, his thoughts far away. Roger watched him, puzzled and uneasy. Alice snapped at him and told him to wake up. They didn't quite know what to make of it. Only Mary seemed to understand. Her eyes were bright and excited, her answers random too.

The ship was moored, the engines silent; hosts of sallow, noisy, Italian-jabbering men had poured aboard. Here was the courier from the Travel Agency: their own private courier, a dapper, knowing little man called Bertrand. He would be with them till they reached Paris, and Roger was secretly relieved to feel that he was there. Like Alice he felt uneasy, unwilling, before the prospect of foreign cities, railway-trains, hotels. They had so much baggage too . . . Yes, he was glad to see little Bertrand come.

Fluent with English compliments to a flattered Mary, fierce with Italian orders to porters, Bertrand saw them ashore. Through the customs, through the scrimmage of touts and hawkers, through a chaos of whip-cracking cocchieri, into the big two-horse conveyance that was waiting for them. Darkness had fallen by now; they didn't see much on their drive to the hotel. Mary and Harold kept up a rapid fire of comments and ejaculations: Jim and Alice scowled angrily as the driver lashed his horses and jerked the reins; Roger—a little homesick for the quiet English steamer —saw only a blur of lights and faces, blowing fountains, ornate buildings, foreign words on posters and shop-signs. The hotel was high up on a hillside, high up above the city: Bertrand again, and bowing porters, bowing managers, English voices in the lobby, a lift, a passage, big bright rooms with french windows opening on to balconies. There was a garden, down there in the darkness, and below it the lights of Naples, the long lines of lights that curved round the bay. Someone was twanging a guitar and singing, there was a scent of flowers, of lemon-trees.   Mary and Harold went out on to the balcony, and stood there, listening and staring : he came and stood beside them, and for a moment he felt something of the romantic spell that was on them. He smiled at Mary through the shadows, remembering those evenings in Mrs. Vance's dusty garden, and Mary's wistful dreams, his promises.

" Well Mary, we said we'd come to Italy. And here we are."

She looked round and smiled and put her hand on his arm : for a moment she seemed to be remembering too. Then Harold said something, and she turned back quickly towards him : when Roger spoke again neither of them seemed to hear.

*   *   *   *

Before long they felt as if they had always been travelling. Always driving through foreign cities and being greeted in hotel-lobbies by bowing managers in frock-coats and *concierges* with gold keys on their lapels. An influx which made the other guests stir and stare. The Klondike millionaire and his family seeing Europe. Mr. Barton, Mrs. Barton, Miss Barton, Mr. James Barton, Mr. Harold Barton. The courier and his assistant, Mrs. Barton's maid. The piles and piles of shiny luggage. The books, the flowers, the luncheon-baskets, Miss Barton's new fox-terrier. And

hard on their heels an ever-changing train of tutors,
language-teachers, hairdressers, dressmakers, guides ;
of chauffeurs and coachmen and grooms ; of people
with things to sell and people asking for money and
people come, apparently, just to look at a millionaire.

They would have dinner up in their suite. To-
morrow they would have a car or a carriage and go
out to see the sights. Then they would go shopping,
and soon the big expensive-looking boxes would be
delivered at the hotel. Miss Barton and her brother
might hire horses and go riding. Mr. Barton usually
sat in the garden reading newspapers most of the day.
In the evening he wouldn't always go with them to the
theatre or the opera.

Naples—Pompeii, Vesuvius, Capri, Amalfi. Lace
and silk and coral and queer, jewelled, twisted things
of silver from those tall, shabby palaces. It wasn't
all sightseeing and shopping. They had letters of
introduction from Mr. Hargraves to Americans who
had a villa at Sorrento. There was a luncheon-party
on a terrace gay with bougainvillea ; among the guests
were some rather loud-voiced people from the white
steam-yacht which lay down in the bay ; they had an
English lady with them, a Mrs. Vane, very well-bred
and elegant and self-assured. One wondered what she
was doing in the soap-king's yacht with his fat jewel-
hung wife and screeching daughters. Mrs. Vane
talked about the London season and Cowes and Good-
wood and the ball given by the Prince and Princess of
Wales last summer after moving into Marlborough
House. She and Mary had a long conversation in a
corner after lunch, but Mary didn't say what they had
talked about.

In Naples, as in New York, life for a millionaire was

a long battle against unwanted visitors. You could refuse all the invitations and presents from people you'd never heard of, though it wasn't always so easy to make Mary distrust a glossy card with a coronet. But you couldn't keep out all the dapper little men in frock-coats with blue-prints and prospectuses. There was an Italian count with mineral-rights in Albania, and a South American with talk of silver in the Andes, and a Belgian who had ideas about rubber and a sheaf of answers to the allegations of atrocities in the Congo. There were others who had nothing to sell but jewels, pictures, family heirlooms, and others again who had nothing to sell at all. " But I was in Leadville back in '85, Mr. Barton, you wouldn't remember me, but I remember you. All I want is a little grub-stake. The price of a steamer-ticket back to God's Own Country."

Rome was sunshine on old red brick : it was the Sistine Chapel and the mediæval colour of the Papal Guard. Up on the Pincio there was a park, where white-gloved officers in dazzling uniforms rode up and down on big black chargers and saluted each other punctiliously. Jim and Alice hired horses and rode there too. Alice eyed the officers' chargers, and the officers eyed her. Jim was conscious of nothing but his own seat in an English saddle, his new English breeches and boots : he even talked of fox-hunting on the Campagna. Roger sat in the hotel lounge and read about the Russians and the Japanese. The American Embassy made polite gestures. There was a Russian count who wanted to discuss some hydro-electric scheme in the Caucasus. Before they left Rome Mary and Harold went and dropped their coins into the Fountain of Trevi, in token of their return.

143

After Rome, Pisa, Florence, Venice : Mary and Harold, as they had always dreamed, sliding in a gondola down the Grand Canal. A gondola with two gondoliers. Then Stresa, Montreux, Paris.

Paris was chestnut trees and fountains leaping in wide, pigeon-breast irridescent squares : it was another huge hotel all gilt and silk and marble, a swirl of gay dresses and frock coats and uniforms. A Grand Duke with Cossack servants occupied nearly all one floor, there was a Rajah with jewels in his turban, there was a dyspeptic Chicago millionaire. There were invitations from people met in Rome and Venice : luncheon-parties and conversation at restaurants under the trees in the Bois : there were tiaras and fans and tedium at the Opera ; dressmakers and modistes and the suite full of big cardboard boxes and billowing tissue paper ; a diamond necklace from Cartier for Mary, and a little string of pearls for Alice, Charvet ties and coloured waistcoats for Harold, and for Jim. That was a surprise, somehow. You wouldn't have expected Jim to want silk ties and amber headed walking-sticks, and to wonder if his New York suits would look all right in London. He was nearly as excited about Paris as his mother . . Alice didn't know what to make of him either. He was quite annoyed when she laughed at that amber-headed cane.

Roger had a visit from a smooth little man with a ribbon in his buttonhole, who had a concession for copper-mining in Morocco ; it was a long story, though, involving a cousin and the cousin's mistress and a will made under the influence of drugs . . . The Chicago millionaire and his wife gave a party for three hundred people, including the Bartons : tables heaped with orchids, marble walls flooded with pink and golden lighting, Italians singing from a gondola that floated in a lily-pond in the middle of the floor. Everyone said it was the biggest entertainment of its kind since Tom Walsh was in Paris as one of the commissioners to the Exposition. He had entertained four hundred people at the Élysées Palace, in a room lighted by candles set in blocks of ice. There was a Camp Bird display in the Palace of Mining at the exhibition, and a whole section devoted to Cripple Creek. Alice was always interested when anyone mentioned Colorado. It didn't happen very often though.

*   *   *   *

And finally London. The glimpse of the grey river, the noisy station, the streets. Crowds, newspaper placards, big two-horse buses, jingling hansoms, old growlers, motor-cars. It was only a few hundred yards to the huge hotel off the Strand. Another lobby, more bowing men, lifts, corridors. Rooms looking out across green trees to the grey river again. Somewhere down there, out of sight round the bends, were the docks and streets and alleys where a lonely boy had wandered one night, just back from India in the old barque *Chester Rows*.

London all blue and gold and hazy with the summer : green trees heavy over railings in quiet squares, flower stalls and scarlet tunics bright against the stone of old buildings. Shop windows gay with silver and jade and crystal : streets brisk with wheels and hooves and barrel-organs. The sleek horses foamed against their bearing-reins ; wheels spun, carriages bright as jewels went past with coachmen and stiff tigers : old men in club windows watched and agreed that things weren't

K   145 what they used to be. There were awnings out across pavements in the evenings, and the sound of music came through tall windows : ostrich-plumes shook and medals glittered in carriages driving down the Mall towards the Palace in the smoky sunset.

He had an introduction to Theo Weisser, head of a big mining company. Weisser asked him to lunch at his club. Statues round a marble hall and old men reading *The Times* in hushed libraries. Theo Weisser, who had made his first fortune in Mexican silver-mines and his second on the Rand, was a sleek, heavy-eyed man with a gentle voice and soft white hands. There was an associate of his there, a Sir James Lancelot-White, elderly and dapper : they lunched off game pie and stilton and talked about racing and European travel, and only at the end of the meal did they let the conversation drift round to gold mining. It was funny, in these surroundings, to hear talk of Cripple Creek and Dawson : surprising how much they knew about Stratton and his Independence and John Hays Hammond and the Venture Corporation, about Nome and the Klondike, Alec MacDonald, little Swiftwater Bill . . . They even knew that Hargraves had made him an offer which was still open, but they didn't know how much it was, and he didn't tell them. When they asked him what his plans were now he said that he hadn't made up his mind.

After that there was a dinner-party at the Weissers' house in Mayfair. Bare shoulders and white ties, a procession into dinner, flowers and silver and wine-glasses in a long panelled room. Mary made friends with a Lady Someone : a Member of Parliament took her into dinner, they talked about the theatre, she told

Roger afterwards that the Weissers were charming.
" No one has any feelings about Jews these days.
The King himself has Jewish friends."

And then onwards their time was full. Luncheons
and tea-parties and dinners, more theatres, more
opera. They went to the Italian Exhibition at Earl's
Court (" For goodness sakes ! " wailed Alice, " Haven't
we just spent *weeks* in Italy ? "). They saw Mr.
Rothschild's St. Amant win the Derby on an afternoon
of crashing thunder and pouring rain ; Mary and
Alice and Harold went to a great charity bazaar and
spent a lot of money and were introduced to people
with titles ; Mary met the American Ambassador at
a luncheon party, and made discreet inquiries about
tickets for the Royal Enclosure at Ascot and presenta-
tions at Court—it was too late to arrange it this year
though—and heard about William Jennings Bryan,
who had been in England recently. She wondered if
they could get Mr. Sargent to do a portrait of Harold ;
she went to another bazaar, and saw the Princess of
Wales there, only a few yards away.

Then Lady Lancelot-White left cards, and they were
asked to dinner there : more white ties and bare
shoulders in a long room with pictures of Venice
round the walls. Mary could apparently hold her own
in the give-and-take of conversation, and even Roger
was beginning to find it a bit easier by now. Among
the guests, this evening, was Mrs. Vane once more ;
she greeted Mary like an old friend, and when the men
went up to the drawing-room, after their port, Roger
found Mrs. Vane and Mary deep in talk again. Both
seemed a little guarded, as if they were sharing some
secret plan, but not till they were driving home at
the end of the long dull formal evening did he learn

what it was all about. Mary tense with excitement beside him in the carriage.

" Oh, Roger, wasn't that a delightful evening ! If only Harold had been there ! That lovely house, those Canalettos in the dining-room !—Tell me, what do you think of that Mrs. Vane ? "

" She seems all right. Who is she ? "

" Oh, she's a cousin of an Earl . . . very top-drawer. She hasn't much money, but she goes everywhere. She—she is very clever about helping people like ourselves who . . . who have come from abroad. Helping them to find houses and servants and so on. Arranging dinners and receptions and dances. Advice about . . . who to ask, and getting their daughters presented . . . she knows all the right people."

So that was it. He'd more or less expected it.

" What does she get out of it ? Commissions from the shop-keepers ? "

" Of course not ! But naturally if she helps people they . . . show their gratitude. It's a recognised thing. She could help *us* a lot, Roger."

" She'll have to be quick about it. We've only got a few weeks more over here."

" Roger ! "

" Oh well . . . no reason why you and Harold shouldn't come back next summer. Alice too, if she wants to."

" That's not the same thing at all. What sort of position would I have as a sort of grass-widow, dragging Alice and Harold round from hotel to hotel ? No— if we do it at all it must be properly. Our own house, our own servants. But not just yet—we're not—ready for that yet."

She drew her breath and went on quickly, before he could reply.

"What Mrs. Vane suggests is another winter or two abroad. In a villa somewhere—she knows of one near Florence—with really good tutors for Jim and Harold and a—not a governess, she's too old for that, a *dame-de-compagnie* for Alice. I think Mrs. Vane would come too, some of the time. And then, later on, we could come back here. . . ."

They went through it all again and again. Before they got to the hotel, in that gilt-and-satin drawing-room of theirs upstairs. Jim's future :

"Jim can have his gold-mines. Only he can do it the way your Mr. Weisser does. Like a gentleman, not like some backwoods prospector." Harold. " He could go to Oxford or Cambridge. It's not too late. Look how quickly he learns and adapts himself." Alice. "You won't know Alice after a year of—of polishing. She can have a proper London season, be presented, we could give a ball for her. She can have jewels and lovely clothes. . . ."

"You'll have her a Princess at this rate." He was heavily jocular, but Mary's reply took the wind out of his sails.

"That might even happen too ! Look at Prince Colonna—you remember we saw him at the Opera in Rome. His mother was the daughter of one of the Comstock Kings you used to talk about ! And they say the Duke of the Abruzzi is going to marry an American girl. And there are dozens of others . . . even in England. Look at Levi Leiter's daughters. But that isn't the point now. What do *you* want us to do ? "

It was no use his trying to answer. To talk about

149

a house in Denver, a house in San Francisco, a place down the Peninsula at San Mateo or Burlingham. It was no use talking of New York, Newport, Washington. For her America would always be Curicanti. She wouldn't listen.

When she began to cry he was driven to compromise. She could have a house in London, to-morrow if she wanted. She and Harold and Alice (and that was treachery !) could stay here, he and Jim could go back alone. But that didn't suit her either. She reminded him of his promises when they were married. She reminded him of Curicanti ; the long, grinding years, the boarders, the kitchen-sink. The years of scraping and anxiety while he was away. " Don't you think—don't you think I've earned a little consideration now ? "

If it hadn't been for the thought of Jim he would have given in then. But he hardened his heart and made no promises. Nothing was settled when at last they went to bed.

*   *   *   *

She would hardly speak to him when he went in to her next morning after breakfast ; she was as cold and polite as if they had never met before. She and Harold were going out together. Jim and Alice were riding in the Park. What were his plans ? He mumbled something about a little business, he wandered back to his own room and looked at the appeals and advertisements on his desk ; finally he got his glossy hat and tight-rolled umbrella and went out. He hadn't slept well and a little air would do him good.

He took a hansom up to Hyde Park Corner and walked along beside Rotten Row, outwardly not too different from the other well-dressed men who walked with big-hatted ladies under the trees. Now and then he stopped and watched the riders; the dapper elderly men and hard-faced women, all so correct, so beautifully turned-out, on their well-groomed, genteel-looking horses, the children no less correct on ponies no less genteel. Even now, though he expected it, it was a shock to see Jim and Alice come cantering along on the horses they hired from the stables in Knightsbridge. Jim and Alice riding in Rotten Row. . . .

They caught sight of him and drew up; he stood by the railing and patted the wide, solid neck of Alice's mare. Alice was still unhappy in riding-habit and side-saddle; she was having trouble with her hat and crop, and had lost a glove somewhere. But Jim, in Saville Row boots and breeches, looked surprisingly at home.

"Honestly, Dad, I don't know what I'm going to do about Alice. You'd think she'd never seen a horse before. I'm going to hire one of those ponies next time, and take her out on a leading-rein. Gosh, twice already I thought she was coming off! And that's the girl who used to talk about riding on Cattleman's Day!"

Even his bantering voice was a little more English already. Alice laughed with him, but it was a bit forced.

"It's all very fine for him to talk. If he had to wear these silly clothes . . . and sit in this dam' saddle . . . Dad, why can't I ride astride?"

"Because, as your mother will tell you, it isn't

ladylike." It was Jim who answered. "Just as it isn't ladylike to swear."

" Is that so ? Well, if you don't like it, Jim dear, you can go to hell. And don't made me homesick talking about Cattleman's Day."

Her laugh was unsteady. She jerked at the reins, before Roger could speak she swung the mare round and jammed in her heel. There was a spattering of earth and she was gone at a canter which was very nearly a gallop ; a red-faced old lady on a sedate grey looked after her and pursed disapproving lips. Jim's eyes met his father's. Then he shrugged his shoulders, turned his horse round and followed. Roger watched them out of sight and went on with his thoughtful walk.

Another letter from Hargraves was waiting for him when he got back to the hotel. He read it carefully, and read it again. Hargraves renewed his offer . . . and not only renewed it, increased it ; he must have heard about the new strike at the Horse-shoe. It was a pretty staggering offer, in black and white like that. So many millions outright, a big block of shares in the syndicate, and a royalty on all the profits of the Klondike holdings for the next five years. Enough in any one of those to keep the Barton family in luxury for the rest of their lives.

He sat in his room looking over the river and tried to think. The Klondike had seemed so near and real and vital in San Francisco and New York even, but here in London it seemed remote and unreal. This letter was real, and the money it represented. Was it really fair to Mary to turn it down ? Jim wanted to see the North . . . but that could be arranged too. Hargraves would give him a job of course. That could be made a condition of the sale. . . .

Mary was in her room, trying on a new hat ; Lucille fussing about her holding mirrors, adjusting pins. She scurried out when he jerked his head at her ; he plunged into that endless discussion—again. And at last Mary had her way, or most of it.

He would never see the Klondike again—but Jim would. Jim would go back to New York and Hargraves would find a job for him. Later he would go up to the Yukon—or to Canada, or to Mexico or South Africa or wherever the Syndicate wanted him to go. He would become an expert, he would be a second John Hays Hammond, and then with his capital he would be able to launch out on his own. And the rest of them would stay over here. France, Italy, then perhaps the house in London, the programme outlined by Mrs. Vane.

"Oh Roger, I know I'm right. You've done enough, it's time for you to enjoy yourself. We'll have such fun . . . it will be like our plans years ago. . . ."

Roger nodded a little wearily. At any rate, he told himself, he would be on hand to protect Alice from the princelings. And Jim, when it was put to him, seemed quite pleased at the idea of working for the Hargraves Syndicate, living in New York, travelling about the world, on his own, without his father's supervision. Alice said nothing. Her look made Roger feel a traitor, but what could he do ?

He would go back to New York with Jim, and close the deal with Hargraves and see Jim settled. Then he would come back and join the others on the Continent somewhere. Mrs. Vane was very helpful.

153

Harold liked the tutor, whose name was Morton,
Lionel Morton, a gentle, rather delicate young man
who had been at Oxford and whose father was a Dean.
And Alice, with reservations, was prepared to accept
the self-possessed, middle-aged Miss Cartwright, who
looked well in a riding habit and spoke beautiful
French and Italian and was fond of dogs. When
you had a lot of money it didn't take long to get things
arranged.

The season was nearly over; soon everyone would be
scattering to their yachts and spas, to their country-
houses and shooting-boxes. Not even Mary could
imagine Harold on the lawns of the Royal Yacht
Squadron or in a butt on a Scottish moor. Not yet.

Before they left they were invited to a reception at
Cauldfield House. The Countess of Cauldfield, who
got up so many charity bazaars and garden-parties,
was some connection of Mrs. Vane. It was all like
something out of one of Mary's favourite novels:
the tailcoats and swishing trains progressing up a wide
staircase, the functionary calling out the names,
Lady Cauldfield all silk and diamonds standing with
her son at the top of the stairs. She gave them a hand
and a murmur, and her son, who was in the Diplo-
matic Service as his father had been, gave them a
murmur and a hand. And then they were adrift in
a sea of black coats and uniforms and bare arms and
waving fans. Roger was aware of polite eyes glancing
at his new evening clothes and Mary's jewels; high
ripples of conversation washed round them, nicknames
and allusions which might have been in Chinese for all
they meant to him. Mary was very self-possessed but
seemed relieved to find Mrs. Vane and her command-
ing sister Lady Hornbeam who was very affable and

pleasant. There were refreshments ; someone from the Opéra-Comique sang. "*Lucia*," said Mary. " I'm always *so* fond of Verdi." People were introduced, people made conversation, Mary waved her fan and smiled and talked. He wondered if she was thinking of the evening at the Church Social in Curicanti, when Mrs. Klein was rude to her.

CHAPTER

IX

BEYOND THE BALUSTRADE OF the terrace, through the cypress trees at the bottom of the garden, the hills and the sky and the roofs and towers of Florence were like the background of a picture in the Uffizi, all brown and red and faded blue and delicate green. Roger lingered on the terrace a little longer, enjoying the warmth of the spring sunshine ; then he turned and went back into the house. Through the hall with its heavy carved Tuscan walnut and its pale blue and white bowls and vases of majolica, into the drawing-room beyond, where the owner of the villa had so oddly contrived to blend Edwardian England with an antique-collector's Italy.

The room was empty, but it still seemed to echo the fluting, chirping, chattering voices of Mary's friends who had been here to lunch to day. Mrs. Vane and dapper little Sir Quintin Quigley and those people from Boston and the Italian Countess and her son. The beaky-nosed, quick-eyed woman in black and white, and the soft-voiced young man in English clothes, with his winning smile and his heavy dark eyes.

They had been very agreeable, both of them, recalling that pleasant meeting at Aix-les-Bains last summer ; the excursions, the dinner-parties. Naturally when they found themselves in Florence they had felt that they must come and see the Bartons. Perhaps later on this summer the Bartons could visit them, at the estate in the Abruzzi. Unfortunately they could no longer live as they used to, but there would always be a welcome for their friends. The Bartons were going back to London for the Season, and later to Germany and Austria? Well then, it would not be much further to come on to the Abruzzi in the autumn.

The Countess had beamed upon a flattered Mary, a flattered, embarrassed Harold; the young Count had talked to Alice about Paris and Italy. When he saw that she was not interested in theatres and pictures he changed the subject and told her about the cavalry school at Tor di Quinta, where Count Polidori was training a new regiment of rough-riders. It all started, apparently, with a certain horse called Skapta, who liked going down the sheer cliff-face of the quarries; gradually, and at the cost of some casualties, they had trained other horses to do the same.

Alice was interested but dubious; it sounded cruel, and in any case she never knew quite what to make of this sleek young man with his background of antique portraits and dusty baroque palaces. He was a famous horseman . . . but Miss Cartwright, who knew about European aristocracy, didn't approve of him, though she wouldn't say why not. Even at Aix, when the Countess and Gino left, there were whispers about the hotel-bill, angry shop-keepers, a cheque . . .

Mary wouldn't listen to that sort of thing; the Almanach de Gotha was enough for her. It wasn't hard to guess what she was half-hoping, even if she never spoke of it. She was annoyed with Alice for not being nicer to Gino . . . but that was an old story, too, by now. In all this plunge into European society, Alice had been her chief disappointment. Shy, awkward, rather sullen Alice, who wore her expensive clothes so badly, and had no small-talk, and didn't want to go to London and be presented . . . she was not only unhappy herself, but she made her partners at dances unhappy too, and her hostesses at dinner-parties. If she went on like this she would ruin everything.

Mary was resting now. The house was very quiet. Upstairs, Harold and Lionel Morton would be busy. Reading Latin or French or English poetry, looking at books on art and architecture, correcting one of the little essays Harold wrote. It seemed a queer way for a boy of Harold's age to want to spend the afternoon, but there it was. Lionel was doing his job well. Harold had all the social tricks and patter already, and old ladies at Mary's tea parties thought he was charming.

It had been a good winter for little Harold Barton of Curicanti ; here in the Fiesole of Boccaccio and Galileo, of the Medici and Fra Angelico.

He had made wonderful progress in his studies, largely because he was so madly anxious to learn and because he had such a burning admiration for gentle, cultured, Oxonian Lionel. When they weren't reading and writing they would go for long walks among the vineyards, or they would go down to Florence and look at churches and picture-galleries. Perhaps Mary would join them there, for tea at Doni's ; later they would go round the antique-shops of the Via Fossi, or stroll in the Piazza Signoria. Lionel would talk about the burning of Savonarola, or show them the Perseus, and tell them about Cellini and how he had to throw in his cups and plates and goblets when the metal ran out that night while he was casting it.

Mary enjoyed all that too. She liked the villa—there was a Swiss housekeeper to look after things for her—and the luncheon-parties and dinners and evenings with talk and music. The English colony had been a little slow in calling . . . but there were plenty of other visitors. The gutteral Duchess with the wig, who knew all the scandals of every capital in Europe, the little Danish painter who had done a portrait of Harold, the Russian nobleman who collected books—he had asked Harold to tea at his flat, but Lionel had advised him not to go—little Sir Quintin cooing over the majolica and helping her with her own antique-buying . . . Yes, Mary was getting what she had always wanted now.

For himself, he reflected, the winter had passed pretty quickly. He had read a lot, and his business correspondence kept him busy, and he had liked poking about the old lanes and alleys, or strolling up to the podere to talk, as best he could, to old Pietro the contadino about his vines and wine-presses. It was pleasant in his deep cellar with its vats and casks and coolness and smell of wine. And there were always letters from Jim to look out for . . . sometimes to receive. Jim was settling down in Hargraves' office, and in his spare time learning his way round the glittering New York of the Waldorf and Sherry's and Delmonico's. About now he should be starting off for Mexico, where the syndicate had interests in silver-mines.

Only Alice had found the winter too long. Trying to make conversation at Mary's parties, and reading novels in her room, and going walks with Miss Cartwright. Miss Cartwright, always so neat and smart in her coat-and-skirt, had found it difficult to know what to do with Alice, who wasn't interested in sketching or learning French or playing the piano, and didn't want to hear about the customs of English society, and was dreading the London season that was being planned for her. Mary had already written to the Embassy in London about that presentation . . . Well, that was a harmless ambition. But this business about young Gino was taking things a little too far.

*   *   *   *

Mary was horrified and angry and disappointed when he told her that he was going back to America this summer and taking Alice with him, but when she tried to argue, he shocked her into silence with a snarl that surprised himself almost as much as her. He regretted it afterwards ; after all, her disappointment was natural enough. She had taken a lot of trouble, writing to the Embassy in London, writing to Lady Hornbeam, to Mrs. Vane. She meant it all for the best—this season she had planned for Alice, the new clothes to be bought in Paris, the lists of eligible young men, with titles if possible, and doubtless not much money, who would take Alice in to dinner and fill her programme at balls. But she saw, for once, that he had made up his mind, and shrugged her shoulders. Very well, then. She and Harold and Lionel would go alone. Afterwards they would go on to Germany and Austria. "You can join us there when you feel inclined."

She was angry and disappointed . . . and yet
perhaps in her heart a little relieved. He knew that
when it came to society, he himself, and Alice, were
more of a liability than anything. Mary and Harold
would get on better by themselves. And even if
those last days at the villa were glacial with Mary's
disapproval, Alice's eager, excited, joy made up for
everything.

*   *   *   *

A British ship again, from Genoa. Forty or fifty
saloon passengers, a multitude of emigrants in the
steerage. Looking down at the shifting crowds on
the foredeck—ragged young men, scared old women,
giggling girls, children beyond numbering—he wondered what would happen to them in the new world
ahead. It was only a little more than thirty years
since he himself stole ashore with empty pockets,
almost as lost and alien as those boys from Piedmont
and Liguria.

He would stand and watch them, while the liner
throbbed Westward, till Alice came almost dancing up
and took his arm and dragged him off to play shuffleboard with her. She was another person now—
gay, talkative, laughing, her cheeks bright in the sea-
wind. As he watched her, his pleasure was not
unmixed with anxiety. This was all very well . . .
but Mary's Europe would be even harder for her
afterwards.

They spent two weeks in New York. Alice had
loathed it when they were here before, but now she
glowed with pleasure at each familiar object, from the
first sight of the statue of Liberty to the first breakfast

L   161

of hot cakes and maple syrup, and while he was busy she pottered happily about alone.

He had a lot of business to talk with his lawyer—little Oscar Judson ; all that money took more looking after than he had bargained for. His block of shares in the syndicate was paying good interest . . . and there were royalties from the mines still coming . . . and on top of that all his new investments, sound, conservative investments, in Government Bonds and railroads and real estate. Lists to be gone over, statements to be read, documents to be signed . . . and after all, he had never been a business man, really. Only a miner, and a pretty unsuccessful store-keeper. It was lucky that Judson was efficient and reliable.

Jim was away in Mexico still, but Hargraves was in town : they talked business, he and Alice were asked to dinner at the Hargraves' great stone house on Riverside Drive. There were statues and Italian paintings which looked less alien and imposing now somehow, and Alice, though she hadn't much wanted to go, went one of her Paris dresses and quite enjoyed herself. Mrs. Hargraves was fat and wore diamonds, but she was a kindly, simple woman really, easier to talk to than the Countess, or Mrs. Vane. Little Hargraves, puffing at his cigar later, said that Jim was shaping pretty well. He had felt his oats a bit at first, but that was natural. This trip to Mexico ought to do him a lot of good.

Roger listened and nodded and had to be content with that. Next day he had another talk with Judson, who was keeping an eye on Jim too, and whose attitude was much the same. Then he went back to the hotel and collected Alice ; they had dinner at a restaurant and went to a theatre. A few days later his business in New York was finished. They took the Twentieth Century Limited to Chicago and went on by the Rock Island to Denver.

The last morning in the train, Roger could see that Alice had not slept at all. She sat with her cheek against the window, watching the brown plains, little farms, barbed-wire fences flicker by, and suddenly she touched his arm and pointed to the mountains that stood against the sky ahead.

Denver and the crisp sunny streets with all their life of crowds and street-cars, horses and automobiles. The Brown Palace Hotel and recognitions, greetings. Alice flinging open her bedroom window and breathing the electric mountain air.

Sam Potter came to see them that same day. His wife and daughter were away : he entertained Roger and Alice in his big, uncomfortable, expensive house, and they talked about Cripple Creek and the Klondike and things here. His son-in-law was helping him to run the store these days : soon Sam would be able to retire and live a life of ease like Roger, only on a smaller scale. Ellen wanted to see Europe ; maybe they would come over some time. What were the Barton's plans now ? Were they going over to the Western Slope ?

Roger shook his head. There was nothing to take them back to Curicanti. Rather to his surprise, Alice didn't want to go back there either. Somehow she too seemed to feel that that would only be embarrassing.

And indeed, as the days passed, there was a vague feeling of anti-climax even about this. The hotel was comfortable . . . but you expected that, you took it as a matter of course by now. People were friendly . . . but rushed and busy and full of their own affairs. Sightseeing was only sightseeing after all, whether you were looking at arrow-heads and eagle-feather war-bonnets in a Denver museum or going round a gallery in Florence with Harold and Lionel. And, after the first thrilling breath of mountain air, the first sight of the mountains, it all seemed flatter and smaller and dustier than you had remembered when you sat and thought of it in Italy.

You'd remembered the mountains, the blue-jays, the smell of sage-brush, Doctor Whitman talking about Zuni and Acoma and the cliff-dwellings of the Mesa Verde . . . You'd forgotten the flies and the mosquitos and the squalid wooden shanties, the raw-boned mules pulling overloaded wagons, the tired, shabby farmers' wives. You'd remembered the busy streets of Denver and Sam Potter, shrewd and friendly and kind. You'd forgotten the back streets and the billboards and the pool-rooms, the tobacco-chewing and the cuspidors. You'd forgotten that people would stare at a suit made in London, a coat-and-skirt bought in Paris, that hack-drivers would try to cheat rich-looking tourists, that the newspapers with their scream ing headlines told you so little about the rest of the world.

You had forgotten, in fact, that all this time you had been changing more than the people and places you used to know.

Letters came from Mary and Harold, in London, full of things they had seen and done, people they had met, music they had heard. The Lancelot-Whites and the Weissers had been kind, and Mary had gone to another big bazaar got up by Lady Cauldfield, and Lord Rosebery's horse had won the Derby, and Lionel had taken them to Oxford and shown them round the Colleges. People were worrying about the intentions of the German Emperor, and Harold had been reading a novel by Joseph Conrad and some poetry by W. B. Yeats.

Roger and Alice read the letters and said nothing. When they had had enough of Denver they went down to Colorado Springs. They drove round the Garden of the Gods, and saw the Cave of the Winds, and drank water from the bubbling spring at Manitou, and, as Alice admired " Ramona," went up South Cheyenne Canyon to see Helen Hunt Jackson's grave. It was all very pleasant, but they were tourists among tourists here too.

Then they visited Cripple Creek, and for Roger that was another anti-climax. Cripple Creek was a flourishing little city now, all big brick buildings and rows of trim little houses and wide streets open to the sun. It was strange to see it, and the mines which still produced their millions, the shafts which went down to depths once believed impossible. They were shown round by guides, like any other tourists. Mine buildings, machinery, mills. Roger made no effort to hunt up old acquaintances. It was only with a brief twinge of envy that he listened to mine-owners and engineers in the lobby of the National Hotel, talking a language he once used to talk. Only for a moment did his fingers itch to handle the samples of ores in glass cases in the souvenir shops.

Portland, Golden Cycle, El Paso with its new drainage tunnel, Stratton's great Independence still a name to conjure with, though Stratton himself, the wild, eccentric, lonely Stratton, had died three years ago. The lawyers were squabbling about his will now, but whoever got his money he himself hadn't found much happiness in all the millions he made.

It was almost a relief to come away from Cripple Creek again.

Their last weeks in Colorado they spent as boarders at a ranch in the mountains, fishing, riding, lazing in the sun. That was better . . . running water, creak of saddle-leather, chipmunks scurrying round the mouths of the old deserted mine-shafts in the baking, glittering hills . . . but even that wasn't all they had hoped. There were too many other boarders ; chattering, giggling school-teachers with bunchy skirts and sun-peeled noses ; the rancher's horses were unexciting even by livery-stable standards, and Alice didn't like the young man who was told off to act as their guide. He was tall and brown and handsome, fond of jingling his spurs and showing off his horsemanship, and he insisted on treating her like another tourist, and telling her tall stories about wolves and grizzlies as if she was one of the wide-eyed schoolmarms. He was pleased with himself in every way, and took it for granted that she would be glad to flirt with him. Roger didn't like him either. Just the same, he was a little surprised at the expert ruthlessness with which Alice snubbed him. Lady Hornbeam couldn't have done it more icily. Alice wouldn't have been able to do that, a couple of years ago. She wouldn't have wanted to do it, either : she would probably have got on with him quite well . . .

But it wasn't till they were back in Denver, packing and getting ready for the journey back to Europe, that she admitted how much her ideas had changed. He had been out all morning, at the steamship office and the bank, and Alice was sitting by the window of her bedroom when he came in. He asked her what she had been doing since breakfast, and he thought her voice was a little too casual as she replied.

" Nothing much. I went out and did some shopping. Presents to take back to Mother and Harold —though goodness knows what one can get here that *they* would want. Just outside the hotel, when I came back, I—I met an old beau."

" Oh? Who was that? "

" Johnny Bishop, from Curicanti. He's been in Denver visiting some relative. It—it was funny seeing him again."

" Johnny Bishop ! Is that so ! I'd like to see him again too. Where is he now? Did you ask him to come in? "

" Yes. He came in and we sat down in the lobby for a few minutes. He's gone again now—he had to catch a train."

Johnny Bishop . . . Roger looked at Alice. She and Johnny used to see a lot of each other. He used to take her out in a buggy in the summer, or in the Bishop's cutter in the winter . . . they used to go skating together, people used to tease them . . . he was a nice boy though, they'd known each other all their lives, he'd been pretty fond of Alice, and she was fond of him. If things had turned out differently . . .

" Gosh Alice, that must have been a surprise all right. What is he doing now? Working in his father's store? "

" No. Someone—some uncle left him a little money and he's bought a ranch. Not a very big one, but he's going to try and built it up. He was talking a lot about his ranch-house and a new pedigree bull he wants to buy and a water-pipe he's laying from a spring somewhere."

" Why didn't you make him wait till I came back? I'd have liked to see him. We could have given him a meal. You must have had a lot to talk about . . . Was he looking well ? "

" Yes, he was looking very well. But—after the first few minutes, we didn't have much to talk about."

She stopped with a nervous little laugh, and then went on again more slowly.

" You know, Dad, he was the person I missed most of all, at first. I used to imagine coming back, and meeting him again. I even tried to write to him once or twice, that first winter, but I always tore the letters up. He and I and Jim and Mollie Bishop—we used to have a lot of fun together when we were children, and afterwards, too. When I saw him in the street there, this morning, I could hardly believe it, it seemed too good to be true. And, just for a few minutes, it was like old times. Hearing about himself, and the ranch, and Mollie—she's married now—and Doctor Whitman, and the Kleins. Hearing about old Tex —he's dead, he died last winter—and Cattleman's Day, and the new schoolhouse on Cedar Street. And then . . ."

" And then what, Alice ? "

" Oh, I don't know. It all sort of died. He began asking me about Europe, and what we were doing, and he obviously didn't understand a word of what I told him . . . it was like talking to someone from another planet. He tried to ask the right questions . . . was it true Englishmen put on red coats and stove-pipe hats to chase foxes, and did the French really eat frogs' legs, and didn't we get tired of living in Italy among a lot of Wops. The more I tried to answer the less he understood. And then I tried to change the subject, and I said something about New York. I happened to mention the Waldorf, and I saw a funny look come in his eyes, he thought I was showing off. And the way he looked at my clothes, and my gloves, and my handbag . . . I wanted to ask him who he was, to look at me like that. Poor Johnny sitting there, holding his hat in his big red hands, wiping his forehead with a red bandana . . . I couldn't believe that he really used to be . . . so raw and crude and ignorant. I could just imagine his little ranch, and the chickens pecking round the door. A few years ago I used to think that it would be heaven to live on a ranch like that. Now the idea of it made me shudder. Then he asked me why we hadn't come to Curicanti, and I didn't know what to say. I just mumbled something about you being busy. So he gave a funny hard little laugh and said he guessed the Golden West Hotel *would* seem pretty uncomfortable after the Waldorf. And that was that. It was rather a relief when he got up and said he had to go."

There was a silence. She bent forward, staring out of the window. At last she spoke again.

"Of course he hasn't changed, really. And we did have a lot of fun together, in the old days. Even when we used to quarrel, it was fun. But now . . . it's different. Maybe I don't belong in Mrs. Vane's world. But I don't belong in Johnny's world either, now."

*   *   *   *

By letters and cables it had finally been arranged that they should meet the others in Munich. They crossed in a German liner, ornate as a palace and efficient as a man-of-war, crowded with Germans and German-Americans. Roger found it all very strange —the unfamiliar language, the rich food, the close-cropped heads, the cigar-smoke and the portraits of the Emperor and the dreamy faces listening to dreamy music over coffee-cups piled with whipped cream.

Mary and Harold were waiting for them in Munich : Lionel had gone back to England for a few weeks' holiday. They were staying at a big hotel in the Ludwigstrasse : it was strange to be back in the European world of Hall Porters and Head Waiters, of little gilt lifts and long French-windowed rooms. At dinner they drank champagne to celebrate their reunion, and Harold chattered away about the Wagnerfeste at the Prinz Regenten Theatre and the Castle of Neuschwannstein, built by the mad King Ludwig. It was like something in a fairy-story, on top of a great rock.

Alice said nothing about Johnny Bishop and Roger didn't either. Mary asked a few dutiful questions about Denver and Mr. Potter. She talked less about her time in London than he had expected, and he gathered that she hadn't enjoyed it as much as she had hoped. Once she was a little sarcastic about Mrs. Vane and Lady Hornbeam, and once she made a slightly bitter remark about the snobbishness of the English aristocracy. She seemed to have given up that plan of buying a house in London : they had taken

the villa at Fiesole again for a few months. Lionel
Morton was going to rejoin them at Venice, and Miss
Cartwright would come back later, to go walks with
Alice among the vineyards. Later on in the winter
they might visit Egypt and Sicily.

CHAPTER

X

EGYPT AND SICILY, SWITZERLAND and Austria, Paris and London, Italy again. Somehow they never seemed to stay in one place very long. Now it was a hotel with balconies above half-tropical gardens dropping to the Mediterranean ; now it was a little Schloss in the mountains, with old stone walls three feet thick, and curtseying maids in picturesque costumes, and heads of roedeer and chamois round the panelled rooms. At Christmas the bagpipes of the Abruzzi droned through the streets of Rome : in the spring the fireworks flared and hung over the lighted boats off the lighted promenades of the Riviera ; the four-in-hands went glittering under the trees of the Bois ; the bands and bearskins passed down the Mall to the trooping of the colour, barrel-organs poured out the waltz from the " Merry Widow," suffragettes scuffled with policemen outside Parliament. Then the Continent again—the silver trumpets calling from the balcony of the Fest-spielhaus at Bayreuth ; parasols and conversation among the tables in the gardens of Mary's favourite spa . . . in the autumn the valleys of South Tyrol with the grapes heavy in the terraced vineyards, and the coloured hats and leder-hosen under the arcades of little cobbled squares. Then winter again and the bazaars and dragomen of Cairo, or the thin pastoral flute sounding through the ruins of the Greek Theatre at Taormina, and tea on a flower-hung terrace looking out at Etna white and perfect in the sky.

One year the Russian Ballet came to Paris, and Harold could talk about nothing but Nijinski and Pavlova, Karsavina and Chaliapin, Scheherazade and Prince Igor. Taft followed Roosevelt as President of the United States, and Bleriot flew the channel, and Sir James Lancelot White, at Henley that summer, spoke gloomily and bitterly about Lloyd George. In Colorado, the Camp Bird Mine was still flourishing : it was a queer echo of older preoccupations to hear about it from an English author who had recently been exploring unknown America . . . and even Mary was interested to read that Tom Walsh's daughter had bought the Hope Diamond with all its legends of ill-fate. Next spring, at Biarritz, King Edward was staying at the Hotel du Palais : he looked old and tired and ill, and it was no surprise, a few months later, to hear that he was dead. Seven kings rode behind his coffin, and Teddy Roosevelt followed them in a carriage, and Mary wore black that summer, while Halley's comet burned in the sky. Next year she bought a lot of new clothes and they went to London for the Coronation. In the autumn Roger left the others and slipped across to New York again to see Hargraves and Judson, and when the time came for him to start back, Jim suddenly announced that he was coming too.

*   *   *   *

The wide dining-saloon was crowded, gay with lights, noisy with laughter and voices and music and the clatter of crockery and the popping of corks. The sea was calm, but there was a slow, slight roll, a slow tilting and recovery, and always the restless throb of engines driving the liner eastward through the Atlantic night.

At this little corner table there were just four of them, Roger himself, and Jim, and the little banker and his wife. Jim had been annoyed because he and his father weren't at the Captain's table, and Roger hadn't confessed that he himself had arranged this with the Chief Steward. He hadn't wanted a lot of company and formality : he had hoped, rather absurdly, that this crossing would give him a chance to get to know Jim again.

But it wasn't turning out that way. Jim spent most of his time playing cards, and at meals he didn't have much to say as a rule. He disliked the Whitings, who came from Kansas and weren't his sort at all. Only to-night for a change he was in an expansive mood : he had ordered champagne for all of them, and was making himself agreeable. Jim in his evening-clothes, fattish, sleek, a little florid, with a charming white smile under a carefully-brushed moustache and a flower in his buttonhole . . . the Whitings were obviously a little impressed by his talk of New York and London and Paris, and apparently didn't notice the faint condescension in his manner.

" Oh yes," he was saying. " I make this crossing several times a year. The old Cunard line do you pretty well. Though the White Star are building a ship which ought to beat the *Mauretania's* record pretty easily. Some of the German boats aren't bad."

The Whitings nodded. This was their first trip to

Europe. They turned to Roger and asked him again about his home, in Switzerland, wasn't it?

Roger said it was. No doubt they pictured glaciers and chamois, but he didn't bother to describe the big ornate villa on the hillside above Lac Leman, with its gardens and flower-beds and the flagpole where Mary made them fly a Union Jack at half-mast when King Edward died. A funny place to think of as your home. But it really looked as if they were settled there for good now, after all the years of wandering from place to place. The house at Fiesole, the palazzo in Venice, the little Schloss in the Tyrol.

Jim was talking about winter sports at St. Moritz; Roger sipped his champagne and listened idly to a description of the Cresta Run, staring about the room. Mouths eating, mouths talking, faces turned politely towards each other, faces bent over plates. Evening dresses, gleaming shirt-fronts, flowers. The quick, deft stewards, the chief stewards watching, the wine-steward with his draped chain. A figure or a group caught his eye here and there. The family at the next table: father, mother, two pretty girls. The leonine old man with white hair, booming away to two old ladies. He tried to pick out some of the celebrities. Mary would want to know about them. The old American millionarie and his lovely young wife. The Prima Donna who had been making a farewell tour in America. The famous artist. The titled Englishmen. She would want to hear all about them, and about the ship itself, with its lounges and garden-cafés and Turkish baths. Nothing would induce her to cross the Atlantic. She would enjoy a ship like this, just the same.

The room was hot and stuffy; he felt suddenly a

little sickish, the voices round him swelled and blared. One rich course, another, another, the thick gilded bill-of-fare, the sharp prickle of champagne against his tongue. Perhaps out there in the darkness somewhere near was some old wind-jammer in whose fo'castle hungry men and boys were dipping maggoty biscuits in washy coffee.

" Well," said Mr. Whiting. " To-morrow is Sunday already. I wonder if we'll dock on Tuesday evening. Are you staying long in England, Mr. Barton ? "

He realised that the little man was talking to him.

" No, just a day or two. I have a little business to see to in London. Then I expect I'll join my wife and my other son in Paris. For the winter we generally go to Sicily."

These trips to America always made him restless. It would be strange to be back with Mary and Harold and Lionel. Mary would have a lot of new Paris clothes, no doubt. Harold would be full of his latest craze . . . it might be modern painting, or Greek art, or the Russian Ballet, or the history of the Crusades. Patient, gentle Lionel, (who was still with them, though Harold's education had been supposedly finished long ago) would be listening and smiling and sympathising and agreeing as he always did.

Alice should be back too, before long, from her yachting-trip in the Mediterranean. Somehow he hated to think of that smartly-dressed, hard-faced Alice who smoked too much and drank a little too much sometimes and played a lot of bridge. Alice who had never married, and accepted, indifferent and a little scornful, the friendship of a lot of shrill-voiced women and pouchy-eyed men with titles, and hadn't even wanted to come with him to America this time. She had drifted into a queer, restless, pointless sort of life. Gambling at Monte Carlo and driving her own car, too fast, along the winding Corniche, and coming back at intervals to sit about the garden smoking cigarettes in a long holder and staring idly at a book, bored and silent and indifferent.

Mary had done her best for her, with all those expensive luncheon-parties and little dances in London, Paris, Rome. Alice had got over her awkwardness and shyness, and had learnt to dance and play bridge and talk about yachts and racing. But she had never looked twice at any of the impecunious aristocrats they trotted out for her. She was still young, good-looking, an heiress—no wonder the old women watched her and whispered behind their fans. Once or twice she had been interested, but there had always been something wrong. There was the Irishman with the farm in South Africa—she could have been happy with him, perhaps, and Mary would have accepted him : he was the grandson of a Peer. But he was married already, and his wife wouldn't divorce him, though he hadn't seen her for six years. And there was the young man whose father owned a huge cattle-ranch in Hawaii : he had been educated at Yale, his mother was the daughter of a British General, his stories of volcanoes and beaches and Hawaiian cowboys roping long-horned bulls had shaken Alice out of her indifference again. But he was engaged to a girl in Honolulu, he and Alice had met each other a few months too late. By now the whispers behind the fans were becoming a little malicious. Mary never heard them. If Alice herself did, she gave no sign.

M   177

Alice was one of Mary's failures, but not the only one. Mary still went to London, and was entertained by the Weissers and the Lancelot-Whites : she still bought her clothes in Paris, and curtseyed to Italian princesses at Charity bazaars in Rome. But neither Rome nor Paris nor London had given her what she wanted ; the right doors didn't open, the right invitations didn't come.

When they took a house, there was always a good chef and an imposing major-domo ; when they were in a hotel, the dinners were always carefully chosen, the waiters and head-waiters lavishly tipped. The flowers and decorations were always splendid, and the wines were vintage, and there was always someone —Mrs. Vane or Mrs. Vane's successors—to help her to arrange the seating and to admire her new dress. But all too often the conversation seemed to flag, however good the wine was and however carefully the places had been arranged. Mary talked as fluently as ever . . . but then a pause, a tiny prickle of awkwardness showed you—and showed her too— that she had said the wrong thing. Perhaps they had set about it wrongly from the start. Perhaps it was just that they had come to it too late.

The liner quivered and thudded ; a steward said : " No ice, sir ? " and took away a plate. Jim was talking about London now : it was worth going there once a year or so, if only to get some suits made properly.

Roger peeled an orange and ate it and dabbled his fingers : there were rose-leaves in the finger-bowl. Jim had finished too. He looked across, and said :

" Well, Dad, how about it ? Shall we go and have some coffee and a brandy perhaps, outside ? "

He led the way, a tall, stout, well-tailored figure, swaggering faintly, down the long dipping vista of carpet between the tables, out into the creaking lobby, up to the smoking-room. The smoking-room was full of faces and voices and noise too.

Half a dozen florid men knew him already; they waved and laughed and shouted at him as he came in.

"Feel like a little more poker? How about a drink to keep that dinner down?"

He hesitated, wavered, looked at Roger.

"Mind if I leave you, Dad? I was playing with those fellows before dinner, and I promised I'd give them a chance to get their money back."

"Of course not, Jim. Go on. I'll have some coffee here."

Jim smiled his white flashing smile and went across to join his friends. Roger found a little table near the door and ordered coffee and lighted a cigar. Jim must be getting on for thirty now . . . funny that he had never married either. He was too comfortable, no doubt, and amused himself in too many other ways. He did nothing much except enjoy himself—he had quarrelled with Hargraves and left the mining syndicate long ago. First-nights and horse-shows and prize-fights; expensive young women from the latest musical comedy; hunting-trips with a lot of whisky and poker in steam-heated shooting-lodges, voyages to Europe, Savile Row suits, the Cresta Run.

He watched them settling down to their game, until a big, red-faced Englishman came and sat opposite him and struck up a conversation. The weather, the crossing, England and America. Steam-heat and ice-water and those ghastly newspapers. "It will be a relief to see *The Times* again. I like to

follow the news pretty closely . . . it is a nuisance
being cut off for six days like this. These little wireless
bulletins are not much use."

Roger shrugged his shoulders. The news didn't
matter to him much. But it was all very fine to
be so scornful of wireless bulletins. If this man had
spent six months at sea, without sighting a sail,
alone in a circle of sky and water, he would
realise better what Marconi had done . . . He
nodded, grunted, finished his coffee. Then he got
up and went away. The red-faced man looked after
him sadly, and then cast about for someone else to
talk to.

The lift went sliding smoothly down : he wondered
what Captain Morris would have thought of this.
He looked at the smart buttoned page-boy and wondered what he thought. The wide white alleyway
opened aft and forward : he went down it, past the
closed cabin-doors. A tired-looking stewardess passed
him, carrying a tray. An old lady in a boudoir-cap
and dressing-gown scuttled furtively into a door
marked "Ladies." Here was his own stateroom.
Wide and quiet and spacious, with its soft carpet,
its deep bed, the radiance of shaded lamps on silk
and metal and polished wood. He opened the ward-
robe and took out his big tweed ulster and his cap :
then he stopped, looking at his image in a long glass,
with a sudden queer shock of incredulity. This
elderly, thin, grey-haired man in evening-clothes, was
he actually the Roger Barton who had shivered under
the arcades of the Goree Piazza and gone trembling
aboard the *Chester Rows* ? What was he doing here,
in this room, in these clothes ? His hair grey and
his back aching a little and his stomach full of rich

food and champagne? For a second he had that
queer sense of dreaming . . . then he laughed at
himself and turned towards the door. Back along
the alleyway. The wide empty lobby. Ring for the
lift.

The cold wind met him as he pushed open a heavy
door and stepped out on to the boat-deck : on to a
vast plateau of lights and shadows and wind. Scrubbed
planking, white paint-work, lighted windows, boats on
davits, ventilators, the four enormous funnels towering
up into the night. Forward were the officers' quarters,
the bridge above them ; aft the lighted domes of
lounges and smoking-rooms. Aft again, the Second
Class deck. Standing here, in the open, you saw how
tremendous this ship was. The wind was cold on
his face and his eyelids and salty on his lips : the sea
gleamed and glimmered dimly ; it seemed a long
way away, far below ; it rushed and swirled backwards and a myriad of reflections ran and skipped on
the foam. He looked forward again, towards the
remote watch-tower of the bridge.

This ship was the size of a mountain ; it was hard
to realise that somewhere up there were a few tiny
men who controlled it all. Eight hundred feet of
metal, driving along at twenty-four knots, with two
thousand human lives and more. Forty-six thousand
horse-power behind the thrust and kick of those great
screws . . . engines beating like huge hearts beneath
the lounges and snug cabins, the gardens and swimming-
pools. Yes, things had changed since a child stood
on the landing stage and watched a clipper-ship sail
with mails for the Colonies. Up in that wheel-house
was one man barely touching a little wheel. And in
the wireless-cabin was another young man, talking

across the dark leagues of ocean to ships and cities far
beyond the curve of the globe.

The wind was cold, but the sky was clear. There
was dancing somewhere : he could hear the distant
lilt of a waltz ; then the quicker beat of ragtime. The
old Black Ball clippers carried German bands, and in
fine weather there was dancing on the decks. They
did their twenty knots too, under full sail. Captain
Morris used to describe it. But Captain Morris,
grumbling at " tea-kettles," would call you a liar if
you found him now and told him about all this. Yet
some of the officers in those cabins forward there had
served their time in sail. He wondered if any of them
ever wished that they were boys still, still in the half-
deck, working and starving and ragging and playing
mouth-organs in the dog-watch, all this undreamed of
and unimagined. For certainly they could never
have imagined a future that would hold this. No
doubt the plans they made in those days were very
much like his own and Tommy's plans.

*   *   *   *

Next day was Sunday. It was clear and sunny
though the wind was cold still. Breakfast—Jim not
down yet. Mrs. Whiting asking questions about
Switzerland. Morning light sparkling on silver and
china ; the smell of coffee, the eggs and bacon ; the
crisp rolls and cold butter and sharp-tasting marmalade.
Afterwards he sat in his deck-chair, deftly swaddled
by the steward, warm and sheltered from that biting
wind. The long rail lifted and sank against the blue
horizon ; people walked briskly up and down the long
stretch of planking in the sun. Men in caps and over-
coats, women in furs, with veils round their heads.

He could hear distant singing, psalms, hymns, and though he had no desire to attend Divine Service he was vaguely stirred by the thought of the quiet voice that would be repeating the quiet, gracious words.

"Almighty God whose paths are in the sea . . ." Then he heard another hymn, and soon the service was ended. People coming out on deck. Stewards carrying cups of soup on trays. At noon he went to the smoking-room. Jim was there, looking glossy and tubbed and cheerful, surrounded by his glossy friends. He came over and said good morning ; " How did you sleep, Dad ? Did you get up for breakfast ? Have a drink, won't you ? The drinks are on me, to-day. I've just scooped a nice little pool on the day's run."

He had obviously had a number of drinks already, and after a moment or two he drifted back to his friends. Loud voices, cocktail shakers rattling, sudden guffaws of laughter, another round.

He didn't come to lunch. The Whitings had apparently been having a family quarrel, and were icily polite to one another, and didn't talk much. After lunch, Roger sat in the smoking-room again. Jim and his friends were back at their table in the corner, playing poker, a cloud of cigar-smoke hanging over them and a steward still busy keeping them supplied with drinks. He sat and watched them for a little . . . Jim seemed to be winning, he was lucky at cards as a rule, though you couldn't say he had a good poker-face. Or would you have to be his father to know when he was bluffing ?

Then Mr. Whiting came and joined him, and a gloomy-looking Englishman with red beard, and one

or two others, English and American. Mr. Whiting
fell into conversation with one of the Englishmen, and
tried to explain about Taft and Roosevelt and the
Republicans : the Englishman tried to explain about
Lloyd George and the House of Lords. Roger listened
for a little, and then his thoughts drifted away : when
he listened again they were talking about the state
of European politics. The red-bearded man was
pessimistic.

" I tell you, there's trouble coming. A dozen
great States, armed to the teeth, each going its own
way without a thought for the world as a whole.
' National Sovereignty '—international anarchy. The
Hague ? Don't talk to me about the Hague ! Millions
of soldiers, great modern guns, dreadnoughts, all that
power in the hands of a few ignorant, irresponsible
men. That weak dreamer of a Czar. The doddering
old wreck in Vienna. The German Emperor riding
about in a silver helmet. The powers of the Twentieth
Century in the hands of a few medieval autocrats. It
makes one's blood run cold to think of it."

The other laughed lightly : the red beard worked
as he argued with them. Economic factors. The
Zeppelin. Aeroplanes. Read Lowes Dickenson. Read
Norman Angell.

" I tell you, Europe . . ."

Europe, thought Roger. Europe was where you
travelled with Mary. Mountains, lakes, cathedrals,
picture-galleries. Tea-rooms, restaurants, Opera
Houses, hotels and wagon-lits. Sunset on the Pincio ;
coffee at Florians ; shopping in the Kaerntnerstrasse
and the Rue de la Paix. Old Monks showing you
round cloisters, porters screeching over their tips.
Bavarian peasants smiling : " *Gruss Gott.*" Bare knees

184

and flowers and oxen dragging haycarts down winding roads past bright-painted Calvaries.

But it was also the Europe of dreadnoughts whose guns could throw a shell—how many miles? Of the draped statues in Paris, and the endless columns goose-stepping over Potsdam parade-grounds to the braying bands. Of armoured cars and Zeppelins and torpedoes. Of power—like the fifty-thousand horse-power thudding away beneath these carpets—which could be so disastrously misued.

The others went away to sleep or read or play cards. He got a book out of the library and went down to his cabin. It was soon time for tea. Then time to go out and stretch your legs again. Up and down, np and down the long straight deck, while the sunset glowed and faded in the West, astern. It was even colder now, but there were other people briskly promenading. Dusk deepening over the sea, and the great steel stem biting into the calm water, and the screws thrusting and churning eight hundred feet behind. Dusk deepening: lights coming on spaced and regular along the vista of the promenade-deck: lights behind curtains in windows and scuttles all along. You could somehow feel the warmth and stir and presence of the fifteen hundred human lives close around you: officers on the bridge, engineers watching dials and gauges, passengers playing cards and writing letters, chefs busy at great shining ranges and stewards setting tables, arranging flowers.

Sunset and dusk. It would be dark in Europe. Europe of the castles and hotels and villas; of the barracks and the Zeppelin hangars and the guns. What would Mary and Harold be doing in Paris now? Dining at the Ritz or the Crillon, perhaps: Harold talking to the waiters in his careful, fluent French, Mary preening herself a little in her newest dress, looking round the room through her lorgnette. On the yacht off Sicily Alice and her friends would be drinking and playing poker, just as Jim was doing here.

In America, in Curicanti, it would still be day. The Kleins and Doctor Whitman and the rest of them dozing through an over-eaten Sunday afternoon. Wintery already, no doubt, with snow on the mountains, but down by the river the bare earth showing through the snow. Queer to think of their lives still going on there, all these years.

He tramped round and round the deck, the wind driving against him, plucking at him round corners, thrusting at him from behind, meeting him again when he turned. It took his breath away a little, but he plodded on grimly, annoyed with himself for minding the cold, annoyed with his back and legs for feeling tired. He was getting soft, that was the trouble. Wouldn't last long now on the trail in the Klondike winter, mushing behind a dog-team in the snow. Was old Lindquist still at it, plodding and freezing up there somewhere? Or was he dead by now?

*   *   *   *

At dinner, Mr. Whiting felt it was his turn to order a bottle of champagne. Jim was at table, flushed and sweaty and talkative, his eyes bright and his hands a little clumsy : he had been playing poker all afternoon.

" I started well, but then my luck changed. I'm a couple of hundred dollars down now. Never mind, I'll get it back to-night."

186

He laughed at Roger's hint about card-games with strangers on steamers : hell, this game was all right, he said.

" I know one or two of 'em in New York. And anyway, I wasn't born yesterday. It would take a better man than any of that bunch to put anything over on me ! No, Dad, you wait and see. By bed-time I'll have made those boys wish they had listened to Mama when she warned them against cards ! "

He gulped his champagne and picked at his food : it seemed to steady him a little, and he addressed himself to the Whitings with heavy, uncertain geniality. That was a charming necklace Mrs. Whiting had on. She must make her husband take her shopping when they got to London.

" Just remind me, before we land, and I'll tell you the right places to go. In any of the best shops in London, all you have to do is mention my name, and they'll lay down the red carpet for you. And if Mr. Whiting is interested in sport, I can help him there too. They know me pretty well at Tattersalls . . . and my bookmaker gives the best odds you'll get, even if he is a nasty little Jew. If you want a pair of really good riding boots I'll tell you where to get them." Little Mr. Whiting, an elderly banker, blinked at that, but Jim went on. " For hunting pinks you have to be specially careful about your tailor. Oh yes, I've tried fox-hunting too . . . but I like something bigger for my money. Next year I'm thinking of going out to Africa, like Teddy Roosevelt, and having a look at all those lions and elephants. Maybe you'll come too, eh, Dad ? Bring along a pan and shovel, and we'll find ourselves another Klondike on the bank of Lake Nyanza . . . What do you call

this, steward ? Anyway, I don't want it. The food
on this line isn't as good as it was a few years
ago."

As soon as he had finished, he mumbled some
excuse and went away. Roger watched him go ;
big, swaggering, a little unsteady, the Jim who used
to brag to his friends about his father's gold-mines,
the Jim who nearly killed himself diving off the railroad-
trestle when someone dared him . . . the Jim who
might have done such a lot with his life, and was doing
nothing. He wished the Whitings wouldn't look so
carefully, politely expressionless.

After dinner he went into the smoking-room again,
but the red-bearded man eyed him hungrily and he
went hastily away. He didn't want another lecture
on European politics.

He wandered restlessly about the huge, bright,
crowded heated rooms. People listening to music.
People playing cards. Mary would never play cards
on Sunday : it was one of her little superstitions. You
couldn't call it piety with her. Any more than her
smartly-dressed church-going. Harold was the only
one who took any real interest in religion even. He
had gone through an Anglo-Catholic phase at one time.
But it hadn't lasted long. He was very much the
sceptic again now.

Old ladies talking together in sofas under the
vibrating leaves of palms. Middle-aged women scribbling letters at jarring tables. People staring along
bookshelves in the library. He took some magazines
and retired with them into a corner : the long evening
throbbed and rattled itself away. Before turning in,
he went out on deck again. Bitterly cold, with stars
sparkling above the flat black sea. There was some

sort of service going on in the second class saloon, a faint, distant sound of hymns again. He turned the other way and walked forward : stood watching the wide bows driving into the starry night. He wondered what they were thinking up on the bridge, up in the crows-nest, with fifteen hundred lives in their care. The rail quivered under his hand ; he felt the thrust and lift and life of the whole vast shuddering machine. And suddenly he heard the sharp, familiar sound of striking bells. Clang-clang, clang-clang, clang-clang, clang ! Seven bells . . . it was strange to hear them. It took him back strangely to those distant nights when he himself had stood watches, struck bells. This drumming steel monster was a ship like the others, after all. Like the *Chester Rows*, the *Lady Mary*, the *Paladin*.

As he stood there, a man in uniform came out of a doorway and along the deck. A stoutish, elderly man, with grizzled hair under a rakish cap and the four rings of a Captain on his sleeve. He was vaguely like the Captain Dobson of the old Cunarder bound for Naples, years ago. This fellow had risen higher in his profession, but he was the same type.

He saw Roger and nodded and said good evening with all the bluff, conscious heartiness of a liner captain greeting a first-class passenger. He must have served his time in sail too, though : there must be moments when he was aware of the contrast. Perhaps being skipper of a crack Atlantic liner was like being a millionaire. Hunting for gold was a sort of dream : the same with sailors. Fighting up the ladder of promotion, dreaming of the top. Waking up to find yourself in command of a ship like this, with old ladies worrying about their poodles, and rich young men being fleeced at poker, and a Board of Directors expecting you to keep the Blue Ribbon, and fifteen hundred lives in your care.

Still, it was a job worth doing. And this man didn't look as if the poodles and the Directors worried him. He went on down the wide, scrubbed deck, quick and assured and purposeful, and up the ladder to the bridge. Roger felt a queer, unexpected pang of envy as he watched him go. Captain Dobson, he remembered, had a son who had been in the *Conway* and was an officer in the P. & O.

CHAPTER
XI

IT HAD RAINED IN the night, but now the sun was out
again and the moisture steaming up out of the lawns
and coppices. The high, sharp roofs and turrets of
the chateau threw their shadows across the gravel ;
wetness dried off the breasts and flanks of the stone
nymphs along the balustrade. In the long formal
garden, old Pierre was trimming the edges of a path ;
he turned round and touched his hat when Roger
came along. He didn't look as if he wanted to talk,
but Roger stopped and nodded.

" Fine day to-day." His French was elementary
but sufficient ; Pierre agreed grudgingly that the
weather was good.

" I am glad that it is fine. My daughter is coming
to stay. You know, she drove an ambulance during
the war. Since then she has been travelling . . .
lately she has been in East Africa."

He wondered again what Alice had found to do in
East Africa all these months. She had been staying
with friends . . . an ex-General and his wife who had
a title, on some huge sun-baked farm in Kenya. Her
few brief letters had told of shooting and riding and
flying and a lot of bridge, but they didn't tell you
what Alice really thought about this post-war world
and her place in it.

Pierre nodded and asked some question about Monsieur 'Arold.

"Yes, Monsieur Harold and his wife are coming too. With their little girl. My elder son is in America, as you know."

Pierre nodded again and said something too quick to follow ; it sounded felicitous, but there was a slightly bitter look in his eyes. Roger wondered if he were thinking of his own sons, one legless and making baskets in an institution for the *mutilés*, the other buried at Verdun. He was conscious of a vague embarrassment as he grunted something and wandered on. Through the opening in the yew-hedge, round the lily-pond where more marble nymphs preened themselves in the still water, through the rose-garden, back across the gravel to the huge front door. Some queer people must have come through this door since the château was built by a profiteer of the Second Empire ; pale, painted ladies of the Opera, swaggering officers whose destiny was Sedan, fat politicians confidential about Panama, old generals snarling over Dreyfus, the American steel-king planning central-heating and new bathrooms, the Bartons and their friends. Perhaps, when you came to think of it, they were the queerest of the lot.

His thoughts came back to old Pierre, clipping the edge of the path out there and remembering his sons. Europe was full of such memories these days. But the Barton family had been lucky, the War hadn't come very close to them.

They were in Switzerland that summer ; they had a house on the hillside above Vevey, looking over the lake to the mountains of Savoy. When war broke out they just stayed where they were—on an island of peace

surrounded by a continent at war. Only Alice, and
Lionel Morton, had broken away. Lionel was the
first to go ; he had always been delicate and gentle
and scholarly, but that first autumn he went back to
England, and enlisted as a private in the Army, and
died of pneumonia in some rain-sodden training-camp.
Alice had never liked him much—but soon after that
she too went off, to work in a hospital in Paris, empty-
ing basins and scrubbing floors. Later she transferred
to an Anglo-American ambulance unit, and drove an
ambulance along the dark roads behind the lines.
She never talked much about that now, and if the
things she had seen and heard had left their mark on
her, she never showed them outwardly.

Harold had worked in a relief bureau in Geneva,
answering letters, checking card-indexes, drafting
appeals. It was there that he met Ruth, the only
daughter of Charles Domney, the R.A. whose pictures
were so popular thirty years ago and who was drinking
himself to death in his big villa on the Italian Riviera
now. She and Harold had all the same tastes in art
and books and Italian travel ; she had once come, as a
child, to tea at the villa at Fiesole, years ago. They
were married soon after the Armistice, and had a little
girl now, and lived in Paris. Tall windows looking
out across the Quai Voltaire and the bookstalls to the
river and the Louvre. It was to be near them that
Mary had suggested taking this château in Normandy.

That was Alice's War, and Harold's. Jim had
joined the American Army in 1917, and had risen to
the rank of Major but had never been sent to Europe,
and was back in his comfortable apartment in
Manhatten now, grumbling about Prohibition and
gambling a little in Stocks and Shares. And as for

N

himself . . . all that he had found to do was to sit
about the villa in Switzerland and read the papers and
write cheques for war charities and go with Mary to
take fruit and flowers and chocolate to the big hotels
along the lake where the sick and wounded soldiers
and sailors lay, who had been sent out of prison-
camps in Germany.

Polished floors and neat rows of beds, neat rows of
faces. Waxy, unhealthy faces ; tired, shrunken faces,
polite thanks for the books and cigarettes.

"Thank you, sir. Much obliged, I'm sure. Yes,
you can do with something to read, lying here all day.
Though after Germany, this is too good to be true."

One eye on the embarrassed old man with the
papers and cigarettes ; the other on that elegant lady,
sweeping round like Queen Alexandra, with the doctors
and nurses being so polite to her.

Mons and le Cateau, prison-camps and salt-mines.
. . . You wondered what they were thinking, but
you couldn't ask them. When you tried to talk to
them, you found you had nothing much to say. But
you felt very old and useless, trailing after Mary down
those long rooms lined with polite, watching eyes.

*   *   *   *

Well, it was over now, and had been over for four
years, and to-day was not the day for brooding over
the past. He stood there in the big hall with its
carvings and its suite of rather tinny-looking armour,
and wondered what to do for the next couple of hours.
Upstairs, on the landing, he could hear voices. Mary
giving instructions to the housekeeper, about to-day's
meals, about the rooms for Harold and Ruth, for little
Sylvia and her nurse. Mary wouldn't be bothering

much about Alice's room, he reflected ; she wasn't
really interested in Alice, she wouldn't have minded
if Alice had stayed in Kenya, she didn't care what
Alice did. Still, everything would be in order.
Madame Comblis would see to that without being
told. And later on, when Mary was back in her
own sitting-room, he might slip up himself and have a
look. There might be some little thing . . . writing-
paper, ink, flowers, a jar of those bath-salts from the
shop in Paris . . . Not that Alice would care about
flowers and bath salts. But it would be pleasant to do
something. After all, it wasn't every day that Alice
came.

He stood there, in a shaft of light coloured by a
hideous stained-glass window, jingling the money in
his pockets and listening to the voices upstairs. In
the library, he knew, there were papers to be read and
letters to be written, but he couldn't settle to such
things to-day. It was no use telling himself that he
wasn't restless and impatient and excited. Alice was
coming, and he hadn't seen her for two years.

    *   *   *   *

Alice reached the château in time for lunch. She
came in a new car she had bought in London, and it
looked as if she had been buying some new clothes
too ; a mannish grey-flannel coat and skirt, expensive,
mannish, low-heeled shoes. She ran up the steps
to kiss her father, and he held her shoulders for a
moment and tried to imagine that this was the same
Alice who used to run out of the house to meet him
when he came back from a trip to Cripple Creek. But
it was no use trying to identify that Alice with this
middle-aged, smart, rather battered woman who

was so obviously making an effort to be nice to her parents. Alice had changed as much as the others—if not more.

He followed her into the hall—she hadn't seen the château before, and her eyebrows lifted a little as she looked round at the carvings and stained-glass and chandeliers. But she made no comment ; she kissed Mary and told her how young she looked and what a pretty dress that was, and almost at once she had pulled out a packet of cheap French cigarettes whose smoke made Mary cough protestingly. Yes, she had a good crossing. Spent the night in a hotel by the road somewhere, and had a short run this morning. Yes, her new car had come along very well.

It was all like that, bright, polite conversation in the drawing-room, Alice dutifully recognising a picture, an old French clock, a china figure from the old days in Italy or Switzerland ; looking out of the windows and telling them that the garden was charming, glancing at the books on the table and asking if they had been reading anything interesting lately. Alice, telling them some little anecdote about an English novelist on the ship coming back from Africa ; a young man whose books were full of sex, daring and outspoken, and who was frightened out of his life when a bored Frenchwoman made advances to him one evening in the Red Sea. Alice, in fact, laying herself out to be agreeable, a stranger, a middle-aged, smartly-dressed woman come to spend a night or two. . . .

It was a relief when another car rolled up the drive ; Harold and Ruth arriving with their little girl and her nurse. More handshakes and greeting ; Ruth eyeing Alice, and Alice polite to Ruth. Little Sylvia brought in in her nurse's arms and Alice poking a finger at her and trying to think of the right things to say. Obviously not much interested, lighting another cigarette and changing the subject as soon as she could.

" I hear you've got a lovely house looking over the river. I must come and see it. My flat? Well, it's comfortable enough, not the sort of thing you would admire. Do you know who I met the other day though? Edith Cartwright . . . do you remember, the Colonel's daughter who tried to do for me what Lionel Morton did for you, Harold? Poor creature—I used to worry her terribly. She's had worse worries since then, though. She must be in the fifties now, and she hasn't a penny except what she can earn, and nobody wants her ladylike talents now. She wept when she saw me . . . it was rather terrible. I'm thinking of taking her on as a sort of housekeeper . . . I could never be bothered with hiring servants and paying bills."

" What are you going to do with yourself now, Alice? "

" Oh, I don't know. Live in my flat. Travel a bit. Get another car—something a little more exciting. I might try driving in trials, or even do a little racing. . . . I'd like to fly a bit too, I started to learn, in Kenya. Horses? Perhaps . . . But I don't think I could be bothered with the huntin' set now."

She refused one of Harold's fat hand-made cigarettes and smoked another of her French horrors ; a little man in white gloves came in with a tray of cocktails ; she finished hers at a gulp and went on talking.

" Kenya? Oh, yes. I enjoyed myself. A great sprawling place in the wilds, with horses and dogs and a horrible pet baboon wandering round the garden. Dressing for dinner at night, and talking about the

197

Derby winners of the 1900s, while the native farm-hands beat their drums somewhere in the darkness outside. It's a good climate . . . sometimes the air and the lights reminded me of Colorado. A lot of riding . . . queer little race-meetings, Gerald generally rides a winner or two . . . Yes, it's an odd place. Natives and Indians and Greeks and hard-bitten old hunters and smooth young men in Old Etonian ties. Shooting . . . yes, any amount, if you want it. I suddenly found I didn't like killing things—God knows why not. Gerald has made a little landing-ground, and got a Puss Moth out from England—I enjoyed messing round with that as much as anything."

At lunch, she ate very little ; her mood seemed to have changed suddenly, and the conversation flagged a bit. More men in white gloves waiting, a vast, ornate chandelier heavy above the table, a profusion of ornate furniture, Harold talking to Mary about Paris and the salon, Ruth looking at Alice and wondering what to talk about. That tea at Fiesole seemed a safe topic ; those wonderful ices, the other visitors.

" There was an old Duchess in a red wig. And a rather charming young Italian with a title . . . I remember he paid you great attentions, and I was consumed with envy . . . I was just a girl then."

Alice remembered that young man too.

" He was a soldier, very brave and dashing. I thought of him when I heard how the Italians ran at Caporetto. I'm afraid I never cared much for Italians or Italy."

Ruth had loved Italy all her life. She had been engaged—and Alice had once known that—to a young Italian who was killed in the War. She swallowed and said nothing. Mary's face tightened with annoyance ;

198

she bent forward quickly and began to talk about the new Duchess of York. " Of course you know the legends about Glamis. . . . "

After that all the conversation was a little forced. They discussed the theatre—Alice picked at her food and pretended to listen ; they discussed politics, the League of Nations, the fantastic state of the mark in Germany. Harold, who worried at times about the ethics of Empire, tried to ask Alice questions about the treatment of the natives in Kenya, but Alice hadn't paid much attention to the native question ; she wasn't interested in politics.

It was really quite hard to find anything to talk about . . . and quite hard to find anything for her to do all afternoon and evening. Get out the car and go for a drive . . . she was obviously impatient with the sedate old Daimler, the careful English chauffeur, Ruth's raptures over lanes and quaint old villages. Back to tea. Too hot for tennis . . . neither Ruth nor Harold played much anyway. No horses in the great rambling stables. Alice liked a game of bridge, and Harold played if he had to, but how to make up a four ? A pity the Lancelot-Whites weren't here— they were keen bridge-players. God, to think that with Alice here after all this time, you wished you had the Lancelot-Whites as well !

They sat on the terrace and Harold talked about the Second Empire. Mary showed Alice some of the Princesses' embroidery, and told her all about the Russians and the ikons and the tea rooms, but Alice said she thought the Russian ruling-classes had deserved all they got.

Roger took her to see the rose-garden. The afternoon light was still hot and the air heavy with scent. There were great red roses and pink roses and yellow roses, white roses and salmon-coloured roses, roses named for cities and empresses and courtiers. They walked up and down slowly on the flagged path ; he made some remark about Curicanti, and she gave a little laugh.

" It doesn't seem real at all now, does it ? And yet I suppose it's still going on, a little modernised but really just the same. My God, when I think how homesick I was at first ! Was I ever as young as that ? Still, we had some fun when we were children. Tell me—do you ever wish you hadn't gone to the Yukon and struck it rich ? "

He didn't answer for a moment. He looked up at the turrets of the château and the windows flashing in the low sun ; he looked at this battered, well-dressed spinster beside him, her hands in the pockets of her tailored jacket, staring up at the château too, her eyes narrowed appraisingly. Alice who used to believe all old Tex's stories about the gunmen and the Trail Herds . . . who was so angry when he wouldn't let her ride Doctor Whitman's sorrel in the Ladies' Race on Cattleman's Day . . . who didn't believe anything much these days, and didn't know what she wanted, and didn't care . . She guessed what he was thinking, and laughed again.

" Oh yes, I know. I didn't mean that. How about you yourself.? Do you really like all this ? "

" I don't know, Alice. I'm accustomed to it now. I felt like a fish out of water at first, but that was nearly twenty years ago "

" Supposing you had your life over again, what would you do ? Stay in Curicanti ? Go back to the Klondike and make another fortune ? "

" I might have lost the one I had. Plenty of people did, you know. Otherwise . . . I don't know . . .I should have tried to do a bit more with my money when I got it. Something a bit more constructive . . . I don't know why I never did."

" Mother's social ambitions got in the way. And anyway, it isn't easy. I've had ideas like that too sometimes. As a matter of fact when I was out in Kenya I nearly bought a farm and settled down to do some honest work. But then—I don't know—it all seemed such a nuisance. Starting from scratch, learning everything, making mistakes, people taking advantage . . . it would never have been the real thing, in any case. So much easier to come back to London and take a flat and let Edith find some servants . . . . Oh well, what does it matter anyway? I suppose it must be nearly time to go and change."

There was nothing more to be said. She had closed the subject. At dinner she talked about Kenya again, and the rich men led by white hunters on elaborate safaris ; motors, and crates of drink and food from Fortnums. . . . "Just the sort of thing that would suit Jim. I'm surprised he's never tried it. But I suppose he's too busy now, being the shrewd financier. I believe he has made quite a lot of money lately, though I don't suppose he knows himself quite how it happened. He offered to double my income for me, but I said no thank you."

Mary didn't like that much. She admired Jim and hated to hear him sneered at. It seemed a long evening altogether, and everyone was secretly relieved when it was time to go to bed.

But lying under a great golden canopy, in his great pseudo-Renaissance bedroom, he couldn't sleep. The château was very quiet, but he could feel its life pressing all around him ; Mary in her room. Alice, Harold and Ruth, little Sylvia and her nurse . . . all those hardly-known, sallowfaced servants ; housekeepers and footmen and cooks and little maids. Expensive clocks ticking and moonlight filtering through brocade curtains of tall windows into tall rooms full of elaborate furniture. Moonlight on the terraces and rose-trees and statues ; moonlight on the orchards and the ponds.

It was for this that he and Charlie and Lindquist had toiled up the Scales and run the rapids of the Yukon in a crazy boat ; for this that they had sweated, frozen all that winter, wallowed in filth, wolfed beans and bacon out of a rancid frying-pan, slept in a stinking little kennel, crawled out at dawn to dig again. Charlie had been dead for nearly twenty years . . . old Lindquist must be dead too now . . . and he was left, lying in a bed that had belonged to a French financier's mistress, and wondering if it had all been worth while.

Hunting for gold wasn't like other ways of making money. You didn't really think of it as money ; it was like tracking a deer, it was like some queer game, or maybe it was like gambling. What you were after was not a French château full of statues, but only that one moment when you stopped the water and saw the gold shining in the riffles and knew that you had won. You didn't have time to wonder what would happen later ; what you would talk about to Countesses at dinner-parties, what would happen to your children, snatched out of a little mountain town into a world of ocean liners and de-luxe hotels. When you did start to think of that, it was too late. They were too old, and you were too old yourself, to make a new life properly. There was nothing for it but to blunder on, spending money, buying things, taking the line of least resistance, letting other people make suggestions, watching Mary and Jim and Alice do the same. A fat, flashy man who knew all the best night-clubs ; a hard-faced middle-aged woman who thought of going in for motor-racing . . . they were strange grandchildren, when you thought of it, for the First Mate of the clipper *Ocean Pride*.

He flung back the bedclothes and got up, stepped off that ridiculous dais on which his bed stood, padded across the room and pulled back the curtain to look out on the moonlit lawns and terraces. Alice's room was in a wing—he could see her window and a light burning. So she was awake—lying there smoking her cheap cigarettes and perhaps remembering that conversation this evening too. She should have been a rancher's wife, and worked, and had a lot of children. Jim should have been a rancher . . . or a sailor, a Conway boy like the son of Captain Dobson on that Cunarder years ago. He must have a ship of his own now, young Dobson, if a torpedo hadn't got him. The war had been over for four years—men like young Dobson had won it—and now a whole new world had to be made, but neither Jim nor Alice nor Harold was doing much about making it. How could they make a new world, after all, when they couldn't even make anything of their own lives ?

He stood there looking out at the moonlight and the shaft of yellow light from Alice's window till the cold reminded him that he was an elderly man who must be careful and sent him back to lie awake for a little longer in that great soft ostentatious bed.

*   *   *   *

Alice went off with Harold and Ruth to spend a few days in Paris ; life at the château returned to normal. The Princess came back—elderly, thin, restless in smart black clothes, talking endlessly and volubly about life in Biarritz before the war and the iniquities of Trotsky. Little Sir Quintin Quigley turned up on his way to Aix-les-Bains, a faded, slightly shabby ghost of another age, inspecting the château through his eyeglass and talking to Mary about the English country houses of King Edward's day. The Marquise de something, born in Boston, came to tea one afternoon with a few of her guests ; she patronised Mary a little and raised her eyebrows, behind her lorgnette, at the tapestries and chandeliers of the Second Empire profiteer ; her own château, though she did not say so, had seen Ronsard and Leonardo da Vinci, Catherine de Medici and Diane de Poitiers. With her was a sharp-eyed little French author, and an English Lady someone who had explored Arabia, and a young American diplomat from Turkey and an elderly French general in a black suit with an empty sleeve.

It was strange, so soon after Alice and the memories of Curicanti, to be in such company. Roger Barton of the hardware store walking in the rose-garden of a French château with a diplomat and a general ; hearing what really happened at the Lausanne Conference, and what the general thought about the Ruhr. The general who had been fighting in Morocco forty years ago, who had sat in a French farmhouse with a map before him and helped to send ten thousand poilus floundering to death . . . he was a simple little man, really, who suffered from rheumatism and liked a good cigar. Roger knew that Mary always

expected him to say the wrong thing. She pricked up
her ears suspiciously when he asked the General what
he thought about the Ruhr. But the General only
shrugged his shoulders. The Ruhr, the Rhineland,
who could say what the politicians would decide ?

"But you, Mr. Barton, you are a practical man ;
you have dealt with realities. If the sea had twice
come flooding across your lands, you would not be
happy until you had built a wall to keep it out. To
me the Germans are like that, a natural phenomenon,
a tide that ebbs and flows, but more incalculable—
shall we say rather a great dry forest that may catch
fire at any moment. Sentiment and reason do not
enter into it. But I am old, I may be wrong. Perhaps
they have changed all that, in their ugly hotel beside
Lac Leman."

He gave another shrug and walked on. Mary was
telling the Marquise about the Gainsboroughs at
Cauldfield House.

CHAPTER
XII

THE WORLD WAS SETTLING down; the French had left the Ruhr and the statesmen had spoken European at Locarno; Italy was peaceful under Mussolini and Mary was tired of Normandy. Liguria was a long way from Paris—but Harold encouraged the move, he had never liked that great vulgar château, and he and Ruth came to Italy once or twice every year. It was Ruth who knew of the Castello on the headland above the little bay near Genoa.

The walls went down to the rocks, the rocks to the clear blue water; when the fishing boats passed into the little piled white harbour the voices and snatches of singing came floating up with the wash of waves through the sleepy air. Pine trees framed views of blue mountains and bays and white villages; the world turned golden in the sunset and Harold talked of Shelley sailing past here on his way to death. On summer mornings the little flagged terrace was warm in the sun; the oaken hall was cool and shady, it was cool in the many-windowed rooms so high above the sea. In the winter there were log fires, and through the glass you watched the clouds on the peaks and the squalls across the water, and now and then you saw a liner or a rusty tramp feeling its way up the coast to Genoa.

It was smaller and simpler than the château; there were no fountains and peacocks and footmen in white gloves. An elderly little butler, Mary's maid, a chorus of plump village girls, a gardener and his sons.

There were fewer visitors, fewer parties; perhaps on verge of the sixties Mary was getting ready to settle down. They had some company of course; people from nearby villas came to call and heard about the château; artists arrived with letters of introduction from Harold and sketched under the umbrella-pines; there were civilities from the consul and the English chaplain and the local dignitaries, Harold and Ruth came . . . They left little Sylvia and Charlie with their nurses in the care of their grandparents while they went off to look again at the mosaics of Ravenna or the tower of San Gimigniano or the moors and paladins of Palermo's marionettes.

He and Ruth were full of interests, always after something new; now it was Crete, frescoes and Minoan vases, now it was Baroque buildings about which one of the Sitwells wrote those books. They went to Austria, and took Roger and Mary with them; they went on to the new Germany where modernistic concrete buildings jostled the old peaked roofs and the Wandervogel went singing through the woods; they came back by Geneva and after that Harold talked about the League of Nations for a week or two. He was always interested, in an academic way, in the Conferences and the pacts, in internationalism and humanity. He read books about the Five Years' Plan and talked of a trip to Russia, he worried a little about Fascism and the *Confinati*, he signed appeals for

Sacco and Vanzetti, and expressed vague sympathy with strikes in England and Home Rulers in India. But then he would read a book about the Etruscans— the unknown language, the long-nosed, enigmatic figures on the crumbling sarcophagi—and he and Ruth would be off again to look at tombs in Tuscany. Later on they would go to Spain to see the Goyas and El Grecos, or to Britanny to watch the Pardons in grey towns by the grey sea. There was such a lot to do . . . the only trouble was that life would be too short for it all.

Roger smiled a little when he heard Harold—in his late thirties—quoting those lines about Time's chariot. He was in the seventies himself now, and Jim must be forty. Who would have dreamed it would all turn out like this?

Sometimes he would try to make friends with his grandchildren, those neat, self-possessed little creatures who played on the terrace in the sun under brisk Miss Beecham's eye. Miss Beecham was a very superior modern Nannie, whose father had been a Major in the Indian Army and who secretly disapproved of Harold's admiration for Gandhi and Ruth's interest in struggling young poets. Sylvia and Charles were as fond of her as they were of anyone; though there were some wild scenes sometimes, for Miss Beecham could be firm on occasion, and both these children liked to get their own way. Sylvia was apt to shrink and wail for sympathy which Harold always gave her, and little Charles, who was four now, would flush and flounce like a little turkey-cock if he was crossed. But on the whole they were wonderfully well-behaved, going obediently through their little routine of getting-up and going to bed, of baths and walks and playing with carefully-chosen toys and eating carefully-balanced meals. Harold was inclined to worry about germs, and insisted on the water being boiled before they even brushed their teeth in it. (Roger used to wonder sometimes if he remembered the rusty old pump, so near the outdoor toilet, in the backyard at Curicanti when he was a little boy.) They were polite under Mary's sudden fits of yearning, smothering affection, and Sylvia, who was fond of display and dressing-up, liked to be shown her grandmother's jewels and opera-glasses and fans. And Charles was tolerant when his grandfather tried to talk to him.

"Well, well, if it isn't young Charles Barton! And what have you got there? A book, eh? And what does the book say? Come and let me see."

Little Charles thrusting out some glossy, expensive picture-book for children, beautifully illustrated, chosen with care by Harold who had ideas about forming the children's taste.

"Rabbits. Foxes. I think they're silly. I like Topolino best."

Topolino—who turned out to be Micky Mouse Italianised—lived in a papery little book Carlotta had given him, much to the embarrassment of Harold, who didn't want to hurt her feelings but was afraid of germs. Topolino in a little aeroplane, flying, burr-burr-burr . . . bang! little aeroplane runs into a mountain—all broken. Topolino not hurt though. Now he's a fireman in a big brass helmet—ding! ding! ding! Harold didn't approve of Topolino, patiently holding out a picture of lambs with ribbons and shepherdesses with crooks and frills.

O

" I think they're silly. Topolino's a sailor now. On a battleship with big guns. Bang, bang, bang ! "

*　　*　　*　　*

Miss Beecham had taken them away, up to their own tea in the big room in the town. Sylvia cuddling a huge, exotic, Rue-de-la-Paix mannequin of a doll, Charlie with Topolino on the warship still, in fancy, bang-banging broadsides that made his peace-loving father wince. The rest of them were having tea on the terrace, in the shade of the big umbrella-pine.

There was Ruth, listening to the fragile old lady who had known her mother :

" I remember coming out with her to visit this very place . . . I forget who had it then. We came in an old vettura, and your mother had on a big straw hat which blew away. . . . "

There was Harold talking to a plump English novelist, about Dalmatia, brown nets drying on the broken marble columns of Diocletian's palace.

" We are thinking of going there next year. Some friends offered to take us in their yacht this spring, but we thought it would be better to go by ourselves. People's tastes differ so. They would probably have wanted us to play bridge all day."

Mary talking to that overdressed woman from Los Angeles, who had turned up with her little husband and a letter of introduction from Jim. They had just landed at Genoa, and were on their way to Rome.

" Yes, Rome is always lovely. But spoilt now, like everything else. I remember when we used to go there before the War, it was so gay and charming. Some dear friends of ours had such a wonderful old

with them, and looked annoyed when Edith tried to pet them.

"Darling, they're not lap-dogs. For God's sake don't let's have any dear-dear-doggie nonsense with them, anyway."

Edith flushed and was silent, but she didn't seem to mind. Her eyes followed Alice adoringly about the room : when they were alone together for a minute she bent forward towards Roger and began to talk of Alice's kindness to her, Alice's charm, her cleverness.

"She is a very wonderful person. I mean that, Mr. Barton. She always was, of course, even in the old days when everything was so strange and unnatural to her over here. . . . Isn't it queer to remember that time ? But now . . . I think it is amazing, all the things she does. She terrifies me at times, with her flying and her motoring, but I daren't let her see it, of course. Not that I think she is really reckless. Only I am not made the way she is. I don't understand about cars and aeroplanes. Only the other day, when we were driving down to the country . . ."

Roger listened to the elderly, eager voice recounting some tale of Alice's prowess : he tried again to understand this brusque, hard Alice with her ugly flat and her ostentatious dogs and big open car. Miss Cartwright had some pictures and clippings out of newspapers. Alice standing beside a racing-car with two young men in flannel trousers. Alice with another woman starting out to drive from Norway to Monte Carlo. Alice in a flying-helmet, standing beside a little biplane. Perhaps, he thought, it was not really hard to understand. The Bentley roaring in the sleet

round mountain-passes was only the modern fulfil-
ment of the dreams she and Jim had dreamed when
they were small. It was the pinto with the silver-
mounted saddle ridden to victory on Cattleman's
Day. Perhaps that was the root of the whole matter.
Perhaps it was simply that Alice had never quite
grown up.

In the afternoon, while Edith exercised the Borzois
in the Park again, Alice took him down to see her
Flying Club. They went in her car, through the
rush of traffic, out along some great ugly arterial
road that slashed across suburbs of little houses with
red-tiled roofs and names on their gates ; she drove
very fast, with a neat, taut assurance, cursing under
her breath now and then at a cyclist or pedestrian
who threatened to interrupt her roaring, booming
progress.

There was a wide green aerodrome at the end of
a side-road somewhere : a hangar, some little wooden
huts, a wind-sock, a club-house very modern and
square and white : people were sitting on a terrace
in the sunshine and watching a few little biplanes
drone round the sky and land and take-off again.
Most of the other members seemed a good deal younger
than Alice, cheerful young men and women who
joked and laughed and called each other by their
Christian names. They waved and nodded at her,
but she didn't pay much attention to them. Only
one man, the brisk little Chief Instructor, came over
and made himself agreeable and asked Alice questions
which Roger didn't understand. What was the news
from the factory ? What had they decided about
those fuel-cocks ? Louis was flying at the moment,
but he should be down at any time now.

Alice answered briefly and evasively : she took Roger round the hangars and showed him the aircraft ; this one had such-and-such an engine, this was a Moth with a hood for blind-flying : it didn't convey much to him. She made him watch the flying a little, and tried to explain what was going on. Somebody doing a first solo, and a little crowd of his friends on the tarmac, watching. Pretty good, but he was using too much rudder on his turns. . . . Now he was coming in to land—that was the tricky bit. Not bad though. His instructor going out, grinning. Drinks all round this evening. Somebody else coming in, too ; doing a bad landing, bouncing.

" Yes, it's good fun at first. But this sort of thing loses its thrill after a bit."

Back in the club-house they had tea, and the mysterious Louis appeared. He was another of the instructors, a thin, dark man in the thirties, with a serious face and a sudden charming smile. He sat down with them and drank a cup of tea and talked a little, most of what he and Alice said was too technical for Roger, but he liked this Louis somehow, and guessed that he would be good at his job but that life hadn't treated him very well. His tweed jacket was well cut but a little shabby, and there were deep lines round his eyes : his face twitched a little now and then.

Apparently he had been in the R.F.C. in the war, and had been flying for some half-bankrupt air service in Northern Canada since.

" I should have stayed there, really. There are a lot of good openings for pilots in the North-West these days. An hour in the air takes you as far as ten days with a dog-team. And there's usually a lake to land on ; it's wonderful what you can do when you try. You feel a bit of an explorer too . . . yes, it's better than living in a boarding-house on the edge of London and teaching stockbrokers' wives to fly. Oh well— who knows but some day . . ."

He stopped abruptly : he and Alice glanced at each other. Then he got up and made some excuse and shook hands with Roger and drifted away. Alice watched him go. Then she ground out her cigarette and suggested starting back to Town.

It was not until they were roaring along the main road, among the cars and lorries and motor-coaches, that she broke her silence.

" What did you think of Louis, Dad ? "

" He seemed a nice chap. Is he a good pilot ? "

" Wonderful. He joined the R.F.C. when he was eighteen : if he hadn't been good he wouldn't be alive now. I suppose there was a lot of luck in that too. But he hasn't been so lucky since. Barnstorming round the world, instructing, flying air-taxis . . . he's too good for that sort of thing."

She was watching the road ahead ; cars flashing by, strings of wobbling cyclists. Roger waited. After a moment she gave a little laugh.

" Yes, he's a wonderful pilot—and navigator. Which is just as well, as I'm going to fly the Atlantic with him before long."

" You're going to do *what* ? "

" Fly the Atlantic—East to West. It's only once been done that way, you know : Huenefeld and Kohl and Fitzmaurice last year. They flew from Baldonnel to Labrador in thirty-seven hours. We plan to go from somewhere in England, if we can. I'm getting

216

a special plane built by Normans . . . a three-hundred horse-power engine, fuel for forty-five hours . . . maximum speed about a hundred and twenty miles an hour. Louis is doing most of the donkey-work. Supervising the building, and seeing about C. of A. and maps and weather-reports and all the blasted formalities . . . he's fixing the Press too. We don't want a lot of ballyhoo if we can help it, but it's not easy to avoid. I daren't tell you what it's all going to cost. Louis hasn't a bean himself, of course. Still, if we bring it off our fortune is made."

" Your fortune . . . for God's sake Alice . . ."

" Oh, I know. I was only joking. It doesn't matter a damn to me. It would make all the difference to Louis though. And I want to try . . . life seems so flat and so dull : it will be a change, anyway. A new experience . . . yes, a thrill, if you want me to be frank. It will be . . . oh, God knows. I nearly didn't tell you. You won't let Mother know, will you ? Or anyone . . . we don't want too much talk. I'll only be a passenger really, though I'll try to help with the navigation, and Louis may let me take the controls a bit now and then. Dad—you're not going to worry, are you ? You don't mind too much ? "

He didn't answer for a minute. The traffic came glittering past along the sunny road between the little houses—it all seemed a bit unreal somehow, as unreal as this fantastic thing she was discussing so calmly —" It's only the take-off with all that fuel that will be really tricky. Modern engines are reliable enough . . ." Something outside his life entirely, something he couldn't imagine, something he couldn't argue about at all.

" The chief thing is to get a good weather forecast. They're fitting a new gadget for de-icing . . ." Alice had been a sort of stranger for years before this. But now she was putting herself in another world entirely. He didn't know what the hell to say to her.

At last he shrugged his shoulders, made himself laugh a little, found his voice.

" It's no good asking me not to worry—you should know that. But if you really want to—well, good luck to you. I won't tell anyone about it. I'll even put up a bit of the money if you're short. But I think you're crazy, and I don't mind telling you so."

Alice laughed too, and didn't answer. She took one hand off the wheel and patted his knee. Queer how that unexpected little pat almost made up for this new bewildering anxiety.

*   *   *   *

Their aircraft wouldn't be ready for some weeks yet, and then they might have to wait weeks more for suitable weather. It was no good his thinking of waiting in London to see them off. He would go on to America and perhaps he would still be there when they arrived : it would be funny to see Alice and Louis driving down Broadway in a shower of ticker-tape. He tried not to show his feelings when she saw him off at Waterloo that day.

He sailed from Southampton in an over-ornate liner full of returning tourists : he didn't mix with the other passengers much, and spent most of his time lying in a deck-chair and trying to read. There was a book about flying in the ship's library . . . it was all as strange to him as a description of the Klondike

would have been to Mrs. Vane or little Quigly :
fuel-consumption, headwinds, fog, icing, navigation
. . . the critical point after which, whatever happened,
you had to go on. He tried to remember what he had
read in the papers about the other people who had tried
this East-West flight against the headwinds in the last
few years. Two women at least with their unlucky
pilots had vanished without a trace. Even from the
deck of a liner the seas looked cruel. Blue seas running
and flashing in the sun, black seas tumbling in the
darkness, grey seas with white caps and rain-squalls
. . . hour after hour, day after day, hundreds upon
hundreds of miles. If there was an aeroplane floating
out there now, who would see it ? How long would it
last—and the man and woman in it—before it was gone ?

It was a relief when the crossing was over and he
could forget the sky and the sea for an hour or two in
facing New York and this new America.

The skyline of New York went glittering up into
the hot morning air : some of the buildings were
familiar, but half a hundred sleek new giants had
dwarfed them since he was last there. They hung
like clouds above the haze : they had nothing to do
with the dusty America he remembered, with Henry
Miggs and Doctor Whitman and the children playing
by the creek. Here again was this fantastic modern
world where Alice and Jim lived and thought like
strangers, in ways he could never understand.

Jim met the boat, and saw him through the customs,
and drove with him to the hotel. His apartment was
being redecorated, and he had a suite in the same hotel
too : he had Roger's rooms engaged and ready, and
a case of real Scotch laid in. Jim was fat and sleek
and a little bald now, but seemed cheerful and well,

joking and laughing and pointing out the sights and talking about musical shows and polo and week-ends on Long Island with important friends. At the hotel there was a flurry of clerks and bell-boys and floor-managers when he swaggered in and introduced his father. The sitting-room and bedroom were smooth and opulent as coloured advertisements in the back of an expensive magazine, and below the windows the beetle-scurrying of traffic was something from a film.

They had dinner upstairs ; Jim ordered the waiter about and opened the case of whisky and talked about prohibition and speak-easies. Then he lighted a cigar and began to talk about Wall Street, the boom, the great Bull Market, stocks and shares higher every day.

" General Electric—390, U.S. Steel, 260. Westinghouse, 289. Over four million transactions on the Stock Exchange to-day. And believe me, that's no flash in the pan. It's going to last . . . it's a real reflection of the state of things. Don't you believe these people who talk about inflation. With modern methods of mass-production, and high wages giving a hundred million people spending-power . . . why, God Almighty, Dad, it's not a ' boom ' at all really, it's just another set of standards. We're living in another era now, that's all."

The whole country, he said, was watching the markets these days. Housewives and bellhops and cowpunchers on the prairie listening to the stock quotations on the radio and ringing up their brokers and getting richer every hour. He had got on the Band Wagon too : he had a lot of friends among the men with inside knowledge, and had gone in with some of them in a pool.

" Why don't you come in too, Dad ?   I know you've got all the money you need, but hell, why leave it salted away in a vault drawing four per cent. when you could double it in a month if you used it the right way ? "

He looked as eager and appealing as the Jim who used to beg for a new rifle. But Roger was hardly listening. He was tired and stiff and old and sleepy, and he still couldn't forget those leagues of water, he still couldn't get Alice out of his head.

Next day he drove down through canyons of stone, through log-jams of traffic, to Judson's office high up in the face of a glass and concrete cliff. They went over lists and lists of investments, and Judson quoted figures which surprised him : even after Jim's talk and his own reading he hadn't realised quite what was going on. Judson took him to his broker's office— there were little brokers' offices in all the clubs and liners and hotels : men and women sitting round in arm-chairs watching the figures change on a big board at the end of the room. The same thing was happening all over the country . . . it reminded him of the old Comstock days, but Comstock multiplied by a million, It was like a great gold-rush without the hardships and the work.

Once, perhaps, he might have had a flutter. But it was all too big and quick and complicated, and in his heart he had a silly little feeling that all the prosperity of margin-speculation and hire-purchase was too good to be true. Perhaps old Judson felt the same, though he didn't say so. He was worried about the figures of brokers' loans, and looked a little dubious at the mention of Jim's friends.

And suddenly, before he expected it, a letter came

221

from Alice to say that the new plane had been delivered
and that they were busy with tests and formalities,
and had begun to pester the weather-experts at the
Air Ministry. He read it with a sinking heart—somehow, up to now, he had never quite believed this would
really come—and tried not to remember the vast
empty skies and empty waves of the Atlantic. He was
tempted to tell Jim—but she had asked him not to
. . . and he didn't see much of Jim in any case : Jim
seemed to have a lot of friends in town even at this
time of year, and was always out lunching, watching
polo, dining, dancing, coming back bleary-eyed and
flushed next morning to grumble about prohibition
gin.

Roger pottered round alone, rode about in taxis,
went and saw Judson again and talked about his will.
Jim and Alice and Harold had their own income . . .
they could have more, some day. Alice could buy
bigger and better aeroplanes. Perhaps, if Jim had
wanted, if they had gone on working, it might have
been much more by now. Steam yachts and special
trains and great estates with parks and polo-fields and
aircraft-hangars : bodyguards with pistols and miles
of barbed wire. Or perhaps by now they would
be back where they started, selling hardware in a
little wooden store and slipping off into the mountains
to do some prospecting on the side. And perhaps, he
reflected, they would have been just as happy as they
were now.

The September days were hot and sunny : straw
hats and flimsy dresses, sweat and dust and smells in
back streets, shrill, ragged children screeching in
alleyways and fat old women huddled on fire-escapes
of dingy tenements. The traffic ground and gleamed

and roared and glittered : they were putting up a
new building near his hotel, and the air shuddered
with the rattle of the riveting-machines. It was hot
at night, and the sky glowed and pulsed with sky-
signs, and all the time the roar of the traffic was
broken by the wailing of syrens and jangling bells of
fire-engines. There was nothing to keep him here,
but he couldn't go till he had heard from Alice . . .
when the cable came at last his hand shook so that he
could hardly open it. Now, at this minute, he thought,
she might be on the way . . .

But she wasn't. He read the cable twice before
he took it in. " Aircraft crashed on test flight,
total wreck, Louis killed, self uninjured, writing.
Alice." At first all he could feel was relief. It
wasn't till much later that he thought at all about
that quiet, tired man with the restless hands and
worried eyes who had been a good pilot but always
had bad luck.

So that was that—he needn't worry any more—at
any rate not until she decided to try again. He told
Jim that Alice had been in an air crash, and Jim said
grimly that Alice was sure to break her neck one
day : she was too old to play round with aeroplanes and
racing cars. Roger didn't answer. He rang up the
travel bureau and inquired about the next boat for
Genoa.

It was a relief to be going back. Jim saw him off :
he sailed in the *Tarquinio* at midnight. Sliding and
banging down under the elevated tracks and across
railroad sidings, going through bare concrete halls
up a gangway into the gilt and glass and little palm-
trees of a big Italian hotel. Queer how familiar it all
seemed now . . . the decorations, the Italian voices

223

of the stewards, almost like coming home. Jim came with him to his state-room, through the clamour of a midnight sailing: music and orchids and tipsy voices and evening clothes. The bar was shut, of course, and would stay shut till they passed the three-mile limit, but Jim had a flask, and they had a last drink of bootlegged Scotch: Jim was amused to hear him talk a little Italian to the steward. Then he shook hands and went away: there was a crowd round the gangway, and shouting and flashlight photographs. The siren blew and the engines began to throb. Roger felt old and tired and suddenly lonely, and went to bed.

The *Tarquinio* with her bands and flowers and swimming-pools went lunging South and East through the sunshine. Again he sat in a deck-chair and watched life go on. He observed the ship—he hadn't thought the Italians could build such good ships—and the other passengers. There was a Papal Count and a Japanese diplomat and a film-star with her latest husband and a French racing-motorist. There were well-to-do families bound for the Riviera, and pretty girls who sunbathed on the imitation beach of the top deck. There were gala dinners with evening clothes and bare backs and champagne and caviare: there were dances and cinema-shows and concerts: the very ship seemed to preen herself as the band played "Giovinezza" at the end of the evening and the officers in their white uniforms gave stiff Fascist salutes to the gilded rods and axes at the end of the ballroom ... there was another broker's office; the market had slipped a little, but it seemed to be recovering all right now.

Sometimes he talked a little to an oil-man from

Texas : a big, slow, red-faced farmer who had made a
million from a gusher in his pasture and was out with
his wife and daughter to see the world. The wife
was impressed by the Papal Count, and the daughter
danced with the French racing-motorist. It was
oddly like the Barton family coming this way a quarter
of a century ago.

They called at Algiers, and the family from Texas
came back to the ship with Oriental rugs and copper
jars : they called at Palermo, and they brought back
brocades and coral and amber : they said they had
bought a tiny Sardinian donkey with a tiny cart all
painted with Moors and Paladins : it was being
shipped back to Texas for them now. At Naples
they went ashore for good. Roger watched them
go, and thought of the Barton family's arrival that
far-off evening : he remembered a luncheon-party
on a terrace with bougainvillea. No doubt there
was another Mrs. Vane waiting for these people
somewhere among the lights up there.

They came to Genoa in the sunset, as they had come
to Naples that evening a quarter of a century ago.
Rich lights on the hills and the high piled city flashing
and glowing so that you forgot the docks and cranes,
and remembered vaguely the palaces and galleys of
the Dorias. Mary was back at the Castello : she had
sent the car to meet him. Sliding through the raucous
traffic and along the coast-rode above the fading silken
sea. It was oddly pleasant to be back. The welcoming
servants, the steep steps through the thick stone walls,
the terrace and the lights coming out in the dusk all
along the great curve of coastline and up in the lonely
villages of the hills.

Mary seemed quite well. She knew about Alice,

who had been bruised and cut and shaken, it appeared, but was all right again now. Yes, she herself had had a nice time with dear Ruth and Harold. Only she had found Paris tiring, and had had a great many horrid headaches.

" I saw Harold's doctor, but he didn't do me much good. But then I found the most wonderful woman who cured them straight away. No drugs or anything . . . it was more like massage, only it wasn't massage, it—it was like a sort of laying-on of hands. She just touches you gently, so gently, and talks to you quietly, and looks at you with her great dark eyes. Yes, perhaps it is a sort of hypnotism. Or a sort of faith-healing really. Only the faith is all hers . . . she seems to *will* your pain away. As if she knew, and could make you know, that there is no such thing as suffering really. Oh no, not Christian Science, her way is quite different. It is a sort of gift she has—some strange, deep quality inside her. She has had such an interesting life too . . . queer, tragic, rather wonderful. She has travelled all over the world, and has helped all sorts of people, in palaces and peasant cottages. Harold and Ruth are a little sceptical, but Princess Mendidoff thought there was no one like her. The Russians are wiser than we are about these strange potentialities. Her husband was Austrian . . . Gregor is her name, Nadia Gregor. She is visiting Italy next month, and I have persuaded her to come here for a few days."

She said it as proudly as if she was announcing that she had persuaded Kreisler to come and play for her. Another discovery, another fad. There had been so many. But she looked old and defenceless, in her long chair under the big lamp. If this woman made her happy, that was the main thing. One more hanger-on wouldn't matter much, one way or the other.

"That's fine, Mary," he said. "I'm glad she's coming. Yes, she sounds interesting, too."

XIII

CHAPTER
XIII

IT WAS SPRING, AND to-day had been windless and warm. The afternoon sun lay soft on the hills, but already the shadows were moulding the valleys ; windows were flashing and burning in the long, low light. A few miles along the coast the towers of the old Castello stood up out of the pine trees : the pines were dark against the white and pink of the fruit trees, the pale green of the vines and pale grey of the olives. Roger lay back in his chair and looked at it, wondering idly what the place was like now that it belonged to the motor-car manufacturer from Milan. This little villa —it was not so little, really—was just as pleasant, when all was said and done. Even Mary had stopped regretting the Castello long ago. She had never said much, really : she had never quite taken in what was happening, but she had felt vaguely that to complain about moving would have been to complain about Jim.

"Warm, peaceful, beautiful." Harold's voice broke the silence. "It is probably raining in England. Raining in Manchester, where the unemployed are queueing up to draw the dole. Raining on the strikers outside the factories round Paris. And in Berlin, it will be cold and grey, and there will be more unemployed hanging round the street corners and Storm

Troopers swaggering up and down jostling Jews off the pavements. In America it is probably snowing. More shabby crowds outside factories, and unemployed selling apples on Fifth Avenue. Even in Italy here . . . you wouldn't notice the sunshine much if a couple of Blackshirts were marching you into some sinister little office for examination. Queer how it goes on, isn't it? Month after month, with a sort of blind inevitability."

The words sounded theatrical, but there was a twist of real feeling in them. Roger looked at him curiously. Harold, who had never troubled his head about such things a few years ago, was worrying himself sick these days about economics and politics. Crisis, crisis, crisis, unemployment, fascism, communism, rearmament, till you never wanted to hear the words again.

And yet, he thought, there was a vague feeling of inevitability about it too. Ever since the Wall Street crash and the cables and phone-calls from Jim and Judson . . . ever since the slump hit Europe, and all the exchanges went crazy, and there were no more tourists, and the big hotels shut their doors. . . . Things would be different, everyone said, after this, after that. Now that there was a National Government in England. Now that the statesmen had made all those decisions at that latest conference. But they never were any better, they were worse. Roosevelt taking office in an America of closed banks and panic : Roosevelt apparently all set to transform the whole economy of the country overnight. And Hitler in power in Germany, turning a million bullies loose in a mad flood of songs and torches and rubber truncheons. . . .

Harold spoke again, suddenly.

229

"Do you remember the little surgeon in Dresden who took out Sylvia's tonsils? She adored him—he had a wonderful way with children. He was a Jew of course. He's in Switzerland now, with one eye gone and his hands so crushed and broken that he will never be able to operate again."

Mary stirred among the cushions, her thin, powdered face wrinkling.

"Harold, don't? You know how I hate these horrors . . . all you ever talk about now seems to be violence and misery."

"That's what the world is like, Mother."

"Oh, but it isn't! Look around you now . . . all this beauty . . . even those fishermen singing away down there, they are perfectly happy, they are not worrying or miserable. In any case I'm sure that half these stories about beatings and cruelties are just propaganda. Jim thinks so."

"Jim . . . !"

"You needn't say 'Jim' so scornfully. He is no fool, after all. He has travelled a lot, and met all sorts of people. People who really know what is happening. At the German Embassy in London . . . and that young man he knows in the Italian Foreign Office . . . and all his business friends, and society friends. Why, only the other day he wrote that he had been lunching with . . ."

As she spoke a flush came to her cheeks. Roger tried to signal a warning to Harold, but Harold didn't notice. His thin middle-aged face flushed a little too, and his voice grew a little shriller.

"Jim and his fascist friends . . . of course he laps up all they tell him. Oh yes, he travels a lot. He likes tearing round Europe in his big car, meeting the richest people in the loudest night clubs. But as for knowing what is really happening in the world . . . I doubt if he has ever read a good paper or a serious book in his life."

" Perhaps he doesn't have to take all his knowledge from books. He is a man of the world. A business man."

" A business man ! Yes, if he wasn't a business man you and father would still be living in the Castello. Father, how much did it cost you to rescue him in 1929 ? If it wasn't for you he would be peddling vacuum-cleaners round the suburbs now. Instead he is still driving round in his Packard and dancing at Ciros and lunching with film stars and laying down the law about finance and politics ! "

Mary had closed her eyes. Her face was working and her voice thin and tired.

" I don't care, Harold. He was unlucky then, but he wasn't the only one. I don't understand all these things, and I don't think you do. But you're making my headache come on again."

" Mother ! I'm terribly sorry. I shouldn't have argued . . . Let me get you something."

" That's all right dear. I like to hear your views you know. But I think I will go in now. Roger, would you fetch Madame Gregor ? She is the only person who can do anything for these head-aches . . ."

Harold had slipped over to sit beside her, looking anxious, worried, penitent. Roger suppressed a sigh. These headaches were more familiar to him than they were to Harold. He got up slowly and went across the terrace. Through the quiet hall and upstairs and along to Madame Gregor's room beside Mary's.

He paused, knocked, a voice said "*Avanti*" and he went in.

It was a small room, blazing with sunset : the light was in his eyes and he couldn't see much, but he got, as usual, an impression of stuffiness and crowding. Furniture, cushions, ornaments, magazines, withering flowers. There were tea-things on the table—she had all her meals in here—and the air was thick with cigarette-smoke. Madame Gregor was sitting by the window : a thick-set swarthy woman in a black dress, with black hair and heavy black eyebrows above those strange eyes. If you dressed her up in red and yellow she would look like a fortune-teller at a circus. As it was she looked like—what ? The *patronne* of some seedy French café, manageress of an expensive brothel, a *sage-femme* in a back-street, a cheap dressmaker perhaps. Except for those queer, shining eyes that made you think of some sleepy animal.

She stood up as he came in, brushing the crumbs off her skirt.

" Mr. Barton ! I am sorry. I thought it was Giovanna coming for the tray." Her English was perfect, only a little gutteral. " What is the matter ? What can I do ? "

" Mrs. Barton has another headache coming on. She wonders if you would help her up to her room."

" Oh, but of course ! A headache . . . she has been in the sun, she has been talking, worrying. Always I tell her not to listen to all this talk, the jangle and clamour of this dreadful world. But a headache . . . soon we will get rid of that."

He followed her downstairs : she waddled a little but she could still move quickly. It was hard to guess what nationality she really was, or to imagine her mysterious, cosmopolitan past. How long was it since she had come to them? Getting on for five years now. Elbowing out poor, disapproving old Lucille, getting a scared little Italian girl as her assistant, and slipping into a place somewhere between a nurse and a companion and a ladies' maid. Soothing Mary's headaches and brushing her hair and making her *tisanes* and talking to her about Bourbon princes and Rumanian peasants and South American millionaires.

Across the terrace again, through the long shadows of the vine-trellis : Mary smiling gratefully as the strong, black-silk arm helped her to her feet.

" A little headache again, hein? But that is nothing. Come, you will lie down and I will cure it, and you will have a little sleep . . ."

Harold's lips were tight with disapproval He picked up his mother's rug and book and stalked behind them, and after a moment's hesitation Roger followed too. Mary's big bedroom, the curtains pulled against the sunset, one shaft of golden light on a brocaded chair. Madame Gregor helping Mary on to a little couch and putting a cushion behind her head. He had seen it all before, but Harold hadn't : he watched Harold watching the queer little scene. Madame Gregor pulling up a chair, sitting down, leaning forward . . . the broad, ugly fingers playing round Mary's temples, then falling to Mary's thin wrist. The unwinking burning eyes, the gutteral voice murmuring, murmuring . . . and all the strain and tiredness slipping out of Mary's face. They heard her whisper : " Oh, Nadia, it's wonderful, it's like cool water," and the deep voice murmuring again, water, cool water, cool water flowing, flowing . . .

Then Mary's eyes closed and her breath was slow and even, and Madame Gregor motioned them to slip away.

They went back to the terrace : Harold's face was thoughtful. Her jerked his head towards the cliffs, and Roger nodded and went with him. They walked slowly up the path fragrant with box : the sun was low on the sea now, and all the sunflowers were turning towards it : it made a glittering path across the shot-silk blueness. On the hillside the pine needles were dry and slippery : beyond the trees was a bare grassy plateau and a little Rotunda with a painted ceiling where dolphins plunged round a dome of cracked and fading blue. Below it the sea was calm, and a fishing boat chugging past, its big lateen sail furled, sent a slow heave of water to break and wash on the rocks. It was strange to think of the boats and ships which had passed his headland through the generations. Greeks and Romans, Crusaders' ships with golden lions on scarlet sails, low wolf-like ships of the Saracens, towering galleys of Pisa and Genoa, frigates of England and French ships of the line. And always the little fishing-boats coming back out of the sunset.

Roger felt a quirk of amusement. He knew he wouldn't have thought about things like that twenty years ago. That was the sort of thing Harold liked to imagine. He wondered if Harold was thinking about Roman galleys now. But Harold flung away his cigarette and said :

" That woman. That horrible woman. Why do you let her stay ? "

" Madame Gregor ? She helps your Mother a lot."

" I suppose she cures those headaches. But that sort of hypnotic mumbo-jumbo can't be a good thing."

" I don't know. If the headaches are nervous . . ."

" Has Mother seen a doctor lately ? "

" Oh yes. I got one in a few weeks ago. I had to fight for it—Madame Gregor was offended, she doesn't believe in doctors. And your Mother listens to her more than anyone. But I made her see him. He didn't find anything wrong."

He stopped. It had been a nasty little squabble before he got that doctor. Madame Gregor was so sure she could do as much as any doctor, and a whole lot more. Well, she could cure Mary's headaches, and make her hot drinks that fixed her colds, and when little Beppo sprained his ankle she had rubbed it and fingered it and stared at him till he got up and walked like a rabbit coming to a snake. His old mother wouldn't let him come near the place now ; she thought Madame Gregor was a witch or something. " What can I do ? If I tried to send her away your Mother would make such a scene that she would be really ill. No, I don't interfere. In case of a real illness I'd step in fast enough though."

Harold nodded.

" No doubt you are right. I'm sorry I brought on that headache this afternoon though. What time is it ? Ruth and the children should be back from Rapallo soon. And the newspapers should have come. My God, it's so peaceful here . . . I never want to see another newspaper."

*   *   *   *

Harold and Ruth and the children went off to Como, with the chauffeur and the governess and the neat luggage strapped on the back of the big, discreet French car. Mary's headaches were less frequent,

and she was able to walk up to the Rotunda and sit
there all morning with Madame Gregor, exchanging
those queer, long confidences. There were no visitors
these days, and Mary didn't want to travel : not even
to go with Ruth and Harold as they had suggested.
In the afternoon she would sleep, and after tea she
would shut herself up in her room with Madame
Gregor and go through boxes and cupboards and
drawers. They would unlock the jewel-case and
Nadia's thick fingers would caress the ornate, old
fashioned jewellery : they would take down long silk
dresses, furs, hats, some new, some bought years ago
and never thrown away. Paquin, Worth . . . Nadia
would know at a glance ; she would stroke the glossy
furs, and perhaps Mary would smile and say " Keep it
if it is any use to you. I never wear such things
now." Then they would turn to other boxes full of
fans and letters and trinkets, albums of old photographs.

" That is Alice when we first came to Europe.
Harold and his tutor, Lionel Morton, when they went
to Sicily. That is a good one of Jim in his uniform
during the War. That one was taken one day at
Biarritz—it must have been about the time King
Edward died. Lady Hornbeam . . . those big hats
and veils had a certain dignity . . . Harold again.
Jim."

Sometimes Roger looked at those pictures too. It
was like looking at a lot of ghosts. Alice in a long
skirt and a shirt-waist with a stiff collar : Jim and
Harold in stiff new suits with fancy waistcoats and
tiepins and flowers in their buttonholes. Funny how
quickly Jim had discovered that he liked buttonholes
and fancy waistcoats ; you wouldn't have expected it
somehow.

236

Jim came to stay at the villa, that summer, on his way to the Lido or Brioni or some such place. He came alone—no doubt he had left one lady-friend in London and had another waiting for him when he arrived—roaring up the hill in his car, swaggering into the quiet little villa like a gust of wind from a larger world. A big, stout, florid man of nearly fifty, a little flabby, rather bald, brown and sleek and sporting in well-cut grey flannels and expensive suede shoes, giving his mother a gay boyish kiss, gripping Roger's hand, smiling upon the servants, almost ignoring Madame Gregor, who, nevertheless, admired him as much as she distrusted Harold.

Mary was always in rather a flutter when Jim came, she put on her best clothes and fussed about the dinner and the wine. By a queer twist of things she was more interested in Jim than in her once all-precious Harold now. Jim could tell her about the Berkeley and the Ritz and the Lido Excelsior, and he never expected her to enjoy cubist paintings or to worry about the unemployed. Jim was cheerful and lively, while Harold was worried and preoccupied. Jim was still hers, in a sense, while Harold was Ruth's. Jim was the ruffling cavalier, the Regency dandy, the Edwardian man-about town. Jim, thought Roger a little sadly, was Mary's idea of a gentleman.

Jim felt that himself, and half-unconsciously played up to her. Coming in to dinner in a white mess-jacket which made him look like an advertisement for someone's cigarettes, flashing his white Douglas-Fairbanks smile across the table.

"When are you coming to New York, Mother? I want you to see my new apartment. I think you'd like it. Alice? Oh yes, I met her when I was in

237

London. Didn't see much of her though—she spends most of her time in the country, with Miss Cartwright and those dogs of hers."

Roger looked away. He didn't want to hear Jim's views on Alice . . . that gruff, unhappy Alice who lived in Surrey with Edith and a lot of expensive, useless dogs. She had given up motor-racing and flying, that crash must have shaken her more than she admitted, and the death of Louis, and the idea she had that it was really her fault. He could hear her now, in one of her brief moments of revelation after a few whiskies, " He didn't want to go up that day. He said there was something wrong with the engine. He didn't really want to try an Atlantic flight at all. He was tired and his nerve had gone a little. But I wanted to, and I had the money, and he had to do something, he was hard up, he was married. His wife knew—she wouldn't speak to me at the funeral."

No, he didn't want to hear Jim's remarks about Alice's dogs and Alice's whiskies. But Jim had already forgotten Alice. He had seen Harold in Paris, and met some of Harold's friends : a writer, a painter, an odd-looking creature with a little yellow beard.

" But Harold wasn't thinking much about paintings. You really ought to do something about Harold. He's turning into a terrible parlour-socialist."

Ten years ago such a slur on Harold would have brought instant rebuke. Now Mary only smiled. As if he felt his ground firm, Jim went on.

" It's mainly Ruth's doing really of course. She was always a bit too intellectual and highbrow for my taste. That's a nice little girl of theirs though."

That was all right too. Mary had never really

liked Ruth much. She adored her prim little grand-daughter. Jim was still critical of Harold's politics.

"Ruth has a lot of Jewish friends who fill her up with horrors about the treatment of the Jews in Germany. I tried to make her see that the Jews who are being turned out by Hitler are the dregs of Eastern Europe, the scum who have always made trouble and always will. The same gang that are responsible for that crazy Communist madhouse in Russia. But it was a waste of time trying to argue with her. As soon as things settle down a little Ruth and Harold will forget all their politics and economics and go back to nergo-sculpture or the study of Chinese or whatever is the latest fad."

He changed the subject : he began to talk about New York, and London and cosmopolitan society. The Colony Club, Voisins, the St. Regis, El Morocco with its cuban bands and zebra-skins. Spotlights and flashlight photographs at night clubs : the new Waldorf Astoria : Walter Winchell's column : Elsa Maxwell's parties, the opening night of the season at the Opera. He knew all the latest gossip about the Prince of Wales and all the right places to visit in France and Austria and Italy. "Nobody much goes to the Lido these days. It will soon belong to the past, like Nice or Monte Carlo, People prefer those little places along the French Riviera . . . just as they prefer villages in the Tyrol to great resorts in the Alps for winter sports. In Berlin I always find the Adlon quite amusing. Full of English and Americans exchanging lurid stories about Goering in low voices. I believe Goering encourages that rather, just as Henry Ford used to encourage jokes about Flivvers ; it's good advertisement. I met rather a nice chap the other day who had been in the Richthofen Circus with Goering."

Mary listened to him as eagerly as she used to listen to that red-wigged Duchess at Florence, years ago. Some of his stories shocked her a little, but she enjoyed that too. She must have known, or guessed, about his women and his drinking, but again she didn't mind, if anything she was pleased. That was part of the man-of-the-world rôle in which she had always seen him . . . it reminded her of the hints and little smiles and well-bred scandals about young Peers and gay Guards' officers of King Edward's reign.

And when he tried, as he was doing now, Jim could be amusing company. A difficult guest in a way : one was always afraid that his trousers wouldn't be pressed right, or that little Giuseppe would scratch the paint of his car when he cleaned it. But if he gave a lot of trouble to the servants he tipped them well and was genial and expansive with them in a lordly way : the white dinner-jacket and the Packard were the sort of things young Italy admired, and when he came up from bathing, his *peignoir* over his arm and his great brown hairy chest and arms wet and bare, you could see little Giovanna's eyes brighten as she slipped demurely past him in the corridor. And you could see that Jim had noticed that too. It was better not to wonder any more about it. But it made Jim's success with bored wives and hard-up mannequins easier to understand.

He stayed for four days, lazing like a great cat under the sun, swimming a little in the mornings, drinking a lot, but never too much, in the evenings : he still played the markets a little and gave Roger advice about investments and passed on one or two little

240

tips. Then he got into his car and drove away again :
little Giovanna went to Rapallo in the bus and came
back with a smart new dress and silk stockings and new
shoes : Madame Gregor, who had been very much in
the background, came into her own once more. She
and Mary shut themselves up again, and she said the
right things about Jim's looks and charm, and heard
again how well he had done in the War and how much
General Pershing had relied on his advice when he
was a staff-officer. Roger read newspapers full of
Hitler and Roosevelt and the World Economic Conference, and the hot, shrill summer days went on.

CHAPTER
XIV

MARY WASN'T VERY WELL that winter. She had several colds, and while Madame Gregor cured them quickly enough with her mysterious *tisanes* they left her run-down and tired. Roger tried to persuade her to come away for a change to Sicily or Egypt, but she wouldn't. She preferred to stay in her own home, with her books and photographs and Nadia.

He wasn't really worried : he had an idea that Mary was a lot tougher than she looked. When Harold wrote and asked him to come to Paris in the early spring he did hesitate a little, but Mary urged him to go. The change would do him good. She was perfectly well and comfortable here. Madame Gregor would wire or telephone at once if he was wanted. He would only be gone for a week or two.

He went off at last, still a little dubious, and wished he hadn't come. Paris was cold and raw and restless, and Harold was worrying more than ever now.

He would draw the curtains as early as possible, as if to shut out the world. The firelight would flicker on the tea things, touch the backs of books, gleam on bronze and glass and china, and the honking traffic would sound faint and far away. But still Harold couldn't relax.

It had been a bad winter for his kind. Germany's

withdrawal from the League had shaken him badly, and on top of that the Concorde riots in January had brought a wave of violence rolling to his very door. Yelling mobs, burning buses, shooting, a litter of broken glass and bloodstains in the Place next day. The whole *affaire* Stavisky had shown him an aspect of French life which he had always managed to ignore up till now.

" There it is," he said. " The broad, shining Place de la Concorde with its obelisks and statues, so serene, so dignified. And then you lift a man-hole cover and find a stinking network of sewers swarming with rats. Only now the rats are out of the sewers, they've got control. Look at Germany, rearming as fast as she can. Aeroplanes, tanks, poison-gas. Look at Italy. Look at Spain."

He stared into the fire as if he saw there flaming cities and toppling buildings and the fumes of the gasses hanging in the air. Ruth, fitting another cigarette into her holder, sounded impatient as she answered him.

" For goodness sake don't be so doleful Harold. The world has never been the idyllic place you think it should be, but that doesn't mean that we are all doomed."

Harold shook his head. Soon the door would be opened and some visitors would come in. Elderly socialists who would sip their scented tea and talk of the downfall of capitalism ; glib journalists hot-foot from Berlin with the latest horrors ; refugees . . . always refugees. The surgeon from Dresden with the patch over his eye and the clumsy gloved hands ; an elderly woman in black, a young musician who would play, rather badly alas ; a girl who kept her

243

feet planted on the carpet so that no one could see the holes in her shoes. Talking of how they got away, and how they kept themselves alive in Paris, and how they hoped to go to America when the formalities were done. Most of them, Roger noticed, flinched a little if the door opened suddenly.

Later Sylvia would come in, small and elegant and grown-up for her age ; she would go round gravely shaking hands and making tiny curtseys and being polite in English or in French. And Charles, who must be ten now, quiet and inclined to be moody . . . shaking hands too, and submitting to affection, and sitting beside his mother on the sofa looking at them all with big, thoughtful eyes.

Harold had been quiet and moody at that age . . . but my God how different their childhoods had been ! By now Charles and Sylvia spoke French as fluently as English, and could get along in German too. They had bathed in the Mediterranean, and tumbled about Austrian hillsides on little skis, and left their tonsils in the best clinic in Switzerland. Miss Beecham had gone now, but there was a new governess, whose father had been an Austrian professor and who had taken a degree at Cambridge . . . their lives were as ordered and hygienic as ever, under her care. The walks among the statues of the Luxembourg Gardens, the little treats of ices in chic tea-rooms full of scent and sables, now and then, as a sort of adventure into rude society, a ride on the little merry-go-round in the Champs Élysées, or an afternoon at a huge glittering circus, or a look at the tigers in the zoo. They were clever, they were sweet, they were charming . . . they were about as human as two little icicles. At that age Jim and Alice were fighting with the Sauers in the

244

back-alley, and hanging about the round-house with the train crews, and listening to old Tex Clarke talking of gun-fights in Abilene . . .

Alice and Jim both turned up in Paris this time, and Roger lunched with them at a restaurant. Harold and Ruth had been asked too, but Harold discovered some other engagement. He had very little in common with his brother and sister now.

The restaurant was small and expensive, and Jim was fussy about the choice of food and wine. He was a little annoyed with Alice, who didn't care what she ate, and smoked her cheap cigarettes between the courses, and was obviously not impressed by his talk of night clubs and high finance. But he didn't let her cramp his style : he ate and drank with a sort of boyish gusto, and chattered away about New York and the *Ile de France* and Paris and the Concorde riots.

" I bet that made Harold sit up," he said. " Too bad in a way that they didn't get into the Chamber and throw the whole gang of double-crossing politicians into the Seine. That's just what they will do, one of these days. And I wouldn't be surprised to see some of Harold's parlour-socialist friends go into the river too."

He talked a lot about Germany ; he had been seeing a good deal of a German airforce officer, the one who had been in the Richthofen Circus with Goering, a very nice fellow, Jim said, who spent a lot of time in England and America now.

" He had a tough spell after the War, but of course he's sitting pretty now. He is one of the Party big-shots that Harold is always talking about. And you wouldn't want to meet a nicer man, well-educated,

245

sensible, reasonable. He wants me to go to Germany in the summer. He says he'll take me boar-hunting and give me some flying and show me what they're really doing there. He suggests I go in time to see the big Party Rallies . . . they ought to be worth seeing, too."

Roger said nothing. Alice looked a little cynical. She said, later, that she had met Jim's Count too, and hadn't cared for him.

" Not that I care a damn about his politics one way or the other. But he seemed a bit bogus somehow, all charm and tweeds and an Oxford accent and a club tie. That sort of thing is bad enough when it's genuine—it's intolerable when it's aped by foreigners."

Her own plans, it seemed, were vague. She was tired of the house in the country and the dogs ; she was on her way to Spain now, and later perhaps to North Africa.

" I want a little sunshine and a little colour. If I find a place I like I might take a house and send for Edith." She laughed shortly. " I can see myself among the English spinsters on the Italian Riviera yet. String bag and parasol and tea with the English chaplain . . . Edith and I—we'll be a fine pair of old freaks in a few years."

*   *   *   *

As usual, now, when he had been away he was glad to go home. Little Giuseppe met him at Genoa with the car. As they screeched out through the rainy suburbs Giuseppe kept turning to smile fresh welcomes and talk about the weather ; there had been much rain, much cold wind, *tempo brutissimo*. All the fruit blossom had fallen down, and *la signora* was ill, she had a cold and was in bed all day.

Roger grunted at that. Madame Gregor should have let him know. Probably nothing much though . . . anyone could have a cold in weather like this. The cloud hung on the hills, rain swept across the sea, rain soaked and streaked the hillsides and the tawdry painted houses along the road, water came cascading down the garden steps of the villa when they arrived. The hall was cold and musty, and little Giovanna, taking his hat and coat, looked chilly and somehow scared. There were other worried faces smiling dubiously at him through the door to the back quarters ; he nodded vaguely towards them and went as quickly as his stiff legs would take him up the stairs and along the corridor. Outside Mary's room he met Madame Gregor, carrying a tray with a cup on it.

" Mrs. Barton ? Yes, she has a bad cold. But I make her this, and to-morrow she will be better. There was no need to bother you. A doctor ? No, I have not called a doctor. She did not wish it. I can do anything a doctor can do."

She tried to stop him from going in ; Mary was sleeping, apparently, and Madame Gregor didn't want her disturbed. He brushed past her and opened the door ; the room was stuffy and reeked of some queer herbs, and Mary looked very small in the middle of her big wide bed.

She was asleep . . . no, she wasn't asleep, but she didn't look at him. Her eyes were closed and her cheeks were burning ; she was moving and tossing restlessly, and her harsh, broken breathing filled the room. A gasp, a little moan, a gasp again. Her wrist was hot to his fingers; when he found her pulse it fluttered and raced. Her dry, hot hand felt very small and old and frail in his.

Madame Gregor was at his elbow, whispering loudly. It had gone to her chest a little; yes, she had complained of pain, the tisane would cure that. Yes, she had a little fever. " No, I have not used a thermometer. I do not bother with all these so-called scientific toys. . . . "

He pushed past her again and went shakily downstairs; there was only one telephone, in the hall. Ringing, waiting, ringing, trying to make the operator understand. The servants were still watching from the door; he heard a little stir when they realised what he was doing. Funny they hadn't said much. They'd always been a bit scared of Madame Gregor. No time to get an English doctor. The local man was said to be good. He was in. He spoke English. He would come at once. After putting the receiver down Roger sat still for a minute. Then he went back upstairs. The room seemed stuffier than ever; it was smelly and untidy, there were dirty cups and withered flowers and clothes and magazines scattered round as if Madame Gregor had been camping in here too. She was bending over Mary now, smoothing a sheet. His sudden fury left him. She meant well; she had nothing to gain by harming Mary, and a lot to lose. She was only a stupid peasant woman from the Balkans who had learnt to wear modern clothes and talk French and English and read magazines. But he couldn't let her touch Mary again.

She caught his eyes and his gesture and knew what he meant. A queer, scared, sullen look came over her face. They stood for a moment staring at each other.

248

Then she turned away and made a pretence of tidying up the dressing-table. Mary's breathing still grated through the room.

The doctor was young and gentle and efficient, but he shook his head. There was no question of moving her. He would send for nurses, for oxygen, for medicines. He would send for the English doctor, if Mr. Barton wished, and for specialists from Genoa. "That *tisane*?" He tasted it. "Harmless stuff. It might cure a cold in the head, who knows? But for this . . . how long has it been now? You have been away, you don't know. I understand. If I had been called in two days ago. . . . But now, I must tell you frankly, Mr. Barton, I have very little hope."

He went away, he came back; there was another doctor, the nurses, the oxygen. The rain pattered on the windows, the pine-trees swung their branches in the wind. Madame Gregor was packing, she was trembling and weeping a little. Roger had said nothing to her, but the doctor had told her what he thought.

Roger sat in his own room. He had sent wires to Jim and Harold; Alice was in Spain somewhere and there was no way of getting in touch with her. The servants had made up a big fire for him; he was cold and tired and aching. Little Giuseppe came creeping in from time to time with more logs, with hot drinks and little bits of food; there were tears in his eyes, though Mary had never liked him much, and he hadn't liked her. It was just Latin emotion . . . but even his sympathy was something when you were sitting there alone listening and waiting for the doctor to come in and shrug his shoulders again. He was a nice little man, and he seemed to know his business.

But oddly enough Roger kept wishing that it was Doctor Whitman in there with Mary now. Doctor Whitman had died fifteen years ago, four thousand miles away.

He slept a little later on; the rain had stopped in the morning, though there were still low driving clouds and white caps on the sea. Madame Gregor had gone. There was a phone-call from Paris. Jim was coming by to-night's train. But Harold—Harold hadn't forgotten, after all, the days when it was his mother and himself against the world. He had always hated noise and speed and danger, but now he had chartered an aeroplane and persuaded a pilot to fly him to Genoa through the storms which were keeping the airliners on the ground.

Just the same, he was too late. Mary didn't regain consciousness, but she lingered on through the morning. Roger sat beside her a little, thinking what a strange road they had travelled together since that afternoon in Mrs. Vance's parlour. He had given her what she wanted in the end; probably that evening at Lady Cauldfield's, the first time they went to London, had been her zenith. But even coming down the hill since then, she hadn't been unhappy. Or—had the whole thing been a failure? Had Mary realised, latterly, that she had always been trying to catch a rainbow? He didn't know, and he could never ask her now.

They sent him away after a time; he went and walked up and down on the terrace, out of the wind. The paving stones were wet and plastered with twigs and leaves. About midday they came to him there and told him that she was dead.

*　　　*　　　*　　　*

Harold arrived, and Jim, and then Ruth came, leaving the children with their governess. Mary was buried in the little English cemetery at the resort along the coast, in an Anglican atmosphere of flowers and hymns and late-Victorian gothic which was familiar only to Ruth who had spent her girlhood in such gentle, decaying English colonies. It seemed a strange place to leave Mary, among the exiles and the expatriates, but after all she had never really belonged anywhere herself. Ever since she was a girl with her father, dragging from boarding-house to boarding-house, she had been without roots, restless, always looking for something and never quite finding it. One could only hope that she had found it now.

Jim went away immediately after the service; he couldn't stand death and funerals and mourning, he had to go tearing back to try and lose the taste of it in his own noisy world again. The rest of them drove back to the villa. Harold made some excuse and slipped away to wander about by himself among the olive-trees. Roger climbed wearily upstairs to his own room and sat there, wondering what he was going to do now and how he was going to spend his last few remaining years alone.

* * * *

Harold and Ruth wanted him to settle in Paris, but he couldn't decide. He would come there for a time at least . . . he couldn't stay here all alone. Times were bad, and they were lucky to find a purchaser for the villa. Most of the furniture was sold, too; Harold took a few of the books and pictures, and there was a great burning of old letters and fans and theatre programmes, a great giving-away of hats and dresses and furs.

Roger's own packing didn't take long. He had collected very few possessions really during all these years. His clothes, a few books, some business papers, a souvenir or two. In the bottom of one old box he found some bits of ore from Cripple Creek and a little nugget from the Yukon ; he hadn't looked at them for years.

To please Harold he finally consented to take a servant of his own now. They found a little grizzled Englishman named Wilkins, with a slightly Cockney voice and a quick, ugly face like a little monkey, who had been, in his time, a ship's steward, an officer's batman, valet to an eccentric viscount and male-nurse to an American millionaire. He could drive a car and was clever with packing and luggage and shoes and hot water ; he had travelled all over the world, and could shop and keep accounts in half a dozen languages. Roger wished that Mary could see him. She had always wanted him to have his own manservant, and she would have liked to hear about the Viscount and the millionaire.

It was late summer before everything was arranged. He had kept the car, and in September Wilkins drove him slowly along the Riviera and up by Aix and Avignon to Paris. Harold could think and talk of nothing but the murder of Dollfuss. Jim was in Germany, where Hindenburg had died and the swastika flags in their millions waved for Hitler. Then it was October, and Harold was shuddering over the assass-ination of King Alexander and M. Barthou. Ruth was tired of listening to him talking politics ; she had fitted up a studio for herself and was doing a little modelling in clay. Alice had taken a house at Malaga, and the faithful Edith had gone out to live with her.

In November Roger found he couldn't stand any more of the rain and the traffic and Harold's politics and refugees. Wilkins drove him South again ; it was cold on the Riviera, but it was bright and hard and sunny ; like Alice he wanted colour and sun. He took a suite in a big, old-fashioned, gilded-gingerbread hotel in Nice, and once he was settled there it was too much trouble to move again.

CHAPTER
XV

BY NOW HE HAD turned into one of the local landmarks. Residents pointed him out to visitors on the Promenade des Anglais, and street-cleaners touched their caps to him, and occasionally—since he gave a lot of money to local charities—a smeary picture of him would appear in the local press. Life slipped into a quiet, monotonous routine.

He slept badly, and was always awake when Wilkins came in with a cup of tea to pull back the curtains and open the shutters and reveal another day. A sunny day, a rainy day, a dusty cold day of mistral—it didn't matter much. He would read for a little after that, and then—he hated breakfast in bed—Wilkins would come back and help him to dress. They would talk about one thing and another gradually he learnt all Wilkins' life-story ; what it was like in the glory-hole of one of the old long-funnelled Cunarders and what an officer's batman saw of the retreat from Mons ; the safari in East Africa with the viscount, the last years of the millionaire in his French château on Long Island. He knew all about Wilkins' married daughter who had two children and whose husband had deserted her and who kept a little hat-shop near Shepherd's Bush.

Wilkins made all the difference. A funny little

chap, with his ugly face and his clipped, cheerful voice, always good-tempered, never familiar, ready to talk if you wanted to talk and silent if you wanted to be quiet. Once a year he went home for a fortnight, and life was a misery of sallow, obsequious hotel-servants ; it was quite an exciting day when he arrived back again with the latest news from London. He would describe the new buildings and the Belisha beacons and the news-reel cinemas ; the Jews and refugees who were filling whole streets in Bloomsbury and Bayswater, the tarts in Piccadilly and the fun-fairs in the Charing Cross Road. All the things that Jim never bothered to describe, and Harold never noticed when he went to England.

" It shook me, sir, when I went in there. All white tiles and painted walls with cows jumping over windmills like a nursery. Two little chits, all red nails and lipstick, in white coats behind the counter. And this old London cabby, with a Mons Star ribbon on his waistcoat, sitting there sucking up ice-cream soda like a Yankee High School-girl at a drug-store. It made me wonder, I tell you sir, what poor old London's coming to."

When Roger was dressed he would have his rolls and coffee by the window, and later, if it was a warm day, he would go out and walk a little on the Promen-ade. Nice wasn't what it used to be either . . . he could remember the old days of Grand Dukes and cocottes and champagne. There were still a few big sleek cars, but most of the visitors were rather shoddy tourists, and a lot of the gilded-gingerbread hotels were shut.

As a rule he lunched in his own room. Sometimes he would go down to the huge, half-empty dining-room with its mirrors and red curtains and gilded caryatids. There would be a few tourists there, and a few old residents like himself. Sharp-faced old ladies with sticks and high-heels and lap-dogs and companions ; faded old men with tall collars and monocles. All that was left of the glittering Europe of the nineteen-hundreds into which Mary had plunged so eagerly. You could see more of them at Monte Carlo, shabby, elegant, elbowed by the Turks and Greeks and South Americans.

In the afternoon he would rest a bit, and then perhaps he would get Wilkins to take him out in the car. Perhaps he would go and see Alice, who had been driven out of Spain by the Civil War there, and had taken a little villa up at Eze. Perhaps they would go up by Vence and Grasse, or along the coast to Mentone and the frontier beyond which Mussolini had just called up another fifty thousand men.

Jim came to see him when he was in Europe, and Harold was here pretty often ; he had friends in the artists' colonies at Bandol and Cagnes. There were not many places left in Europe that Harold and Ruth could visit now. They wouldn't go to Nazi Germany of course. Harold wouldn't even go to Italy, since the Abyssinian war. He could only go to England, really, or stay in France, and wherever he went he couldn't get away from the newspapers and the wireless bulletins.

He had been all quivering fury about the Hoare-Laval offer, and non-intervention in Spain ; about the gassing of Abyssinian tribesmen and the bombing of Guernica. During the Munich crisis he had been, literally, physically, sick with nervousness. When Daladier came back to Paris and Chamberlain returned

to London to announce peace with honour, he had
gasped with relief and relaxed for a day or two. Then
he had thought again, and been more wretched than
ever. Listening to the radio-commentators, reading
the articles of Madame Tabouis, devouring, with a
sort of sickened fascination, book after book on modern
warfare. Bombs and gas and bacteria ; bacteria, gas,
bombs.

Ruth shared his fears but wouldn't show them ;
she shut herself up in her studio and slapped away at
an unresponsive lump of clay. Sylvia, seventeen now,
laughed at them. She went to a smart little finishing-
school at Passy, and her friends were the daughters of
French soap-kings and aeroplane-manufacturers who
were not greatly concerned about Hitler but had
troubles nearer home.

" Lucille's father came to see her yesterday. He's
a funny fat little man with a shiny face, but he has
the most wonderful, pale-blue Hispano-Suiza. They
say he's lost a lot of money lately, with all these awful
strikes and troubles in his factory. Just think, the
workmen actually shut themselves in and refused to
move, and when he went and tried to argue with them
they jeered and booed and sang the ' Internationale.'
Lucille says it is because he has always been much too
easy-going with them ; she says things will be different
when he retires and her brother Denis takes charge.
He won't stand any nonsense. I saw him too the other
day—rather a nice-looking young man. He has a
scar on his forehead . . . he doesn't talk about it,
but everyone knows he got it in a fight with some
communists. He was in the Jeunesse Patriotes,
and was out in the Concorde riots. Lucille says
that he says that Hitler is quite right in many ways.

R   257

The real danger is Communism, not National-
Socialism.''

Harold would listen sourly and try to argue, or perhaps
just give a hopeless shrug.   He didn't approve of
Sylvia's school in any case, but Ruth liked it . . . and
no doubt it was better than some hockey-playing nest
of amazons in England, which was the only
alternative.

The school in Switzerland where Charles went now
was more to Harold's taste.   International, co-educa-
tional, self-governing, encouraging the fullest expression
of personality . . . Roger grunted a little dubiously
when they described it to him and showed him photographs.   A noisy, shock-haired mob of little cosmo-
politans wandering round an old château near Geneva,
chattering in a dozen languages, hammering on pianos,
painting in the manner of Picasso, bathing naked in
the lake.   It seemed a queer, undisciplined business,
where the children and not the teachers decided what
was to be done.   Not that he would have had much
confidence in the decisions of the teachers, with their
beards and sandals and dirty flannel trousers, if it
came to that.   He made no comment.   It was none
of his business, and no doubt he was old fashioned.
But he couldn't help feeling that what the world
needed most to-day was something that you had to
work for . . . something you wouldn't just find lying
about, in a sort of treasure-hunt round a garden by a
lake.   You had to work for it, and suffer for it perhaps
. . . he couldn't explain what he meant to Harold,
but old Captain Morris, and Doctor Whitman—for
all his poker and his Bourbon whisky—and even little
Wilkins, would have understood.

And yet Charles, when you saw him, was a simple,

rather solemn boy who showed no traces of all the
exuberant experiments for which he had always been
a guinea-pig. Harold brought him to Nice for a few
days, in the spring. Harold himself was as worried
as ever, but he seemed to have something special on
his mind this time, though he didn't bring it out.
He talked, inevitably, of politics, wandering restlessly
about Roger's sitting-room that first evening after
dinner.

" What did you think of Mussolini's Easter greeting
to humanity ? I suppose he will be looking this way
next. ' Corsica, Tunis, Nice ! ' He's got the other
end of the Mediterranean as he wants it now. I
wonder what the Moors are doing in Barcelona to-
night. But after all, it isn't Mussolini or Franco really,
it's Hitler. I met a man the other day who had
just escaped from Prague . . . Yes, it's coming, the
avalanche is poised, a cough will bring it down now.
You know, when Lord Stanhope was addressing the
ratings in the *Ark Royal* recently, he let slip the fact
that the anti-aircraft guns are manned night and day.
They tried to hush that up, but one London paper
let the cat out of the bag. Conscription in England
now . . . and trial black-outs, gas-masks . . . Everyone waiting for Hitler's next move. I can't forget
Chamberlain's words during the Munich time. ' How
horrible, fantastic, incredible it is. . . . ' "

He gave a little shudder and made a brave effort
to change the subject, looking at the gilded pseudo-
Empire furniture and saying something about the old
Nice of the Grand Dukes.

" Cannes used to be the quiet place, and Nice the
gay one. Now, if anything, it is the other way round.
It would be amusing to write a social history of the

Riviera, from Lord Brougham to the Greek Syndicate. Portrait of a civilisation in decomposition . . . the irridescent colours of a dying shark. Osbert Sitwell would do it rather well."

Roger nodded. He was hardly listening to Harold ; he was studying young Charles and wondering what to make of him. A silent, rather untidy boy in a blue suit, sitting in a gilt chair looking at a magazine. He had Harold's thin, nervous face, but it was browner and healthier than Harold's had ever been. His wrists were thicker, he didn't blink and flinch the way Harold used to do when you spoke to him. What had they made of him, really, the schoolmasters and tennis-professionals, the psycho-analyists and elocutionists ? He was always so self-possessed and reserved and polite and silent. It was impossible to tell what was going on in his head.

"Well, Charles," he said. The boy looked up courteously. "What do you think of things ? How do you like it at school ? "

"Oh, it's all right I suppose."

Harold looked annoyed.

"You don't sound very enthusiastic. Don't say you've been reading *Tom Brown's Schooldays* and wish you had gone to Rugby."

"No. It's not that. Only . . . well, we spent nearly all last term getting up that Persian play. Everyone squabbling about who was to have the leading parts and who was to produce it and how it was to be staged. Arguing and wrangling and chopping and changing . . . and at the end it wasn't very good. It seemed such a waste of time, somehow."

"At Rugby you'd have been arguing about football. Would that have been any better ? "

" No, I suppose not. I suppose it has to be one thing or the other. But neither seems very important, somehow."

Roger cleared his throat.

" What do you think is important ? What are you going to do when you leave school ? "

It sounded very elderly and pompous. Years ago he had asked Harold that. Harold had flushed and stammered and babbled about art, music, literature, travel, seeing everything, experiencing everything. But young Charles only shrugged his shoulders.

" I don't know, really. It's rather hard to say."

No doubt it was. He'd seen nearly everything already . . . not like poor little Harold poring over books at the kitchen table and driven out to do the evening chores.

" You've never been in America yet ? "

" No. I'd like to go there."

Harold looked round sharply, started to speak and stopped himself. Roger floundered ponderously on.

" Like to live there ? "

" No, I don't think so."

" Don't you know at all what you want to do ? "

" Not very well. Did you know, when you were my age ? "

The question surprised him. How old was Charles now ? Fifteen, sixteen ? At that age . . . He laughed.

" I thought I did, Charles. I was at sea by then. Cleaning out a pig pen and planning to study navigation and get my Ticket and end up with a ship of my own. It wouldn't have been a bad life, either. I remember, there was a boy from London in my last ship . . ."

Charles looked at him oddly.

"Tell me about it, will you? I've been reading quite a lot about the old days at sea."

Roger hesitated.

"Oh well, that's a big order. And after all these years . . . I shipped as a boy in an old barque, the *Chester Rows* . . ."

He hadn't thought about the *Chester Rows* for years, and yet it all came back with surprising vividness. The Hoogly, Garden Reach, the long line of ships at their moorings, yards trimly squared against the hot sky. He remembered the smell of the brown river water, and a hundred other smells and tastes besides. Bilges and paint and Stockholm tar and slush : the warm greasiness of Sunday duff, the thin, welcome heat of coffee, even the taste of those imagined meals with which your mind was busy in the hungry watches. The gravy-eye watches before dawn. He remembered the thrust of the wind and the kick of the wheel and the voice of an old man giving hints to a youngster. "Gently does it, gently. Just keep the weather-clew of your royal quivering." He remembered the mud on the anchor-chain, and the chanty, and the click of the pawls. He remembered those other voyages, the light winking off Cape Otway, the clippers so spick and span round the Circular Quay.

Afterwards he wasn't sure just what he had said, or how long he had talked. He couldn't be sure that Charles was really interested and not just polite. But he did seem to have read a lot of books about it . . . he asked a good many questions, and sensible questions too . . . and he looked regretful and unwilling when Harold began to fidget and consult his watch and hint that it was nearly time for bed. After all those surging vivid memories of youth and action it was strange to come back to the present, to a tired old man, his veined hands unsteady, his back aching, who waited in a big ornate room for Wilkins to come and help him to undress.

*   *   *   *

Next day they left Charles to amuse himself and drove up to visit Alice at Eze. They started about ten o'clock, and went by the Lower Corniche to make the drive a little longer : both of them knew that it was no good descending on her too early in the day. As they went through Villefranche they stopped to look out on the wide, grey-green, shifting expanse of the Roads, with the villas dotting the green slopes on either side. There were yachts and motor-boats and little steamers, and out in the harbour, clear and bright as a big model in a shipping-office window, the Italian liner *Imperatore* was lying at anchor, tenders tiny under her huge sides. Harold looked sourly at the squat streamlined funnels and rakish cruiser stern, and said that people underrated the Italians—at any rate their air force and fleet. But Wilkins, to whom the remark had been addressed, wouldn't agree.

" All very fine, sir, but not a ship at all. More like one of those new super-cinemas in Leicester Square. Did you ever travel on the old *Mauretania ?* Now she was ship, for all her palm-courts and swimming-pools. And some of the smaller Cunarders round about that time . . . the old *Caronia*, now, or the *Carmania* that fought the *Cap Trafalgar* in the War. I'd like to see them make an auxiliary cruiser out of that thing there."

" She'd do to carry troops in."

" Not if our Navy was about she wouldn't, sir."

263

Roger gave a little chuckle. He was glad Harold had heard that, the way Wilkins said it. Harold would never remember that if a war did come there would be two sides fighting it.

But Harold only smiled tolerantly. He must have realised, though, that Roger was tired of his jeremiads about politics : he began to comment on the scenery, the villas and hotels, the wedding-cake architecture of Monaco.

" Did you know that Zaharoff, the armament king, when he was planning to buy the Casino, wangled a clause about Monaco into the Treaty of Versailles ? "

Roger hadn't know it. Harold was full of such odd little scraps of information, he collected them just as he used to collect scraps of Parian marble and Roman coins when he first came to Europe. The story of Zaharoff kept him going all the rest of the way, by Rocquebrune and up the Grande Corniche, the wide view opening and widening like a panorama in another tourist-office, pink and white towns and green headlands and that liner diminished, tiny, bright and toylike, far below.

Alice's villa lay down the hill a little way from the road : Wilkins parked the car and they left him with it and went down a path, through a gate in a high stone wall and little garden full of cactus-plants and bougainvillea all oddly neglected and overgrown. It was a square, modernistic little house, scarlet-painted woodwork and rather dirty white stucco : Harold rang and rang the doorbell but no one answered and at last he turned the handle and stepped in. You came straight into a living room whose far wall was one huge sheet of glass filled like a picture-frame with sea and coast and mountains. It was stuffy, smelling of stale drinks and cigarettes and neglected flower-vases, and the glass-topped tables were littered with tumblers, cigarette ends, plates of half-eaten sandwiches, all the debris of a party which had gone on too long.

Harold's nose wrinkled. He went across and opened a window . . . looked into the next room, shrugged his shoulders, called out : " Anybody there ? "

Funny that Miss Cartwright wasn't about. And there must be some servants . . . After a long time a voice answered. After another long wait Alice herself appeared.

She was wearing a long house-coat and a pair of sandals, her hair was untidy, her face pale and puffy, with a careless smear of lipstick on her mouth. She stood in the doorway staring at them dully for a moment ; then she came forward.

" Dad ! Why didn't you tell me you were coming ? And Harold—how goes it, Harold ? Hitler still keeping you worried ? "

She pushed back her hair and looked round the room.

" Christ, what a mess ! I told Edith to tidy it up a bit before she went. Our blasted servants all walked out on us this morning, and she's gone to try and find some others. And to bring back something to eat . . . not that I feel like eating. We had a bit of a party last night. Some revolting people I met somewhere . . . I don't remember much about them."

Her eyes were still blurry and stupid, but she was trying hard to pull herself together.

" Get some chairs and sit down. Would you like a drink ? I need one. If there's anything left to drink, that is. There was a fantastic old Irishman who took charge of the drinks last night, and I expect he finished off the lot. A dapper, horsey old boy with a red wig who talked about the Dublin Horse-show. He was going to tell me an infallible system for the Tables . . . I wish to God he could. Where are those blasted cigarettes ? "

They sat in their chromium chairs and watched her : a shaky hand holding a lighter, a deep puff and another : that seemed to steady her a bit.

" You're looking well, Dad. The Riviera seems to suit you. I can't say the same for myself. Do you know, Harold, even here people insist on talking about politics these days ? There was some sort of writer from Cagnes last night, spouting away about crypto-Communists and crypto-Fascists. No doubt you're a crypto-Communist. And Jim's a crypto-Fascist . . . I must tell him that when I see him. And that should be in a few weeks, thank God."

Roger looked at her sharply.

" What do you mean ? Is he coming over again ? "

" No. I'm going. Next month I think. Back to ' God's Own Country.' Only I'm not going to stay there—I'm going to Mexico. Why Mexico ? God knows. It should be interesting—bright and violent and sunny. Plenty to drink, all sorts of odd people to talk to, bullfights . . . you didn't know I was *aficionado-aficionada* is it ?—did you ? I used to worry when Italian cab-drivers beat their horses . . . I still do for that matter. But a good *corrida* is as picturesque as your Russian ballet, Harold. And a damn sight more exciting . . . both the bull and the matador have got a lot more at stake than any ballet-dancer. And on the west coast, at Acapulco, there are little

266

modern villas just as bogus as this one, and bathing beaches and Casinos, and you can watch Indian boys diving off the cliffs. If they time it wrong they kill themselves. That should be exciting too."

Harold said nothing. After a little Roger asked : " How about Edith Cartwright ? Is she going with you ? "

" I suppose so. She isn't very keen, but she's a faithful soul, you know. Anyway, she's nowhere else to go."

Her voice was indifferent, trailing away. She closed her eyes, opened them again, swallowed and crushed her cigarette.

" Dad, I've got a horrible headache. Do you mind if I go and lie down again for a bit ? I'm sorry to be so inhospitable . . . if you like to wait till Edith comes back she'll make you some coffee or something. And I'll come down and see you to-morrow or the day after. Oh yes, God yes, I'll be all right now. Edith will be back in half an hour, anyway. Good-bye, good-bye, Harold. Got your gas-mask yet ? They tell me the Germans have got some new gasses that no mask will keep out . . ."

Roger got up slowly. He ought to say something . . . he ought to do something. . . . But somehow they were out in the sunlight again, climbing up the path to the car.

*   *   *   *

" My God," said Harold. " I'm sorry for Edith Cartwright."

There was no answer to that, either. He sat back against the cushions, feeling very old and tired.

Harold's face was bitter. Roger wondered if he was remembering a big, gay tomboy of a girl who used to make fun of him and scold him and fight tooth and claw to protect him from the Sauer boys and the Kleins.

The road went looping down again, past the villas and the little cafés and the rocky olive-groves. It was Harold at last who broke the silence.

" Funny that Alice should have announced her news like that. I've been trying all the time to tell you— we're going to America too. All of us. Almost at once."

Roger started.

" To America ? Good God, Harold. I thought you hated it over there ? "

" I don't like it much. But I can't go on living here, in this powder-magazine. I want to get Sylvia and Charles out of it in time."

" What does he think about it ? "

" We haven't told him yet," Harold swallowed. " We had thought of England, but if war does come, England won't be much better off than France. Jim knows of a house on Long Island where we can stay for a little, while we look round and find ourselves some little Shangri-La somewhere. In California perhaps. If other highly-civilised people can stand it we should be able to. And—we want you to come and live with us. We can't go off and leave you here, like this."

" This will be safe enough."

" Will it ? But I wasn't only thinking of safety in any case. To go away and leave you all alone in that great gilded mausoleum, the rest of us thousands of miles away . . . You needn't actually live with us,

if you don't want to. You can find some little place
of your own."

Roger hesitated. He had nearly refused . . . for
he didn't want to hang on to Harold's coat-tails, he
dreaded the upheaval, yes, and he hated to look as
if he was running away. But then he saw himself
alone here, alone in that hotel, alone in Europe,
waiting for the end like some poor old spinster in
a pension.

"All right, Harold. I'll come with you. It's nice
of you to want me."

Harold looked pleased : for a moment his face
was almost cheerful. Then it changed again, as he
bent forward and stared out at the sea and the pale
grey mountains tumbling away into the soft midday haze. A little café with red-checked cloths on
the tables, a fresh green arbour throwing a pattern of
shadow, two fat men drinking and talking, an old dog
dozing in the sun.

"Europe," he said. "It will be strange to leave
it. It has always had a sort of fascination for me,
ever since that first evening at Naples, do you remember ? I keep remembering things these days. Going
through the Uffizi with Lionel . . . the swallows
whistling round the towers of Siena . . . the banners
spinning and leaping before the Palio. And Paris—
I remember the first time I saw the Winged Victory,
standing there, poised and triumphant—it was all
I had ever read or imagined about Ancient Greece.
And then, I remember, I discovered the Leonardos
and the whole Renaissance . . . you know, I still enjoy
reading what Pater wrote about the Mona Lisa, even
though I don't believe a word of it now. Well, I'll be
able to bore my grandchildren with my reminiscences.

How I saw the first season of Russian ballet at the Châtelet in 1909, and how I met James Joyce at Sylvia Beach's bookshop, and how I met Gertrude Stein and Picasso, and how I saw Isadora Duncan dance. You know, one of the things I shall always regret is that I didn't go to her funeral. So few people did . . . we were all trying to avoid an American Legion jamboree that day. But we've had some good times. Were you with us when we went to Aigues Mortes and saw the Church of the Three Maries and the gypsies and the horses ? Salzburg, Buda, the up-lands of Spain—long glaring roads when you expect to meet Don Quixote—the little fierce hill-towns of Sicily, the Piazza delle Erbe in Verona, the Place de la Concorde at dusk with all the lights coming on. . . . There was something about it all—it was one civilization, or should have been, could have been. And I *wanted* it so, I wanted to understand it and be part of it. And now it is all going. It seems so—so *unfair* somehow."

His shoulders drooped : he looked, suddenly, an elderly, querulous, bitter little man, sitting there. Roger didn't answer. By now, after all these years, he more or less understood what Harold had been after in his restless journeys, his jackdaw gathering of books and pictures, Russian ikons and Greek amphoræ. But what had Harold done to save it ? Signed a few petitions, subscribed to a fund or two, talked a lot, no more. And, now that he came to think of it, what had he himself done either ? What had he done for his own kind, the ones who had not been so lucky, the ones who had stayed in the slums and the dole-queues, or in the fo'castles of the tramp-ships ? Queer how as time went on, you forgot the things you used to

270

know. And when you remembered them again it was too late.

*   *   *   *

Alice, with her tired, faithful Edith Cartwright, came to say good-bye and sailed from Villefranche on her way to Mexico. About the same time Harold and his family, after a hectic packing and a heartbroken farewell to Paris, were sailing from Le Havre. Roger would join them in July or August : he was going to England first, and planned to sail from Southampton. There were one or two things he had to do in London, and it would give Wilkins a chance to see his daughter and his grandchildren.

Wilkins was coming to America too, of course : he seemed quite pleased at the prospect, he was a bit of a rolling-stone, and was tired of this dull life in Nice. He would still be able to come back to England for his holidays, unless there was a war. And in any case he would be back some day. He wasn't saying good-bye to the old world, as Roger must do this time.

Whatever happened, he knew, this was his last long journey. It was strange to be leaving Europe like this, sunny and summery under the threat of doom. You felt almost guilty, somehow, parting from the hotel people, the worried little waiters, and wondering what the next few years had in store for them.

They took the old car and drove in slow stages, by Avignon and Orange and Montelimar, and he felt almost as sentimental as Harold must have felt, leaving the brown, dusty fields, the vineyards, the harsh cliffs and white villages of the South. In the little hotels where they stopped along the way the radios were blaring the agitated voices of the politicians : Frenchmen listened, and grimaced, and shrugged their shoulders ; they heard, with a twist of amusement, descriptions of the first conscripts in England, the militiamen as they were called, going off in their flannel trousers with their neat little suitcases.

Paris, for all its swirling hooting traffic, was oddly alive with memories of that first visit so many years ago. The Grand Dukes and the Rajah in the hotel by the Place de la Concorde : Harold discovering the Mona Lisa, Mary shopping in the Rue de la Paix, Jim buying amber walking-sticks and Charvet ties. The papers were full of the Maginot Line and the Polish corridor : there was an English Military Mission holding talks in Russia, and British bombers were making practice flights to France. Outside Wimereux, on the way to Calais two days later, Wilkins suddenly fell into a mood of reminiscence too. He had been here in 1914 for the first time . . . in a Base Camp somewhere round here, there was an estaminet he used to fancy . . . later he was here again, there was a big hospital . . . it was strange to think of that younger Wilkins, with a waxed moustache and a drooping Woodbine, trudging along these roads here with his pals, whistling " Tipperary," waving to the girls. There were a lot of his kind here still, under their neat white stones in those quiet, endless cemeteries.

They spent the night in Dover and drove up to London next day. He had booked rooms in a hotel in Piccadilly, looking out across the Green Park to-wards the Palace and the hazy towers of Westminster. It was a warm sunny afternoon, all blue and green

and grey and smoky gold : when he was settled in he
sent Wilkins off to see his daughter and sat by the
window looking out across the busy street at the
park with its children and dogs and couples strolling
arm in arm under the trees, among the raw new
air raid shelters.

It looked peaceful enough to-day, in all conscience,
with the great scarlet busses and doddering old taxis
and the gay summer dresses of the girls : somehow
you couldn't believe that it was really threatened with
the apocalyptic horrors which Harold read about in
all those books and magazines.

If Mary hadn't been quite so ambitious the Barton
family might have settled here in England, and have
some roots down now. It could have been done . . .
but not the way she wanted it, not with white-wigged
footmen and Royalty at her parties. Poor Mary . . .
spending so lavishly at Lady Cauldfield's bazaars, and
pestering Mr. Choate for tickets to the Royal Enclosure,
and furious with Alice who said she didn't want to be
presented anyway. He had never quite known what
made her finally give up her effort to break into London
Society. A snub here, a rebuff there, a general sense
of discouragement, hopelessness. He'd been just as
well pleased himself, when she did give up. After
all, the England she was out to conquer wasn't an
England that had ever meant anything to him.

You couldn't go back on sentimental pilgrimages
to the roaring streets and clanging docks of a Liverpool
that had changed out of all knowing since a boy walked
with Captain Morris down Water Street on a rainy
afternoon.

It was generally raining a little, as you remembered
it now. The cobbles thundered to the hooves of

8   273

great grey horses and the crash of iron-rimmed wheels. Down by the river the gulls would be turning and screaming, and the figure-heads would look down on you as you walked along beneath them, and out in the stream, where the buoys strained and ducked in the muddy water, a little black tug with slapping paddles would be towing in one ship more, home from the sea.

To-morrow, he told himself, he would have to send Wilkins to the Cunard office to make sure their reservations were all right. The *Queen Mary* to the America of Roosevelt and rumbas and streamlined trains and Wall Street and the New York World's Fair. America had been his country too, once, but he had never felt specially patriotic or American. He had liked the smell of the sage-brush, and the colours of the leaves in the Fall : he had liked trout-fishing with Doctor Whitman, and arguing about William Jennings Bryan with Mr. Klein. But the only thing he had really thought about was finding gold or silver. Perhaps if he had thought of a few other things too he wouldn't feel so rootless now.

He looked out of the window again : it was cool and comfortable here, and he felt tired, he hated the idea of more travelling. Luggage, tickets, passports, staterooms, customs. He would have to do something about selling the old car too. They'd had it a long time, Mary had helped to choose it, it would be a wrench to part with it. But you couldn't take a 1928 Daimler all the way to California : it would be cheaper to buy something else out there. Jim would know what was the best to get . . . He was still brooding over that when Wilkins came in again. Little Wilkins in his neat dark suit and hard white collar . . . he looked worried too, what was wrong now ?

" Well, Wilkins, how's your daughter ? "

" All right, sir, thank you. Will you be having your dinner up here ? "

" Yes, I think so. I'll turn in pretty early. It's been a long day."

" Yes, sir." Wilkins swallowed. " I'll have to go to a registry to-morrow, sir, I'm afraid."

" Wilkins ! What the hell do you mean ? "

" I'll have to find you someone else to go with you, sir, that's all. I hate to tell you. Only my daughter . . . she's worrying something cruel, sir. About all this war-talk, and the children. I hadn't quite realised . . . well, you know how things are, sir. If there is a war, the kids will be evacuated to the country of course. That's all fixed up . . . labels to tie on to 'em, and everything, all ready. Two little handbags, two little gas-masks . . . well, that's civilization for you, I suppose. Only of course, she would have to stay and look after the shop. She was reading a pamphlet they sent round, all about gas-proofing a room. And . . . well, while it's like that, I can't leave her here and go sailing off to America, can I, sir ? Maybe later on, when all this blows over, I could come over. We could easily find you someone for a month or two."

His little red face twisted with anxiety. Roger looked away.

" No, Wilkins," he said slowly. " You couldn't run out on her now, I see that. But while you were gone, I was thinking . . . I don't know that I feel up to that journey, just now, myself. And you know, somehow I'd like to stick around and see what happens here. You go out and cancel those passages, to-morrow, and I'll write an air-mail letter to Mr. Harold. He'll think I'm crazy, but never mind that. . . . Did I ever tell you about the first time I came to London ? Just a boy, I was, off an old barque called the *Chester Rows*. . . ."

Wilkins was saying something, surprise, doubt, relief, eagerness and expostulation all stammering out at once. Roger closed his eyes. He didn't want to argue and he didn't want to listen to arguments. He only wanted to rest now, with the knowledge that to-morrow he needn't bother about the car and the luggage and the steamer-tickets, that he could stay in bed all morning, or all day if he wanted to. But perhaps in the afternoon he would go out, and sit in the Park across there, and watch the children playing and the young men strolling with their girls.

CHAPTER
XVI

THE DUSK WAS CLOSING in now, and London was settling
ponderously down for another night of darkness.
Wilkins had drawn the black-out curtains and taken
away the tea-things ; the little flat was warm and silent.
Roger lay back against the pillows, in the pool of
light from his reading-lamp.

Just a piece of fuss on Wilkins' part to make him stay
in bed like this . . . still, the doctor wanted it, and he
hadn't ever felt much good since that attack of influ-
enza a month ago. Shaky, breathless, weak as water,
his heart thumping and skipping oddly in the night.

Well, when you were nearly ninety you couldn't
expect much else. He looked at his big blue-veined,
papery hands against the quilt, and tried to remember
them grappling with canvas on the weather yard-arm,
or swinging a pick in a Colorado mine. If a bomb
landed here to-night it would only hurry up something
which was bound to happen before long, anyway.

He picked up the evening paper and looked at it
idly. The Russians were holding the Germans in
front of Moscow and at Tula, but had lost ground in
the Crimea, and the Germans had taken Kursk.
There was more about the sinking of the *Ark Royal*.
Emden bombed again. Something coming in the
Western Desert . . . the forces there were to be called

the Eighth Army now. More Canadian troops had reached Hong Kong, and the Japanese envoy had started talks in Washington.

Queer to imagine it all going on at this moment, while you lay here in the lamplight in this warm, quiet room. The darkness sifting down like snow over the great wastes of Russia, dusk over the rock and the wire round the Tobruk perimeter, engines roaring and flashing as the Wellingtons took off from aerodromes in England . . . the little ships going out in convoy, with the destroyers whooping round them and the last signals blinking from the shore.

In America, he calculated, it would still be early afternoon. Late autumn sunshine on the little house among the woods in Connecticut where Harold (they hadn't gone to California after all) would be trying to tune-in to London, or sitting in front of a log fire dreaming about Paris, Salzburg, Rome. Still, he was settling down all right over there now ; his letters were calmer than they used to be. When he felt too homesick for Europe, so he wrote, he went into New York and lost himself among the Italian pictures in the Metropolitan. Ruth was getting on well with her sculpture, and Sylvia had made a lot of friends, and they had found a school for Charles, near Boston, which was run on the same lines as the one in Switzerland.

Charles must be nearly eighteen now—Harold had been right to get them out of Europe when he did. They saw Jim sometimes, when he could tear himself away from El Morocco and the Colony Club. Alice was still in Mexico. She had her bogus little villa at Acapulco, and her scrawled, erratic letters told of the bathing-beaches and the diving boys.

And here an old man was dreaming away his last days, through the Phoney War, and the fantastic Dunkirk time, through the Battle of Britain and the Blitz.

They had been lucky so far, not even windows broken. Wilkins' daughter had had her shop damaged, and Wilkins himself had nearly caught it, in a pub he favoured somewhere off Oxford Street. Wilkins always had plenty of news to bring back from his outings these days . . . it was a change from those placid years in Nice! Bomb stories, shelter stories, Home Guard stories, all the latest war-rumours, queer little anecdotes about the night-life of war-time London, the Free French, and Poles and Canadians with their girl-friends. . . . Lying here listening to him was almost as good as getting out and seeing it all for yourself. Only in those bad raids last winter it hadn't been much fun being old and useless. Letting Wilkins fuss you down to the shelter in the basement, among the rugs and stools and nervous conversation of the other residents. Or lying here defenceless while the whole world rocked and glared.

It was silly, really, to stay on in London. Harold repeated that in every letter, Wilkins himself hinted as much sometimes. But Wilkins wanted to be near his daughter, and you couldn't face life in a country hotel without him, and, anyway, now that you were here you didn't like to let yourself be chased away.

You spent a lot of your time in the past, when things were quiet and sane. A little boy watching his mother sewing in the lamplight, or walking with Captain Morris by the docks. (Those streets and docks had caught it too, last winter.) Captain Morris had thought, even then, that the world was going crazy—

279

he wasn't far wrong, either. Still, it was a pity you couldn't get him back to hear about something like the *Jervis Bay*. . . .

Those were peaceful times to remember, and there were many others. A summer evening at Curicanti, with water tinkling in the ditches and Jim and Alice playing while Harold and his mother read a book about Venice in the old hammock on the porch. And later . . . sunny mornings at the villa at Fiesole, when it was warm enough to take your morning coffee on the terrace. Coffee and rolls and honey, and Harold talking with Lionel Morton about the love-affairs of Shelley, and the newspapers all excited about some little trouble in the Balkans, or some aviator who had flown from London to Manchester.

Now you could turn a knob and listen to Churchill or Roosevelt speaking, hear Hitler ranting in Munich, hear a reporter describing a battle, even hear the machine-guns and the shells.

The last war had been fantastic enough, but this one was even stranger, and would be more incredible still no doubt before it was done. It was hard to imagine those nightmare happenings in places which had been familiar for years. The Germans in Paris, staff-cars with swastikas in the Place de la Concorde, fat generals in the restaurants where the waiters used to know Mary, Gestapo hunting men and women of the Resistance along the lanes and alleys where Harold used to hunt the quaint and the picturesque. British aircraft bombing Genoa, where you used to go and shop from the Castello, where you used to land, at sunset perhaps, from a liner full of tourists. High explosive and fire and avalanching rubble in the prim squares of London where Mary used to call on dowagers;

steel helmets and writhing fire-hoses in the streets where the Edwardians drove in glittering carriages. It was lucky that Mary hadn't lived to see all this. She had never admitted that such things could happen ; even during the last war she had never really taken in what was going on, however much she talked about atrocities, and hated Germans, and subscribed to charities. Perhaps they none of them had, except Alice. It hadn't touched them much ; the nearest it came was when they heard of the death of Lionel.

His mind drifted sleepily back to those sunny mornings when Harold and Lionel used to read on the terrace, and Alice went her walks with Edith Cartwright, and old Pietro was pottering about among his vines. That horrible sour wine he made from them, and produced for you to drink when you went to have a chat with him. Even though you didn't speak a word of Italian in those days, you managed to get along with him all right. A little French, a lot of gestures, a few words of the Spanish you had picked up from a Mexican in Santa Fe. When she was a girl, Alice had always wanted to go to Santa Fe, and Zuni, and Acoma. She could go now, if she still wanted to, but that wasn't the sort of thing she did want now. Jim might go there some day, on his way from New York to Hollywood or Honolulu. In his last letter he had written that he was thinking of going to Hawaii this winter. Some people, he wrote, were worried about the war spreading to the Pacific, but that was all a lot of nonsense. The Japs had their hands full in China, and wouldn't take on any more.

Alice, Jim, Harold wandering round, lost and nostalgic, among the Italian pictures in the Metropolitan Museum, Mary's grave in what was now enemy soil. Sylvia with her smart new friends and Charles at a school in Massachusetts where they encouraged self-expression. That was the result of a man on a ship's deck talking about silver-mining. It was strange how things turned out.

Still, it was too late now to wonder if it might all have been better some other way. Everyone in the world to-night could stop and ask themselves that and get no answer. They had all taken a wrong turning somewhere, but perhaps when all this was over they would find themselves on a new road that really led somewhere. Or perhaps they wouldn't. Anyway, some of them would remember the essentials they had seen and the values they had regained in the little ships out in the darkness and in the dark streets under the bombs. It would be interesting to know what young Charles was thinking about things these days. . . .

His thoughts drifted idly on ; he must have slept a little—for he was apt to fall asleep at odd moments now—for suddenly he was aware that he had been dreaming about Charles. Charles—who didn't know what he wanted—and Jim as he used to be as a boy in Curicanti ; and those young sea-apprentices scuffling and tilting their caps in George Street in Sydney, and Tommy . . . and somehow old Captain Morris was in the dream too, and there was an old clipper ship that might have been the *Paladin*, and a little grey ship out of a picture in a modern paper going down a wide grey river under a grey sky. . . . That had been oddly vivid ; the streaked paintwork on her sides, and her wash slipping across the water, and a signal lamp blinking as she melted into the dusk. But what it had all been about, he couldn't remember at all.

He lay for a few minutes trying to remember more

of that strange dream, but soon it had all blurred and faded away ; and he looked round for something to read till dinner-time. Usually about now he felt depressed and lonely. But somehow it was different this evening. Perhaps the sirens would go again to-night, and Wilkins would make him come downstairs. He would argue a bit and finally give in, but he knew it didn't really make much difference. Anyway, he thought, whether a bomb did get him or his unsteady old heart just stopped beating, at least he was back among his own people at last, at the end of the long journey which had taken such a strange turning that night in San Francisco Bay, and little Wilkins was as good a friend as any to have beside him when the moment came.

He found his spectacles, and a book, and started to read. The little flat was very still, as if it was waiting for something or someone.

EPILOGUE

THE DRIVER HAD ROLLED himself a wisp of cigarette and was sitting back smoking philosophically. Ruth was staring out at the mountains that tumbled to the sea. Harold shrugged his shoulders.

"Well," he said. "There it is. I'm glad I did bring Charles to see him before we left. I think seeing Charles consoled him a little for that very unpleasant visit to Alice, and he approved of Charles, though he didn't like the way we were bringing him up. That school in Switzerland—the encouragement of self-expression—it wasn't his idea of things at all. He liked things orderly and . . . and ship-shape. I suppose, by the way, when we get to London we'll have to go and see that his grave is in order. I've always hated cemeteries. Gravestones, crosses, decaying flowers . . . well, that's one thing Charles was spared."

Ruth said nothing. After a moment he went on.

"The encouragement of self-expression . . . Charles expressed himself in a way we didn't expect, didn't he? No doubt he would have been caught up in the maelstrom somehow. It was always futile to think you could keep him clear of a war like that one just by taking him to America. But I should never have expected him to choose as he did . . . and so, so eagerly. After all, his upbringing had been so *continental*, if you know what I mean. It seemed such a waste too. With his knowledge of languages, his knowledge of Europe . . . I thought he was joking, when he told us first."

What made him choose as he did? Was it only the sea-stories he had been reading, and his grand-father talking that evening, and something seen in a news-reel or a film? Or was it something deep and unexpected in him suddenly coming out? There had been all those others before Charles, and before Roger Barton; obscure English sailors whose stories one would never know. Anyway, Charles was with them now.

"I wonder . . ." he stopped.

"What do you wonder?"

"Nothing."

He couldn't express it, but what he had been wonder-ing was clear enough in his mind. Charles had always been a strange, withdrawn, silent boy, who seemed to want something you couldn't give him however much you spent on books and travel and theatre-tickets, on psychologists and tutors and summer-camps and boarding-schools. Had he found what he was looking for at last, in those few crowded months at sea? If so he had been lucky after all . . . luckier than his elders who had never found it.

For one who still had Ruth and Sylvia and Sylvia's children, life still had some meaning, though most of the things one used to dream of seemed to have lost their value, books and pictures no longer thrilled one as they used to, and this Mediterranean sun had lost its magic now. But Jim . . . elderly, fat, florid, clinging on to his youth, hunting it through gymnasiums and Turkish baths, squash courts and night-clubs, a pot-bellied playboy who couldn't even buy himself the admiration he wanted now. Or Alice, (where was she now? Cuba, Bermuda, Florida?) an elderly, haggard woman in a mask of make-up among the empty glasses and withered flowers and half-eaten sandwiches. Charles was safe from that. And, in a glimpse at least, he had seen realities of night and sea and human nature which you didn't find in all your books and dreams and journeys in padded First Class carriages. And he would never be a lonely old man like his grandfather, ending a long and puzzled life in a little service flat.

"You know," he said suddenly. "I can't help wishing father had lived long enough to know about Charles. I think he would have—understood it better than we could, or ever can."

"Perhaps he does know about him."

Ruth's quiet words startled him a little. He had never expected her to say a thing like that. There was an awkward little silence. Then he shrugged his shoulders.

"Oh well, we'd better get along."

He rapped on the glass again, and the driver, having crushed out his cigarette and put it away carefully, started up the car.